The Advance Man

Rick Robinson

Publisher Page
an imprint of Headline Books, Inc
Terra Alta, WV

The Advance Man

By Rick Robinson

copyright ©2015 Rick Robinson

Publisher Page
P.O. Box 52, Terra Alta, WV 26764
www.PublisherPage.com

Tel/Fax: 800-570-5951
Email: mybook@headlinebooks.com
www.HeadlineBooks.com

Publisher Page is an imprint of Headline Books, Inc.

Cover design by Kevin T. Kelly
Cover photo by Brandon Knopp

ISBN 13: 978-1-882658-06-0

Library of Congress Control Number: 2015936223

Robinson, Rick
    The advance man / Rick Robinson
    p. cm.
    ISBN 9781882658060

PRINTED IN THE UNITED STATES OF AMERICA

Behind every successful man are surprised In-laws.
The late- Jack and Jeanne Brewer allowed me to take their
daughter's hand. And Jim and Kathy Brewer, Wade and Robin
DeHate, Jenifer Deiters, Tom Staley and Glen Singleton have been
questioning it ever since.

"You don't need to be straight to fight and die for your country. You just need to shoot straight."

—Barry Goldwater

"Every time I try to get out, they pull me back in."

—Michael Corleone, Godfather III

Prologue

"I'm paid for this."

The time he was spending in the blustery weather under the cover of the old monument was quickly reinforcing the determination of his mission. This was a difficult situation – none of it his own making. But a lot was at stake. No one told him what to do. No one had to. People in his position instinctively know how to handle these things without seeking approval. It was part of his job. He knew it was squarely on his shoulders to make things right.

A steady rain was falling and frigid water streamed down the domed Doric temple housing the District of Columbia's World War I Memorial. A man in a dark coat stood tightly against one of the dozen 22 foot tall, fluted columns, trying to avoid the frigid mist blowing inside the white-stone bandstand. As the cold spray tormented his face, he listened to the wind whipping through fall foliage. The man shuddered as he silently concluded there is nothing quite as miserable as an autumn rain storm in Washington, DC.

Tucked back in a small grove of trees off Independence Avenue in West Potomac Park, the World War I Memorial is the only non-federal monument located on the National Mall. It was built to honor the 499 residents of the District of Columbia who died in World War I and it was dedicated on Armistice Day, 1931 by President Herbert Hoover. Designed to be a bandstand to hold an 80 piece military band, the monument is rarely used today. Wedged between the newer WWII Memorial and the stables for the Park Police horses, it was out in the open and yet secluded all at the same time.

Many current tour maps don't even list the old structure as an attraction. The fact most tourists never visit the secluded location made it the perfect place for this meeting.

As the bitter rain lessened slightly, the man pulled a handkerchief from his pocket and wiped the misty water from his face. Under the cover of the monument for only about 15 minutes, he spent nearly an hour darting in and out of the shadows of the Mall. His plan of walking in one direction and then erratically doubling back around proved an effective method to insure he was not followed, but also soaked him through to the bone. His trench coat keeping the wet cold off most of his upper body, rain soaked through the lower pant legs of his Brooks Brothers suit and his feet squished around in his leather shoes. As he watched his warm breath steam the damp November air, he stiffened his back in a futile effort to keep his body from shivering. The occasional chatter of his teeth was an unpleasant reminder he was, in fact, cold.

The rain was hitting the dome of the monument in a loud rhythm, changing beats as the wind changed velocity or direction.

Standing in the shadows, he glanced down at his Breitling watch. It was 3:10 a.m. He began to wonder if he should have cancelled the meeting because of the cold downpour. But the weather made the location all the more perfect. No one was around. The Park Police were huddled up in their headquarters at the Survey Lodge Ranger Station. Even the homeless huddled somewhere better sheltered from the storm.

Between the branches, he could see a shape approaching. Shifting his position to remain hidden, he turned and looked towards the grove of trees. As he strained his eyes, he pushed his frame tighter against the column. As it got closer he could see it was female and alone. Although separated by distance, he could clearly make out a short, pudgy figure appear from the tree line. The form was walking guardedly towards the bandstand. Once the man recognized the moon-faced woman, he stepped away from the protective cover of the column just enough to reveal his own identity. The woman walked up the steps to get under the cover of the dome.

"Good evening, Ms. Kenady," the man said in a hushed voice. "Did anyone follow you?"

"No," the woman said, her voice deep and manly. She looked around and then shook her head. "No one followed me."

"Are you sure?" he reiterated, blowing hot breath into his hands following the question.

"Jesus. Give it a rest," the woman said, her patience quickly fading. She was as unhappy as him to be out on such a bad night. Still, rather than snapping at him again, she took a deep breath – as if counting to ten – and continued. "I've walked around the Mall for forty-five minutes, just like you told me to do, then stopping and sitting on wet park benches every ten minutes or so to look around." She shook her head. "I feel like a complete idiot."

"And you're sure no one followed you?" he sneered.

The woman waved her hands in the air. "Take a look around you. There is no one out here tonight. If it wasn't for this, I sure as hell wouldn't be out in this godforsaken weather." She was about to explode yet again at the arrogance of the man, so she stopped, closed her eyes and inhaled deeply. Before continuing, she took off her Washington Nationals baseball cap and knocked it against a column. Water sprayed off the cap onto the platform. She needed to redirect the conversation before she snapped at him and ruined the deal. "How about you?" she asked. "Does anyone know you're here?"

The man was puzzled by the question and he cocked his head. "No," he replied. "I wasn't followed and no one knows I'm here."

"Good." The woman reached in her large purse and pulled out a manila file folder. "Because, considering who I stole this from, if anyone figures out how you got this file, my best case scenario is I just end up in jail instead of dead." Her tone was matter-of-fact as she waved the folder in front of him.

The man paused for a moment and considered the comment. He decided to indulge her and, at the same time, amuse himself. She did not know the level at which she was playing. And in the end, it would not matter. "Fair enough," he replied, nodding toward the darkness of the trees. "There's no one out there. I worked the tree line back and forth. I wasn't followed either."

"Good," the woman replied, nodding as she handed over the file. "Here's what you came for. Everything you need is in there."

The man snatched the folder from the woman's grasp. He pulled a small pen light from his pocket and shined it on the single piece of paper in the file folder. It didn't take him long to find what he was searching for. "Fuck me," he growled disgustedly. "I can't believe he's doing this."

"I told you it would be good," the woman said smugly. "I didn't lie."

"No, you didn't," he said, closing the file folder and stuffing it inside his trench coat to protect it from the rain.

"I got really freaky with your pal," she said. "He's a special kind of weird."

"Just keep your mouth shut." He patted the outside of his coat. "What's in this file could start another Cold War."

"I don't really give a damn," the woman replied in a scathing tone. "I'm only doing this for the fee we agreed upon." She paused, nodding back at him. "You did bring the money, didn't you? I told you there would be no negotiation on the fee."

"Yeah." The man reached into his outside coat pocket and retrieved a pair of leather gloves. After he slipped them on, he moved to the breast pocket of his jacket and pulled out an envelope filled with one hundred dollar bills. He handed it to the woman. "No need to count it. It's all there."

"If it's short, I know where to find you," the woman quickly replied. She took the envelope and put it in her purse.

As the woman turned to make her way back down the steps of the memorial, the man quietly unbuttoned his coat and carefully pulled a serrated knife from a waistband sheath. He locked his glove-covered fingers into the brass knuckles on the blade's handle and drew in a sharp breath. His pulse quickened and his eyes narrowed.

Just as the woman prepared to take the first step down from the bandstand, the man grabbed her hair and snapped her head back. Before she could scream, he plunged the point of the knife into the side of her neck and quickly pushed it forward through her throat. Blood immediately spurted out the cavernous gash and its splatter was lost in the mist of the cold fall night. With a shocked look on her face, the woman gurgled and crumpled down the steps, rich red blood flowing from her neck as she rolled downward. She came to rest in a bloody heap at the foot of the monument, her head making a hollow thud as it bounced off the slate walkway.

The man walked slowly down the steps to admire his work. He retrieved the penlight and shined it on her face. He watched emotionlessly as the woman grabbed at her throat, gasping for air. Her face contorted as she tried to speak, but the excessive flow of blood made words impossible. Her legs twitched uncontrollably in the final contortions of death. He lovingly held the knife out in front of him as the rain washed her blood from its blade.

Confident no further action was necessary, the man placed the knife back in its sheath, reached down and grabbed the woman's purse. He removed the envelope of cash and her wallet. Before tossing the purse back onto the ground, a small piece of paper – a business card for a transsexual escort service bearing the woman's name – caught his eye. He stuffed the money and the card into his pocket, looked sideways at the woman and waited for the twitching to stop.

Chapter 1
(four months later)

With his white starched sleeves rolled up and red tie slightly loosened, David Unger typed away on the small keyboard attached to his work pad. He looked up as the middle-aged, brunette flight attendant brought him his second ginger ale on the flight from LAX to Dulles.

"Here you go, Mister Unger," she said, as she placed the drink on his open tray table. "You sure you don't want something stronger."

"No ma'am," Unger replied, feeling his face redden a bit at the sheepish response. "I don't like to drink on the job." He nodded his head in the direction of the computer screen waiting for his attention. Blaming it on the job was an easy excuse, but the fact was he rarely drank. Raised by tea totaling grandparents, there was never any alcohol around the house. And when he moved from North Dakota to Washington, DC, he promised them both he would not succumb to the temptation.

"Okay then," the woman replied. "You have just about enough time to drink this one down before we serve dinner."

"Thanks, Mrs. Bach," Unger replied, trying to look nonchalant as he glanced at her name tag in order to make sure he got it right. "I sure am hungry."

"I know I must seem old enough to be your mother," Bach replied. "But please call me Bridget."

"Sure thing, Bridget," Unger smiled. Ever since he joined Vice President Paul Shelby's advance detail, he learned to call flight attendants by their name. It was only one of the tricks-of-the-trade he learned from others at the office. Most of them called air plane staff by their first name, but Unger thought it impolite and never used first names until so instructed. Others dropped names to get special attention, but not Unger, who did it out of respect. He was raised to believe it was impolite to call an elder by their first-name until permission was properly granted. Rather than a work gimmick, Unger just considered it proper, and since his black leather carry-on luggage was emblazoned with the Seal of the Vice President of the United States, it never took long for the flight crew to figure out his employer.

Being overly friendly was easy for David Unger. It was simply part of his nature. Just out of college and barely twenty-three years old, his dark black hair drooped lazily onto a baby-face still often mistaken to be in its teens. His eyesight was not too bad, but he wore black, horn-rimmed reading glasses in an attempt to look at least a year or two older.

"It's been a long couple of days on the road," Unger continued. "This tastes really, really refreshing right now." He nodded at Bach as he took a sip. Despite his humble motives, it was hard not to enjoy the extra attention the woman was bestowing upon him at the expense of other passengers. "Thank you."

"It must be really exciting, you know, doing what you do," Bach said as she reached down and grabbed the empty glass from the previous drink. "I mean getting to travel around with Vice President Shelby, and all."

"It's an absolute blast," Unger replied, placing the fresh drink on his tray table. "But I'm traveling a lot more than I ever expected."

"I bet you get to meet some really interesting people."

"I'm working my dream job," he replied, flashing his naturally boyish smile. "But I don't really get to meet any of the big celebrities."

"No?" Bach was surprised.

Unger pondered how to reply and not sound like so many of the other self-absorbed young staffers he worked with at the White House. "As the point man on the Vice President's advance team," he said, "I just make sure all the details are in place for a visit. Then, almost as quickly as I get to one town, I'm off to our next event. By the time the Vice President's stop is over and Air Force Two loads up, I'm in the next town setting it all up for the next event."

"So an 'advance man' is the ultimate trip planner?" Bach asked.

"Yes ma'am," Unger replied. "Basically, I make sure it all goes exactly as scheduled. I'm the guy who makes sure all the big and little details come off without a hitch."

"Like the flags…," Bach said.

"Excuse me?" Unger did not know what she meant.

"You know," Bach replied, moving her hands in a smooth manner from top to bottom. "Every time you see the President or Vice President on television, the flags look perfect – no wrinkles and each hung precisely like the others."

Unger now understood the reference. "Coat hangers," he laughed.

"What do you mean – coat hangers?" Bach replied.

"We take a wire coat hanger, bend it just right and attach it to the flag pole." Unger said, smiling as he revealed one of the instructions in the advance manual which was his Bible. "After we iron the wrinkles out of a flag, it hangs over the bent coat hanger perfectly. Each flag ends up draping down just like the others."

"Funny," Bach said. "So you're the guy who puts coat hangers in ironed flags for the Vice President."

"Yup," Unger said as he took a drink. "My big job. If the flags look bad on television, my cell phone starts ringing immediately."

Bach made a motion at Unger buttoning her lips to secure the knowledge. "My lips are sealed," she said.

"And I'll let you in on another secret," Unger raised his eyebrows and whispered mockingly as if revealing the code for a nuclear launch.

"What?" Bach leaned in.

"The homemade signs being held up by supporters along the route of the motorcade…"

"Yeah?"

"Did you ever notice how they all seem to be in the same handwriting?"

"Yours?

"Not all the time," Unger smiled, leaning back. "But I've stayed up many a late night making those homemade signs." He made bunny quotes with his fingers as he said the syllables "home made."

"I guess no one's job is as glamorous as other people think," Bach laughed. "It's like being a flight attendant."

"How so?"

"Well," Bach replied. "At first, the travel is exciting and glamorous. And then one day you realize it's just part of the job – going someplace fun becomes ho-hum."

"I'm sure I'll get there someday," Unger replied. "But right now I have a lot of fun ironing flags and making signs."

"And I suppose with the other side getting ready for the primary process right now," Bach said, "you're going to be making a lot more signs."

Unger smiled. "It seems like I haven't slept in my own bed since I took the job back in January."

"Lots of travel, huh?"

"You can't even imagine," Unger replied. "I'm probably on a plane as much as you. While the other side is jockeying for position in the early primary states, the Rohman-Shelby ticket is out on the road shoring up our base."

"Shoring up your base," Bach replied as she put her hand on her hips. "Fancy phrase for raising money, right?"

"Of course," Unger responded. He took another drink. "I was in Los Angeles for a fundraiser. We have a big one there tonight." He looked at his watch. "In fact, the Vice President should be starting his remarks in less than an hour."

"And you're sneaking home early?"

David Unger traveled with the Vice President on Air Force Two in the past and totally enjoyed the experience. However, Vice President Shelby's Chief of Staff, Jon Dosser insisted Unger fly commercial when on purely campaign trips. This trip involved mixed duties, so Dosser accompanied Shelby across the country and got what would normally be Unger's seat on Air Force Two. The explanation seemed way too long to try to convey. "Kind of," he said. "I'll be in DC for a couple of days, but then I'm on the road again."

"There are worse things than having missed winter in DC, right?" Bach suggested.

"Hey," Unger replied with a self-effacing grin, "I'm from North Dakota, ma'am. DC can't be any worse than winter back home. I grew up on my grandpa's snow plow. So I'm pretty used to lots of snow in the winter."

"Personally, I hate the stuff," Bach said. "People in DC have no idea how to drive in bad weather. This is my home base. I moved outside the beltway, just to be closer to Dulles. I'm glad spring is finally here."

"I don't mind the winter," Unger replied. "And I grew up driving in it. But, I'd like to be in DC long enough to see the cherry blossoms."

"Never seen them before?"

"No ma'am. I moved to DC right before Christmas – running and gunning for the Vice President ever since. I think they're supposed to be at peak next week. I want to go down to the Tidal Basin and get some good pictures to send back to my grandparents."

"Speaking of work …" Bach nodded up the aisle. "I've gotta go do mine."

Unger went back to working on his advance report for the Los Angeles trip while Bach assisted other passengers in the First-Class cabin. He caught glimpses of her as she filled the drink orders of his fellow travelers. He thought briefly about how pretty she was and then remembered her comment about being old enough to be his mother.

Unger went to the photo files on his tablet and pulled up a grainy picture of his mother and him holding hands at a playground. He did not mind fighting back tears every time he looked at the picture. Tears were the dues he paid for being the surviving son of a single mom who died way too young. Unger was deep in thought about his mother and what she would think of his success, when Bach came back to his seat. He quickly minimized the picture on the screen.

"How about the Vice President?" Bach asked. "What's he like? Do you get to spend time with him?" Rolling her eyes at the ding signaling a passenger's call button, Bach leaned against the seatback in front of Unger.

"He's the one celebrity I see a lot."

"He seems like a good guy," Bach said. She was enjoying the conversation as much as Unger.

Unger decided to momentarily forgo working on the report, disconnected the key pad and powered down the tablet. "Vice President Shelby is a great guy," Unger replied enthusiastically. "At every stop I have a lot of one-on-one time with the Vice President in his holding room to go over all the details before he heads to the actual event."

"Holding room?"

"Yeah," Unger rubbed his chin. "Once the Vice President gets off the plane, the Secret Service takes him somewhere to chill out for a couple of hours prior to the event. Our events are usually at hotels, so they get him a nice suite to relax in. I'm there waiting for him when he arrives."

"And you take care of things for him?"

"Yeah," said Unger. "Sometimes it's important stuff. Other times it's just dealing with the little things he can't handle."

"Little things," Bach asked. "Like what?"

"Like today, his Chief of Staff sent me out to the store to get him a new tie."

"A new tie?"

"I guess he spilled something on the one he was wearing," Unger replied, shrugging his shoulders. "Anyway, I went out and got a new one for him. The Vice President just can't go out to the mall like we do."

"I guess," Bach said as she shook her head. "I don't know if I could do it though. I'd want to be there, you know, to see the fruits of my labor. Doesn't it bother you to not be there?"

"No ma'am," Unger replied. "It's called 'advance' work for a reason. Once I hand the Vice President the final version of his speech, I'm out the door."

"Really?" Bach exclaimed. "You aren't annoyed you don't get to see the finished product?"

"Nope," Unger said in a matter-of-fact tone. "By the time the event starts, I'm usually off to the next city to do it all again."

Another call bell sounded. "Well," Bach said. "You certainly lead an exciting life for such a young guy."

"It's fun," Unger replied, "but the job is like a lot of others." He nodded at the tablet sitting on the tray table in front of him. "There's a lot of paperwork."

"Oh, sure, Mister Unger," Bach smiled as she got the hint. "I'll let you know when we're ready to serve your meal." She moved to talk to the impatiently waiting passenger several rows back.

Mister Unger, he chuckled to himself. *If my old high school classmates could just see me now – flying first-class with a pretty older woman callin' me Mister.* He took another sip of his drink and pondered how a skinny, non-descript kid from the corn belt, living with his grandparents was suddenly working for the Vice President of the United States, traveling the world and garnering the attention of people who would have not looked twice at him six months ago.

Unger thought back to his childhood and how he moved from Rhode Island to North Dakota to live with his maternal grandparents after his mother died in a horrible car accident. The transition was tough, even for an otherwise independent latch-key kid. His new classmates at school taunted him for his east coast accent, and he learned how to be alone. Even through high school, he pretty much kept to himself at school and worked on his grandparents' farm on the weekends.

In the fall, after his graduation from the University of Iowa, Unger responded to an ad on an internet job board seeking a personal assistant to a high ranking, but unnamed, public official. He submitted his resume with little hope of making it to the next level. Surprised when a head-hunter called and offered to fly him to DC for an interview, he was literally shocked when he discovered the "high ranking government official" was Vice President Paul Shelby. Less than ten days later, Unger was living in a small studio apartment just off DuPont Circle and working only steps away from the White House at the Old Executive Office Building. When Unger read a story about his appointment in a local North Dakota newspaper, he smiled, knowing it would have made his mother proud.

Unger quickly discovered advance work was not quite as simple as he assumed. The level of minute detail he was responsible for in the final execution of an event was overwhelming at first. Everything from coordinating security with the Secret Service to making sure the stage risers were secure and could not collapse were on his checklist. Chief of Staff Dosser accepted his mistakes – explaining what he needed to do different next time, but insisting the mistake should not happen a second time.

Unger determined quickly Dosser was a good guy who wanted him to succeed at his job. Dosser's military background shown through in the regimented manner he dealt with the office, and he spent a lot of time teaching him the political ropes. When Unger was looking for a place to live, Dosser appointed someone to assist Unger in getting to the top of the waiting list for an apartment at The Cairo, a classic old condo building located blocks from the White House. He even fronted Unger some money to buy a couple of nice suits, so he could "look the part" while on the road.

Constant travel was the down side of being an advance man. Even for a twenty-three year old, life on the road was grueling. The Vice President fired several advance men in his first term in office and it was expressed to Unger, once the ticket won a second term, he was expected to serve at least two additional years on the road before he could ask for another job in the administration.

The major perk of the job was Unger got to spend about an hour of one-on-one time with the Vice President on every trip he advanced. When all of the details were set, Unger would meet Shelby's motorcade and escort him to his suite. There the Vice President would unwind before the big event, have a single dirty vodka martini – containing precisely three blue cheese stuffed olives — and chat with Unger about the details of the day's event. Once Shelby was sufficiently advised, Unger would usually hitch a ride to the airport with a campaign volunteer and catch a flight to the next city on the schedule. The next day, he would do it all over again.

The post-event report for the Los Angeles fundraiser was somewhere in the memory of Unger's tablet, calling out for his immediate attention. As he sipped his ginger ale, his mind began to wander. His eyelids were heavy and when he closed them he suddenly realized how tired this trip had made him. He plugged his ear buds into his iPhone and leaned his seat backwards. As Patrick Monahan, the lead singer of Train, began singing "Drops of Jupiter," he closed his eyes. He was asleep by the end of the song.

Chapter 2

The Roosevelt is an old, classic hotel located on Hollywood Boulevard's Walk of Fame, directly across the street from Grauman's Chinese Theater. The dark look of the interior harkens back to an older day in Los Angeles when Humphrey Bogart frequented the bar in the front lobby, chain smoking cigarettes and guzzling scotch. California's indoor smoking ban changed the odor of the place, but the mahogany walls and tall ceilings still gives off a nostalgic vibe. In the shadows, one can almost hear Bogie talking about the wood on the bar being worn down by the frequent distribution of shot glasses filled with cheap liquor and broken dreams.

Vice President Paul Shelby is one of those rags to riches stories which so often found their way to the silver screen. His rise from a middle-class, Midwestern family to VPOTUS was anything but fiction. Brought up on a generational family farm still operated by his two brothers, Shelby's interest in politics sparked while playing football during college. Forgoing the family business in favor of public service, he became one of the youngest members ever elected to the Kansas State Legislature. His fights against oppressive federal and state regulations gained him the reputation as a no-nonsense leader and catapulted him to state-wide prominence.

Three years earlier, when Jake Rohman was cruising to his party's nomination for president and looking for someone to join him on the ticket, Paul Shelby was not even on his radar screen for the number two spot, let alone the short list. Rohman served as Governor of Florida and initially he was looking for a Congressman or Senator with foreign affairs experience.

At the time, smart money was on Senator Mack Wilson, ranking Member on the Senate's Foreign Relations Committee, Wilson visited the Middle East seemingly as often as he visited his home state of Kentucky. His office on the Hill was adorned with pictures of him meeting with world leaders and the gifts they bestowed upon him during those visits. As the primary progressed, Senator Wilson was often found on the campaign trail introducing Governor Rohman to throngs of campaign supporters.

Still Paul Shelby believed, despite his lack of foreign affairs experience, he could help the ticket. So he methodically went about trying to convince Rohman as much. As the Governor of Kansas, Paul Shelby balanced his state's budget by reforming the state's tax code and getting the state legislature to agree to substantial state pension reforms – something other state chief executives failed at passing. And Shelby worked several different angles to get his pitch to Rohman.

Despite the strong push, Rohman was initially wary of Shelby. Rohman saw no benefit to having two governors on the ticket, especially one better than Rohman himself was on fiscal issues. The fact Kansas only controlled six electoral votes was also not lost on Rohman.

Yet, as the convention got closer and closer, Paul Shelby seemed to will his way into being Rohman's pick. While Senator Wilson went about acting as if he were the presumptive running mate, Governor Shelby worked hard to stay on Rohman's radar screen. A Sunday morning interview in which Shelby successfully dissected an anti-Rohman talking-head seemed to get him to the table, though a heated internal battle within the campaign's inner-inner circle of advisors ensued. Most of those from Inside the Beltway were pushing Wilson. Yet the strength of their push inadvertently caused an equally strong silent reaction from Rohman, who was also looking for a way to assert his independence over the DC crowd. In the end – and over the objection of several key advisors – Rohman chose Shelby.

The final meeting before the convention announcement between Rohman and Shelby was choreographed by Jon Dosser, a military veteran turned lobbyist and confidant to Rohman. Dosser pushed Wilson for the Veep spot. When he saw the resolve Rohman was showing in choosing Shelby, he dropped his support for Wilson and began whispering the name of Shelby into Rohman's ear. Despite thinking it was the wrong political move, Dosser decided to make the most of the situation. Prior to the meeting, Dosser agreed, in the event the ticket won, he'd leave K Street to be to be Chief of Staff to Shelby. Rohman seemed happy to have someone so close to him keeping an eye on his Veep.

Tall, good looking and always immaculately dressed, Paul Shelby drew every eye when he entered a room. The Secret Service noticed the detail he paid to his appearance and gave him the code name of Brooks Brother. A former college football standout, his square jaw and broad shoulders gave him a movie star like appearance and he possessed a charismatic personality which drew attention in a crowded room.

Shelby's wife, Donna Forrest-Shelby, was a strong force in American politics with her own set of impressive political credentials. The pair met at a Governors' conference when Donna Forrest served as Secretary of Transportation during the previous administration – a job she continued into the current one. When their romance became public following the inaugural, they became Washington's premiere power couple. Vice President Paul Shelby and Secretary Donna Forrest were on everyone's A-List of invitations. Shortly after the election sending the Rohman-Shelby ticket to office, they were married at a private ceremony at the National Cathedral, just across the street from the Vice President's residence at the Naval Observatory.

During the ensuing three years, the couple fell into a pattern of making appearances separate or together depending on the importance of the event. Occasionally, but only occasionally, Shelby's wife accompanied him on trips. On this particular trip to L.A, however, he was joined by his Chief of Staff, Jon Dosser.

In his finely-appointed contemporary suite at the Roosevelt, Vice President Paul Shelby stood in his white boxer shorts and tee shirt and stared out the window. He sipped at his dirty martini and gazed down at the tourists mingling along the Walk of Fame. He pointed with the glass at the iconic "Hollywood" sign in the distance. "LaLa Land," he mumbled. "I hate this place."

"Come on, Mr. Vice President," Jon Dosser replied. "It's not so bad."

"You aren't the one standing behind the podium," Shelby shot back. He pulled a stuffed olive off the skewer with his teeth before putting it down and slipping on his shirt. "I get to play nice with a bunch of rat bastards who fought against us last time and who now want to suck up to me in an effort to hedge their bad bet," Shelby said.

"Don't sugar coat it," Dosser replied laughingly. "But instead of rat bastards ..." Dosser let the comment hang for a moment.

"Yeah?" Shelby asked.

"Let's refer to them as second-chance contributors." Dosser knew the Vice President's disdain for those late to the Rohman-Shelby political bandwagon. Shelby used the term "rat bastard" so often to refer to them, Dosser was afraid one day Shelby would actually let the crude comment slip out in public and generate a YouTube moment.

"You can call them what you want," Shelby said as he put official Vice Presidential cuff links into the button holes on his shirt cuffs. "They were late to the party, but they still want to go home and fuck the prom queen."

"And all you have to do is make them feel like you really wanted them all along," Dosser replied.

"I know what my job is, Jon." Shelby replied briskly as he walked across the room to take another look out the window. "I'd rather be with those folks," he said, pointing to people on the street standing behind the bulky metal barricades located across the street from the Roosevelt. A small crowd gathered, hoping to get a glimpse of the Vice President when the fundraiser was complete. "I'd rather have dinner with them. Those people out there are real. The people we're about to get checks from are all a bunch of phonies."

"Well sir," Dosser replied, "the money we get from the phonies lets us stay in office and help the folks in the street with our agenda for another four years."

Shelby was tired of repeating what seemed like the same conversation he argued with Dosser on countless previous occasions. He looked in the mirror as he tied his new light blue tie. "Unger has good taste," he nodded as he admired the perfect Windsor knot he crafted in the tie. "Thanks for having him run out and picking up a new one for me this morning."

"He's a good kid," Dosser replied. He got up and started to mix a drink for himself. "And he's loyal as hell. He's done everything we've asked of him. I think if we asked him to run through a brick wall for you, he'd do it."

"I like him," said Shelby, sitting down on a chair and then bending over to tie his shoes. He licked his thumb and rubbed it across the leather to remove an unsightly smudge. "I always offer him a drink and he never takes it."

Dosser walked to the bar, popped some ice in a glass and poured himself a scotch. "Is that why you never ask if I want one," Dosser laughed. "Because you'll know I'll take it?"

"Lighten up, Jon," Shelby instructed. "You always seem quite comfortable in helping yourself." Shelby paused. "Still, Unger hasn't fallen into the DC trap of power yet. I gather his strict upbringing kept him fairly grounded."

Dosser ignored the initial comment. He knew Shelby originally wanted his own man as Chief of Staff and that Shelby therefore made a dig at him every so often in retaliation. "His grandparents sent me a hand-written letter asking I keep their grandson on a straight and Godly path."

Shelby chuckled at the idea of there being any Godly men in the nation's capitol. "Make sure he gets a seat at the National Prayer Breakfast next year. It will make him feel part of the team."

"Speaking of team," Dosser added, finding the moment to slip this into the conversation. "I think the President is going to want you to go lead the delegation to the annual meeting for the Organization of American States this summer."

Shelby stopped what he was doing and rolled his eyes. "You're kidding me?" he asked. "Right? It's a joke. Please tell me you're making a joke."

"No sir," Dosser replied. He knew the conversation was not going to be comfortable, but President Rohman personally requested Dosser raise the topic.

"Where's it located this year?" Shelby asked in an exasperated tone.

"Nicaragua."

"No shit? Nicaragua?" Shelby shook his head in disbelief. "How come I don't get to go when it's someplace like Belize or Barbados?"

"Luck of the draw, I guess," Dosser replied.

"If I'm going someplace where the people hate our guts, I'd at least like there to be a nice beach involved." Shelby put on his jacket and looked at himself in the mirror, checking each detail of his appearance. "Last month Poland – in a few months, I get Nicaragua in the summer," he said. "Such a glamorous life I lead."

"You've got your own plane," Dosser joked.

Shelby frowned at Dosser, "Call Senator Wilson's people. Let them know I'd like for him to accompany me on this important foreign policy mission."

Dosser laughed at the thought of the burly senior Senator from Kentucky sweating his way through the hot summer streets of Managua. "He won't want to go," Dosser said, taking a sip from his glass.

"He won't have a choice," Shelby grinned and nodded. He gave one final look in the mirror at his appearance and announced, "Let's roll."

"Already?" Dosser asked, looking at his watch. "We're still a little early."

"Yeah," Shelby said. "I want to walk the rope line – shake a few hands – sign a few autographs."

Dosser knew it was coming. Despite never being on the formal schedule of movements prepared by the Secret Service, Shelby liked to walk the rope line. When Shelby started talking about the folks in the streets, he already decided he wanted to go there first.

"You're not going to take the cap of the marker off with your teeth, are you?" Shelby liked to put the cap of his marker between his teeth in order to pull the cap off whenever signing autographs. "Your wife hates when you use your teeth," Dosser said. "She says it looks like you're smoking a cigar."

"You're my Chief, Jon," Shelby replied. "And we're business partners. But you're not my wife."

"Still, sir," Dosser continued, "the Secretary insisted ..."

"The Secretary of Transportation isn't walking the rope line," Shelby interrupted as he took the final gulp from his martini. "I am. Let my detail know there's a change of schedule."

"If you put a mark on your face again, Secretary Forrest will have my ass," Dosser pleaded.

Shelby smiled. "She'll have your ass, but I always have your back."

"The Secret Service will object," Dosser said. It was almost perfunctory for him to say so.

"Of course they will," Shelby replied. He could play the game too. "They always object."

"But ..."

Shelby walked into the bathroom and unzipped his pants to use the john. "Tell the head of my detail I'll be starting five minutes early with a grip and grab along the rope line across the street. There aren't many out there. It will only take a few minutes. And then we'll head inside so I can pretend to actually like our paying customers."

"Guests, Mr. Vice President. Please call them our guests."

As Shelby washed his hands and gargled some mouth wash to get rid of his vodka breath, Dosser went outside the room and told Kathy Fuller about the Vice President's plans to shake hands with people along the street. Fuller was an experienced veteran of the Secret Service and head of the Vice President's security detail. The diminutive red-head held a reputation as a no-nonsense agent. Dosser got the response he expected. Fuller, her face reddening, was not happy. Like always, she planned every movement of Brooks Brother down to the nanosecond. She put up a slight argument about inadequate time to set up the proper security, knowing all the while it would be to no avail. Shelby liked to wander from the script. In fact, he did it so often the Secret Service started anticipating unchoreographed movements. A quick announcement on the radio and agents scrambled to the street to ready for the arrival of the VPOTUS.

When Shelby exited the room he greeted Fuller who advised him the street would be ready for him when they reached the lobby, adding she advised against it. As the short red-head expected, Shelby insisted on heading outside and they proceeded to the elevator.

"Brooks Brother is moving," Fuller advised everyone on the secure radio.

As the freight elevator expressed its way to the kitchen, Fuller explained the route they would be taking to the street. Shelby listened and watched the display over the doors as they descended, adjusting his tie as the main floor neared. "It's game time," he said just before hearing the ding announcing the opening of the doors. Shelby threw his shoulders back and walked into the hotel kitchen to the applause of workers who were preparing food for the reception.

After shaking hands with the people in the kitchen, Shelby and his detail exited the building out a delivery door where they were met by two other officers. Briskly, they all walked past the pool area to an opening between two buildings leading to the street.

The crowd began applauding wildly when Vice President Shelby rounded the corner. Someone began chanting, "Four more years! Four more years!" and others joined in.

Shelby went about doing what he did best – owning the crowd. While Secret Service and LAPD followed Shelby's every move, he shook hands and posed for pictures. People were shouting questions and offering support, and Shelby attempted to acknowledge each and every one, if only with just a smile and a nod. At one point, in a move he mimicked numerous times before, Shelby grabbed someone's iPhone, adjusted the view and took a selfie of himself and the phone's owner. The crowd cheered with delight at the move.

Near the end of the rope line, a young blonde woman held out a Rohman – Shelby campaign sign from the previous campaign. "Can I have your autograph, please?" she pleaded.

Shelby smiled and pulled a marker from his pocket. He held up the marker and winked at a laughing Dosser. Then Shelby grabbed the sign with his left hand and raised the marker to his mouth to remove the cap with his teeth. Smiling at the young woman, he pulled back slowly on the marker.

The sound was not much louder than a good-sized firecracker, but the explosion was lethal. Paul Shelby's head snapped backwards suddenly and blood sprayed from his face and neck onto the blonde and others nearby. Shelby's body tossed violently to the ground, making a sharp thud.

Fuller's eyes widened, adrenaline screaming through her veins. Driven by years of training, she leapt towards Shelby and she was on top of the Vice President almost as soon as his body hit the pavement. "Stay down, Mr. Vice President," she mumbled. "I've got you." The smell of explosives and burnt flesh filled her nostrils. She grabbed her hand microphone. "Brooks Brother is down," she shouted. "Repeat. Brooks Brother is down. This is not a drill."

Still forcing her torso over the chest and head of the Vice President, Fuller looked to her left and saw the blonde lying just beyond the barricade. Knocked to the ground by the concussion, she was covered in blood. Fuller could not determine whether the blood was from Shelby or the woman herself.

With her blood pumping, time for Fuller suddenly seemed to move in half-seconds. Her body supine over Shelby's, she tried to steady her breathing. As she heard the combined screams of the crowd and shouts from on-rushing police and Secret Service, she kept her head down and readied herself mentally for what she assumed would be a second assault by an unknown threat.

Within seconds of the blast, a black Escalade pulled onto the street from a nearby alley. The car sped to within a few feet of the Vice President and squealed to a quick stop. Five members of the Secret Service's exclusive Emergency Response Team jumped from the car and surrounded Fuller and Shelby. From the corner of her eye, Fuller could see the officers in their black camouflage, their ominous SR-16 automatic rifles aimed out like the four corners of a compass rose.

Sirens began to shriek in the background, but Fuller maintained her tense position on top of Shelby. She could feel his warm blood seeping into her own uniform. The sirens got closer and Fuller pressed her body even tighter to the ground.

"Get up," a voice commanded.

True to her training, Fuller held her ground and remained on top of the Vice President.

"Agent Fuller," the voice repeated. "Get up." Fuller suddenly recognized the voice as of one of the other officers on the detail.

"Brooks Brother is down," Fuller said

"Brooks Brother is dead," the voice responded.

"How do you know?" Fuller asked.

The agent leaned down and whispered in Fuller's ear. "Look to your right."

When Fuller looked to her right, she saw the top crown of Shelby's skull lying in the street.

Chapter 3

Awakening, Unger noticed Bach moving his tablet aside and placing his meal in front of him. The clatter of plates and glasses startled him abruptly awake. "I guess I dozed off for a bit," he said, looking at his watch trying to determine how long he was out. Concluding an hour or more, he saw others in first-class were nearly finished with their meals. "Thanks, Bridget," Unger mumbled, wishing she had awakened him when she began serving everyone else.

Bach nodded at Unger as she straightened back up. Her inviting smile was gone. Jaw set, her expression was deadly serious and she offered no apology for the errant fork landing on his crotch. Unger wiped his mouth in fear he was drooling while he slept and looked at his pants to make sure they were properly zipped up. With the most obvious social faux pas covered, he wondered if he was acting otherwise inappropriately to change her friendly manner.

As he gobbled down his meal, Unger brushed aside the concerns about Bach's change in demeanor. He had more important items to attend to and quickly turned his attention back to his report. After he fired up his tablet and reconnected his keyboard, he typed up his notes from the Los Angeles event and was still working on his report when Bach announced over the speakers the plane was making its final approach to Dulles.

"Just a cab ride from home, and tomorrow the cherry blossoms," Unger said to Bach as she stoically walked through the aisles collecting garbage and empty glasses. She ignored his comment entirely. "I wish Reagan National allowed late flights." Still there was no response. Unger shrugged it off and concluded she was simply back to conducting her regular duties.

Unger shut down his devices and began packing them away. Minutes later the wheels of the big main-liner screeched down on the runway at Dulles. The plane started its normal route to the terminals, slowed and then suddenly stopped. Bach sat stoically in her jump seat as she announced there would be a short delay before the plane docked at the terminal and all passengers should remain in their seats. Unger looked at Bach and smiled. Bach averted her eyes and looked down.

The plane sat still for several minutes and most of the passengers did not notice a set of mobile stairs wheeling up to the plane. A single car approached and stopped by the steps. Passengers were looking around at each other when Bach opened the front cabin door and two men dressed in business suits entered the plane. They followed Bridget into the first-class galley. As she spoke to one of the men, she pointed to Unger. Then, the other man entered the first-class section and stopped at Unger's seat.

"David Unger?" asked the man.

"Yes," Unger replied.

"I'm Detective Scott Proctor with the United States Secret Service. My partner up there is Detective Stanley Wicke."

Unger's eyes shot toward the other man, a grey-haired, African-American agent he recognized from the White House. "What's wrong?"

"Will you come with us?" Proctor nodded to the other man.

"Sure," Unger stuttered. He stood up and started to go to the overhead bin for his bags.

"Leave your gear," Proctor instructed. "We'll make sure everything is secured for you. Let's just exit the plane now."

As Unger started to walk with Detective Proctor, he noticed Wicke's obvious tension observing his every move. All eyes in the plane were on him and he shrugged his shoulders to telegraph to the passengers his utter confusion at what was happening. He wanted to thank Bach for the service and he looked back over his shoulder to where she was standing.

What Unger saw next stunned him — Bridget Bach visibly shaking and weeping into her hands.

Chapter 4

Richard Thompson paced back and forth in front of his government class at Gateway Community and Technical College, loosening his tie and pondering the next point he intended to make to his students.

It was four years now since Thompson decided not to seek reelection to his seat in the United States Congress – a decision neither he nor his wife, Ann, regretted for a minute.

In fact, following retirement from Congress, Thompson almost reveled in the decision to abruptly cut short a promising political career most in Washington predicted for bigger and better things. Turning down big paydays as a lobbyist, he instead returned home to practice law with his friend and confidant Joe Bradley, affectionately known as The Fat Man because of his portly build. Even though Thompson returned to a law office, he spent more time making rain for the firm than actually going to court. His reputation in the community kept a steady stream of new and substantial clients beating a path to his office.

The law practice was doing a great job paying the bills, and his reputation as a renegade former-pol allowed him to follow his true passion – teaching.

Most days, Thompson spent a good portion of his time and energy preparing for several classes he taught as an adjunct professor at the local university and an inner-city community college. His formerly sandy hair was now liberally sprinkled with gray and, like most of his colleagues who escaped from politics, allowed it to be cut a little bit longer than when he walked the halls of the United States Congress.

Adding to his look as a full-fledged academic, he shed over twenty-five pounds from his short frame.

There was always a waiting list to get into Thompson's classes. His experience as a Congressman coupled with a quirky classroom presence worked well and students liked he did not make them pay for a textbook. Instead he taught from class outlines he prepared himself. And, like those who experienced Thompson's proclivities during his political days, word quickly spread around campus he might break into song in the middle of class. A student's question could be answered by a line from a Meat Loaf or Warren Zevon tune.

This particular evening, Thompson's government class was discussing the influence of money on the political process – the title of the lecture, "Send Lawyers, Guns and Money." He dressed in boot cut jeans and a long-sleeved flannel shirt with the sleeves rolled up. The wooden heels on his snake skin cowboy boots – a retirement gift from his former campaign consultant, Michael Griffith – clicked on the floor as he paced.

"So, Ms. Vaughn," Thompson said as he turned and pointed at a student, a middle-aged African American woman. "Do lobbyists have too much power in Washington then?" he queried.

"I think so," Vaughn replied, her chin held high indicating her resolve.

"Why?" Thompson nodded his head as if thinking about her position.

The woman put her pen down on a pad of paper and looked at him as if the answer was obvious. "Because of the money."

"Send lawyers, guns and money," Thompson sang out, energetically mimicking a Warren Zevon guitar lick as he sang. He lifted his eyebrows feigning embarrassment to the class at his rock and roll outburst. "Sorry," he said. "I assume by 'the money' you mean campaign contributions."

"Yeah," Vaughn said. "Lobbyists give lots of money to politicians. It's what Washington is all about."

"Shouldn't lobbyists be allowed to support for office whomever they want? Don't they have rights, too?"

"I suppose so," said the woman, not wanting to disagree too much with the crazy man playing air guitar as he lectured. After all, he was responsible for her final grade in the class. Still, she shifted in her chair a bit and stood her ground. "But, you know, they want something in return for their money."

Thompson smiled. The woman was headed down the path he hoped. "So, you believe lobbyists and Members of Congress have some sort of quid-pro-quo. The lobbyist gives money and, in return, the Congressman gives favors."

"Yeah," Vaughn nodded. "Something like that."

"What kind of favors?" Thompson continued.

"I don't know," Vaughn responded. "Votes, I guess. Access."

"So, in return for political contributions, the lobbyist gets access to the Congressman's staff and influence over his votes," Thompson summarized. "Firm in your position?"

"Yeah."

"And that's scummy," Thompson added.

"Yeah."

"And the people who do that are scummy."

"Yeah."

"I was in Congress and my campaign took money from lobbyists who spent time with my staff," Thompson cocked his head as he made eye contact with his student. "Am I scummy?"

The class all focused on the pair waiting to see if their fellow student would insult their professor. She paused, not knowing how precisely to respond. "Uhhhh …" she stammered.

"You don't have to answer," Thompson smiled softy. Having set the trap and received the response he wanted, he let her up. Turning his attention to the rest of the class, he said "Ms. Vaughn just fell prey to what happens in real life politics. People hate Congress, but somehow seem to like their own Congressman. At least I hope Ms. Vaughn still likes me. After our last exchange, I'm not too sure."

Heads nodded and Vaughn smiled sheepishly as Thompson continued. "It's how people like me get reelected despite taking money from scummy people. So let's explore if there are any answers for ridding politics of scummy people like me."

As Thompson readied to launch into the next point in his lecture, there was a light tap on the door before Russell Hughes, president of the community college, entered the classroom. When Thompson left Congress, Hughes approached him about teaching government to the non-traditional students at Gateway Community and Technical College. Entering the room with graying red hair and wearing a sport coat with leather patches on the sleeves, Hughes definitely looked the part of a community college president. He looked apologetically at Thompson for interrupting his class.

Thompson dramatically swung his arm in Hughes' direction. "Speaking of scummy people who supported me when I was in office," he declared in a loud voice. "You all know President Hughes." The class laughed and Hughes smiled, but raised an eyebrow in Thompson's direction at the introduction.

"Sorry to interrupt," Hughes said to the class. "But I need to borrow Congressman Thompson for a minute."

"Professor Thompson," Thompson corrected. "I don't do politics anymore."

"Don't be so quick," Hughes replied. "Better dismiss class, Rick. You've got a call in the office I suspect may take more than a few minutes."

After quickly giving the students an assignment for their next class, Thompson followed Hughes down the hall to the President's office. "What's up, Russell?" he asked. "Who's on the phone?"

"The Governor," Hughes declared.

The response made Thompson wince. As the pair walked silently down the hallway, Thompson pondered why Governor Robin Latimer would call him. While the two were in the same party, his only real tie to Latimer was his old Phi Delta Theta fraternity brother and political consultant, Michael Griffith, who was her hired gun, having run her last two bids for office. Out of his loyalty to Griffith only, Thompson followed Latimer's career, but he was not particularly close to her. In fact, since choosing to leave Congress, he was not particularly close to anyone in politics except Josh Barkman, a protégé who succeeded him in the House of Representatives.

They entered Hughes' office. "This ought to be interesting," Thompson said to Hughes before picking up the phone. He cleared his voice. "Good evening, Governor."

Hughes started to leave in order to allow some privacy, but Thompson nodded his head towards the couch, indicating it was okay for the college president to stay in his own office. Hughes sat down.

"How's it going, Richard?" she asked in a very business-like tone.

"Very well," Thompson said. "Sorry I missed your last fundraiser up here. Teaching evening classes keeps me pretty busy." He knew it sounded shallow.

"I'm not insulted," Governor Latimer replied in a tone indicating to Thompson immediately she certainly felt otherwise. "Griff tells me you don't make too many events anymore."

"Ann and I made it clear when we got out, we committed to staying out," Thompson said, referring to his wife and the joint decision they made for him to not seek reelection to the United States House of Representatives. The pair married long ago when they were staffers on Capitol Hill and spent much of their married life balancing their personal lives with politics. When the time came to leave the arena, they dedicated themselves to getting out of politics entirely.

"So I heard," replied Latimer.

"It wasn't easy," Thompson continued. "But, after more than a couple of decades in the game, we went 'cold turkey.'"

"A lot of people say such nonsense as a way to bide their time before their next election," the Governor challenged.

"Not me," Thompson assured Latimer. "I even got an earring to seal the deal. No one will vote for a grey-haired candidate with an earring."

"Griff told me you'd never put your name on the ballot again," she said. "Until this call, I wasn't sure I believed him."

"Believe him," Thompson said.

"At this point, I do," she replied.

Thompson's curiosity got the best of him and he decided to push to the point. "The direction of this conversation leaves me wondering why you're calling me, Governor."

"Well then, let me cut to the chase," said Governor Latimer.

"I'd appreciate some candor."

"It's unfortunate what happened in LA," Latimer said.

"Devastating," Thompson replied. She was clearly avoiding the point of her call, but he decided to play along. "I only met the Vice President once, but he seemed like a nice guy. It's a very sad episode in American history."

"And despite the fact you've declared yourself out of the game, I'm sure you've also heard the rumor President Rohman is considering Senator Wilson as Shelby's replacement."

"I have," Thompson said. He heard the rumors, but assumed they were just the normal political scuttlebutt surrounding such events. "It seems logical. He was the one everyone thought would be the pick originally, anyway. He's already vetted and everything."

"Well, Wilson threw a curve ball today," Latimer sighed.

"How so?"

"Senator Wilson submitted his resignation from the Senate," Latimer huffed.

"He resigned before the President announced he'd be appointing him to the Vice Presidency?" Thompson replied. He was a bit shocked. Rumors fly so often in politics, but this time the rumors appeared to be true. Hughes looked at Thompson quizzically. Thompson shrugged his shoulders in silent response. "The dirt on Vice President Shelby's grave is still warm. Hell, they just buried him today. It seems pretty early for posturing."

"No, Richard," Latimer said. "Wilson simply resigned. He's walking away."

"Wow, I didn't see that one coming," Thompson said scratching his head. "He's one step away. Why would he resign?"

"I've no earthly idea," Latimer said. "He hand delivered a letter to the Majority Leader, one to me and disappeared."

"You haven't talked to him?"

"No," Latimer sighed.

"The President is quite disappointed," Latimer continued. "A Vice President has never been assassinated before in our history. President

Rohman wanted to get someone in place quickly to calm the fears of the American people. Wilson's a good guy with a little personal baggage, but who is well liked in the Senate. The President thought he could get him through confirmation relatively quickly."

"Probably could have," Thompson said, contemplating the appointment. He was not very close to Wilson. In fact, a personal run-in with Wilson caused him to distrust the man. His response was measured. "It would be good for our state to have one of our own in the White House. We've not had anyone at the White House since Alben Barkley was Vice President." He was still having trouble following where the Governor was going and rubbed his brow. "But what does this have to do with me? If you want me to try and talk to Wilson, we're really not very close."

"No," Governor Latimer laughed. "I don't want you to talk to Wilson. He's out. The letter's accepted. I want you to fill his unexpired term."

"What?" Thompson replied, suddenly rigid with shock at the request.

"Wilson has time left on his term and I want to appoint you to the seat."

Thompson shifted nervously from side to side as he pondered Governor Latimer's proposition. The offer caught him off guard. His response was almost automatic. "Thank you, Governor," he muttered. "I'm truly humbled, but I have no desire to run again."

"I'm not asking you to put your name on the ballot," she said. "I want you to be a caretaker until the next election."

"You want to send me to the Senate and then step away?"

"Precisely."

"But I detest the United States Senate," Thompson declared. It was a bit of an overstatement, but he was rather outspoken in his contempt for the current presidential administration as well as the upper chamber of Congress, having written several recent op-eds blasting both.

"Which is precisely why you're the perfect choice," Latimer replied. "I can appoint someone in the interim to go up there and

...se a little hell. Then when the term is over, you come home. You can vote and express yourself without the pressure of an election staring you in the face."

When Michael Griffith ran Thompson's political operations, he did so according to what he called the Godfather Rules – observations of power gleaned from the trilogy of Godfather movies. It suddenly dawned on Thompson this conversation had nothing whatsoever to do with him spending time in DC, and everything to do with Latimer wanting to run for US Senate. She was drooling for the job and she needed a marker to hold the seat for the unexpired term. *Keep your friends close and your enemies closer,* Thompson smiled, thinking of one of Griffith's favorite Godfather Rules.

Thompson decided to toy with the Governor a bit. "Why not appoint Congressman Barkman to the seat?" he asked. "He'd be the perfect choice. And he already has a political operation in place to get ready for a state-wide race."

"Too young," she replied curtly. "And I've already spoken to the Congressman. He agrees he doesn't have enough statewide name recognition to win a primary following the appointment. Congressman Barkman actually agrees with me. You are the perfect choice to complete the term and then leave the party nomination to an open primary."

"You've done your homework," Thompson replied. He was not surprised Barkman was consulted. He, too, was a Griffith campaign client. "I can assume then Griff thinks this is a good idea."

The Governor held the phone away from her mouth and shouted, "He wants to know if you think this is a good idea." Governor Latimer was clearly addressing someone who was in the room with her and not Thompson.

"Damn right I think it's a good idea," came a familiar voice shouting a response in the background. It was Michael Griffith.

Thompson drew in a heavy sigh. "I should have known Griff was there with you," he said, exasperation in his voice. "Put him on the phone."

"Hey, boy," Griffith greeted. "Sorry to get you out of class."

"You could have warned me," Thompson said curtly. He was a bit miffed Griffith did not give him a heads up.

"Couldn't do it on this one, brother," Griffith said. "Paying customer made the call. We're keeping this on the down low, just in case you say no."

"And why should I say yes?"

"Are you kidding me, man?" Griffith exclaimed. "For two years you get to be on one of the country's biggest stages to say whatever the hell you want with no strings attached and no pressure of a reelect. You don't have to raise a dime. You can tell every contributor and lobbyist comes-a-calling to kiss your fuzzy ass and vote your conscience."

"And, when it's over?"

"Then you can go back to class and tell students the difference," Griffith replied. "Write a book about it. Hell, write a song about it for all I care. But this deal is custom-made for you."

With the voice of Michael Griffith on the other end of the line encouraging him to say yes, Thompson was starting to soften his stance just a little. "I'll think about it," he said.

"There's nothing to think about, man." Griffith was nearly shouting into the phone.

"There's a ton to think about, Griff," Thompson replied. "Ann and I have a new life now."

"Godfather Rules," Griffith shouted into the phone. Known for considering all campaign decisions with guidance from the Corleone Family's choices in the trilogy of Godfather movies, he possessed a rule for every situation. "Michael went away before he came back to be the Boss of Bosses."

"Yeah," Thompson replied, rolling his eyes. "And Barzini blew up Mikey's new wife in the process."

"Technicality," Griffith laughed.

"Explain to Ann she's a technicality."

"You may not want to admit it," Griffith changed the subject, "but you miss the game. You can't be in it as deep as you were and not miss it a little bit. I see it in your eyes when we have lunch. You want to talk about something else, but we always end up talking about politics."

"Maybe," Thompson said in a noncommittal tone.

Griffith was not about to let up. "How about all your 'citizen legislator' bullshit you're always babbling about?"

"Yeah," Thompson replied. "What about it?"

"Well, here's your chance to become one," Griffith argued. "Prove the Founders right. Go to DC. Do your job. Go home and live happily ever after."

"I said I'll think about it." Thompson repeated his promise to Griffith.

"I hate to do this to you buddy," Griffith said, "but you have until the morning."

"Come on, Griff," Thompson replied. "I can't make a decision this big overnight."

"The Governor wants to have a name ready when the news hits the press tomorrow." Griffith paused. "If you don't call by the morning with a yes, the Governor is going to call State Senator Marcum with the offer. He'll jump at the chance."

"Marcum?" replied Thompson incredulously. "The same ass ..." he paused remembering Latimer was listening, "a-hole who filed against me for a primary after my first term because he said I wasn't conservative enough for him? Are you kidding me?"

"The one and same," Griffith replied.

"He'd be a disaster." Thompson thought a minute. "And he'd never agree not to run for the full term. He'd file for sure."

"And you've already shown he's beatable," Griffith said. "The Governor could claim she made a bad choice for the seat and the only way to make it right would be to challenge him in a primary. She appoints him and then she kicks his ass in a primary."

"I hate Marcum," Thompson assured.

"I know you do," Griffith replied with an impish tone in his voice

"I'm starting to hate you, too."

Griffith laughed out loud at the comment. "I'll call you in the morning." And he hung up the phone.

Thompson hung up the phone and sat down in one of the chairs in Hughes' office. He leaned back and put his hands behind his head. He knew Hughes very well and trusted him as a friend. He waited a while before he spoke. Then he looked at Hughes. "She wants to appoint me to the United States Senate." He paused and let the words sink into his own psyche. "The United States Senate," he repeated.

"Damn," replied Hughes. "Tall cotton, man. You gonna do it?"

Thompson shook his head. "I don't know," he said. "Griff's right. I do miss it. I hate to admit it, but I do miss it. It sure is tempting."

Hughes heard the trepidation in Thompson's voice. "But?"

Thompson smiled and continued. "But I'm playing right into the Governor's game. This isn't about me. It's about her and the path she's plotting to power. I'm not sure I want to be a pawn in a game leading to her coronation."

"What's wrong with being a pawn? Every business has them. They're just more frequent in politics."

"It's one of the reasons I got out," Thompson replied. "I don't want to be a part of games like this anymore."

Hughes leaned forward and placed his hand on Thompson's knee. "Richard, do you play chess?" he asked.

"I played a little bit in college," Thompson replied.

"Well, I play a lot," Hughes said. "I've learned a lot about life from playing chess. But do you know the most important lesson I've gleaned from playing the game?"

"What?"

"At the end of the game ..."

"Yeah."

"The kings and the pawns all get put away in the same box."

Chapter 5

Tourists normally flock to the Walk of Fame in Hollywood to track down names of people they've followed on television and the silver screen or to place their hands and feet in the cement imprints of their favorite stars in front of the Chinese Theater. But for the past several days, people instead spent time building a makeshift memorial of flowers and flags to the late Vice President Paul Shelby, assassinated along the rope line in front of the Roosevelt just before a scheduled fundraiser. The street, usually filled with out of work actors dressed as super heroes hawking pictures for $5 a snap, now contained a steady stream of men and women in dark t-shirts with FBI or Secret Service emblazoned on their backs. Today there were no tourists with cell phone cameras, but instead an army of production vans bearing the logos of every major local and national news operation. Some of the yellow "crime scene" tape originally encircling the entire block was still in place, but now only encircling the front entrance to the Roosevelt. The hotel announced a limited re-opening and all guests temporarily entered through a back door off the small parking lot.

FBI Agent Leo Argo flashed his identification to a Los Angeles policeman before ducking under the tape blocking the entrance. It was a by-the-book, quick open and close move. The young officer did not need to look too closely at the credentials. Everyone, even the rookies on the scene, knew Leo Argo as the man sent in from Washington to head up the Federal investigation into the death of Vice President Shelby. His burly Cuban physique seemed to cut its own path as he walked through the press corps to the front door.

"Vultures," Argo mumbled under his breath as reporters shouted questions. "I don't answer questions, people," Argo said to no one in particular. "Public Affairs will be out later to update you."

"Leo," a familiar voice shouted out.

Argo turned and saw Alberto De La Caverone from his hometown newspaper, *The Miami Herald*. He smiled and nodded at the reporter. *"Que pasa,* Alberto?"

"Same for me and you," De La Caverone replied. "We're both a long way from home, amigo."

"How's the family?" Argo asked. The pair knew each other for decades, but not talked for several years.

"Great," De La Caverone said. He was pleased Argo remembered to bring up his family. "The youngest is in her last year at University of Florida. The wife and I are empty nesters now."

"Good for you," Argo said sincerely. "But, a Gator?"

"How about this, Leo?" De La Caverone asked, nodding towards the busy street.

"I got nothin' for you," Argo replied. "I'd love to give you a name and a motive, but we're a long way off right now."

"Sure," De La Caverone nodded. "Keep your old pal in mind if you get anything."

The men shook hands before Argo turned and headed inside. Sipping at a bottle of water with one hand while looking at his watch on the other, Argo moved his strong frame down the lobby's main corridor to one of the Roosevelt's conference rooms. The on-site team investigating the assassination of Vice President Shelby met in an impromptu command center at regular intervals to discuss progress, or more importantly the lack thereof, into the crime gripping the nation. Argo was in California as a direct report to Rob Cicero, the Director of the Federal Bureau of Investigation. He knew Cicero bristled at reports indicating no progress in the investigation and craved something new to send up the chain of command. Argo was headed back to DC on the red-eye following this meeting and desperately needed something fresh to take back to headquarters.

When Argo entered the room, the team was already seated around the table. He kicked a chair free with his foot and plopped down in the seat. "Please tell me there is something new in the investigation," he said, rubbing his right hand over the short stubble on his head. "Izzy, you got anything on the foreign connection?"

Izzy was Jim Izzocenzi, a wiry, quick-witted Italian from the Central Intelligence Agency with a heavy Jersey accent. "Three more groups have claimed responsibility for the assassination of the Vice President, including one claiming to make the marker explode by offering prayers to Allah."

Argo shook his head. "Anything credible?"

"They're all credible, Leo," Izzocenzi leaned forward and placed his elbows on the table. "The kooks who want to convince their followers this happened because of prayers to a higher source have access to explosives just the same as anyone. They blow him up and it shows their prayers to Allah were answered."

Argo nodded his head, unconvinced. "Any chatter or movement to back up the claims of responsibility?" Argo asked.

"Nothing." Izzocenzi shook his head. "All significant movement we were tracking is on the east coast. We doubled back and looked to see if we missed anything, but I've got no listed suspects within a thousand miles of LA the night of the fundraiser."

"How about the local cells?" Argo asked, referring to possible California-based suspects.

"We're running them all down, Leo," Izzocenzi replied, leaning back in his chair to show he was done. "But, there's not much there to indicate this is terrorist based – foreign or domestic."

"Keep at it," Argo insisted. "And ask the Director to cut loose a few more CIA resources."

"Why don't you ask her?" Izzocenzi snapped, making a reference to the fact Argo and CIA Director Jane Kline were living together back in DC. When Argo shot him a cautionary stare, Izzocenzi backed down. "Sorry, Leo. I was out of line. I'll talk to Director Kline after the meeting."

Argo looked at Roberta Biggs, an African-American female FBI special agent tasked out of the LA field office. "Biggs, where are we with the incendiary device?"

"Grab the lights," Biggs instructed as she opened up a Power Point projected onto a screen at one end of the room. "Here's what we know."

Everyone in the room leaned forward and looked at the picture on the screen. "It was really a very rudimentary device," Biggs continued. "Think of a rifle, except on a mini scale – a round small enough to fit into a marker."

Biggs clicked to an enlarged animation of a Sharpie. "The place in the pen to hold the ink was filled with a high powered explosive." She clicked a button and the animation of the pen showed the cap being slowly removed from the body of the marker. "The cap acted as a firing pin," Biggs said as the animation showed an explosion.

"Interesting," Argo mumbled. "What kind of explosive?" he asked.

"Good question, Leo," Biggs said. "They used a plastic resin not available commercially in the US, but readily available via the black market in certain overseas countries."

"So you don't know the origin?" Argo queried.

"Not yet," Biggs said. "We're checking it out now. It's also stored at several military bases. We're checking those inventories now as well as the companies supplying the military."

Izzocenzi looked puzzled. "I don't understand how the explosive didn't just blow off his hand."

"At first, I thought the same thing." Biggs clicked forward to enlarged photos of fragments of the marker lying on the ground with evidence tags placed next to them. "Take a look at this picture," she said as she aimed a laser pointer at the picture on the screen. "It occurred to me the fragments from the marker were exceptionally large for the force of the explosion. I sent off a fragment for analysis and the plastic was reinforced with metal fibers. It worked like a rifle barrel, sending the force of the explosion forward instead of outward."

"So if he would have pulled the cap off with his hand instead of his teeth, the explosion would have simply shot into the air?" Izzocenzi continued the logic.

"Precisely," Biggs responded.

"And it also means the casing was custom made," Izzocenzi remarked.

"Once again," Biggs said. "You're right on the mark."

"Any prints on the fragments we found?" Argo asked.

"None," Biggs replied. "Well, none other than the Vice President's."

The wheels in Izzocenzi's mind continued to turn. "There couldn't be too many people close enough to the Vice President to get a pen to him," he interjected.

"Well, it certainly narrows the list of possible suspects," Biggs said. "But he walked the rope line a lot. One theory is someone could have given it to him, he used it to sign a few autographs, put the cap on – activating the firing pin, before placing it in his pocket ready to go off the next time he used it."

"Widens the circle," Izzocenzi said.

"Boss," Biggs looked at Argo. "Back in DC we're working with the Secret Service to review the schedule and to check every place he signed autographs over the last week. We're reviewing tapes to see if we can spot anybody who might have come to the rope line with their own marker."

Argo shook his head and took a big swig of water. None of the new information would make Director Cicero particularly happy. He looked up at the only person left at the table, Will Baechtold of the Secret Service. "Willie, please tell me you've got something for me."

A short, red-headed German, Baechtold was straight out of central casting for a detective. "As I told you at our previous meeting, the President and Vice President always have a certain number of active threats we're investigating. We are continuing to push through those and we're following up on a handful we find credible."

"How about the kid?" Argo asked, referring to David Unger.

Baechtold nodded. "We've finished our interrogation of the Veep's advance man, David Unger."

"And," Argo prompted with anticipation.

He pulled out a sheet of paper Argo assumed was a report from Secret Service Headquarters at the White House. Baechtold scanned the report and summarized. "He's one of the people to keep on the short list of suspects. He was with the Vice President hours before the explosion and he took a commercial flight to DC, which gives him cover when the explosion occurred."

Argo frowned. "I feel there's a Kim Kardashian coming on."

"What?" Baechtold looked up puzzled.

"A big but," Argo said.

Baechtold did not smile but nodded his head. "We tore the hell out of his place and ripped his computers to shreds," he said. "Nothing."

"He's an advance man," Argo said. "I assume he was pretty well vetted. Any motive?"

"We have suspicions but we don't have enough to hold him. We cut him loose about an hour ago."

"Fuck me." Argo paused. He hoped the interrogation of Unger would lead to something. "What are the suspicions?"

"I can't really say right now," Baechtold said reluctantly.

Argo stared. "What the hell do you mean, you can't really say?"

Baechtold looked down to avoid eye contact. "It's just speculation," he stammered.

"I don't give a damn if it's about the alien from the *Weekly World News*," Argo shot back. "I need to know everything, man. If it's a rumor, we'll run it down. But, I need to know everything right now."

Baechtold thought for a moment, slowly forming his answer. "Well, some suspect he is gay."

"Sexual orientation doesn't mean a goddamn thing, Will," Argo said shaking his head. "Unless it has something to do with motive, it just doesn't matter to this investigation."

"Some people are developing a theory in which Unger was obsessed with the Vice President," Baechtold replied. "Brooks Brother was wearing a tie the kid gave him as a gift."

Argo lowered his chin and stared at Baechtold while speaking to the entire group. "Okay, strike what I said before," he said slowly. "No speculation. Unless Unger hung naked pictures of Shelby on his apartment walls, I don't want to hear some silly scheme."

Argo slammed his open meaty palm on the table, largely for effect. He closed his eyes for a moment, and then took in a deep breath he exhaled as almost a sigh. Then he made eye contact with all of the others in the room before saying, flatly, "I need facts!"

Chapter 6

Ann Thompson lay in bed with a book on her stomach, wondering when her husband would be home from teaching his evening class. The television was on and he was almost always home in plenty of time for the 11:00 news. In fact, he usually came home right after class, but he was running late tonight. She flipped through a few channels before landing on CNN. She watched a bit of the coverage about the investigation into the assassination of the Vice President before returning to her book, assuming her husband would be home shortly.

She liked the fact she and her husband decided to leave politics. The relaxed lifestyle meant Ann no longer worried about being engaged by angry constituents every time she went to the store. The life of a Congressional spouse can be fun and exciting, but the public exposure also adds stress to a marriage. When they left politics, Ann decided to pursue her own dream of working with women in recovery from drugs and alcohol. Using her influence as a former Congressman's wife, she was able to raise funds as well as awareness for a rising plague effecting women from all socio-economic levels in their community.

As she anticipated her husband's arrival, she slid her right leg from under the covers of the bed and gazed at the scar. For the most part, Ann aged much more gracefully than her husband. Her blonde hair exhibited only a hint of grey peeking through, and a personal trainer at the gym kept her in relatively good shape. Yet, no matter how good everyone said she looked, she was still coping with the damned scar.

The result of a shooting incident in Ireland which ultimately led to Thompson's decision not to seek reelection to the United States House of Representatives, the physical wound healed, but the enduring scars were mental. Long after surgery grafted new skin over the physical wound, nights spent wide awake intertwined with restless sleep haunted by nightmares of rainy Irish roads, gunshots and blood. It took some serious psycho-therapy to put the entire episode behind her – mostly.

Ann rubbed the scar and smiled gingerly at how the whole thing now seemed like one of those bad dreams occurring a lifetime ago. She had moved on, or so she had convinced herself.

A few minutes later as Ann heard the garage door open, she looked over at the bedside table to see it was 11:11. After the garage door came back down, Ann could hear her husband rustling through the kitchen cabinets before finally making his way up the steps to their bedroom. As Thompson walked into the bedroom, Ann noticed he was carrying a dozen pink roses in a vase he retrieved from downstairs.

"For me?" Ann pressed her hands against her chest as Thompson entered the room.

"Of course," Thompson replied. "Who else would I bring flowers?"

"Oh, I don't know," Ann replied, taking the vase from Thompson's hands and smelling the roses. "Maybe the young coed you were out carousing with for two hours after class."

"Yeah," Thompson laughed. "Because so many young girls look at grey-haired, community college professors and think 'wow, I wanna get me some of that.'"

Ann looked at her husband slyly. "You never know what goes through the minds of desperate women," she said.

"Desperate?" Thompson replied, a mock hurt look on his face. "Gee thanks. Have I gotten so old the women who may find me attractive are scraping the bottom?"

"You know I'm still desperate for you," Ann smiled. "But seriously, what's up? You never stay out this late after class."

"I went out for a sip of Michter's with Dr. Hughes from the college," Thompson said as he began to unbutton his shirt. "Well, maybe two sips. Then I picked up the flowers."

"Well, they're beautiful," Ann said. Thompson slid across the bed and kissed Ann deeply and soulfully. Her response was immediate. Still, after only a few moments of passionate kissing, Thompson pulled back. Ann looked at him in surprise. She certainly thought the kiss was going to lead to more. "What the hell?" she smiled. "When did you start playing hard to get?"

"We need to talk." Thompson chuckled lightly to himself. Normally, it was Ann uttering those words to signify the onset of a serious conversation. He was used to being on the receiving end. Those same words coming out of his mouth suddenly seemed odd.

Ann sat up a bit. "Talk – about what, baby? Is something wrong?"

"No," Thompson replied. "Nothing is wrong. In fact, things couldn't be more right." Thompson searched for the right way to tell Ann about Governor Latimer's offer. Now, in the midst of executing his plan, he was getting cold feet. "Well ..." he stammered.

Ann cocked her head. "Your eyes are squinting," she interjected. "Whenever you get nervous, you squint your eyes."

"Yeah," Thompson sighed. He could not argue the point. "You're right. So let me be straight with you. Remember when we got out of the game and we swore I'd never run again?"

"We agreed," Ann replied slowly. Now she was squinting. "Don't even tell me you're thinking of running for something." When Thompson did not answer immediately, she repeated the question louder. "You're not are you?"

"Not really," Thompson continued. She was not making this easy. He got out of bed.

"What do you mean – not really?"

"Well," Thompson replied as he started to pace around the bedroom as if he were back in his community college classroom. "What if I got back in the game, but we didn't have to run?"

"Okay," Ann said with a hint of doubt in her voice while shifting nervously in the bed. "I'm not really following you, but go on."

Thompson sensed the opening and dove in. "So, here's the situation. Wilson stepped down today."

"Wow," Ann replied. When Thompson and Ann originally met, both worked on Capitol Hill. Ann knew her politics. Mack Wilson resigning was huge. "Why? Wasn't Wilson being considered to replace Shelby at the White House?"

"So I heard," Thompson said.

"Think it's his health?" Ann asked.

"All you have to do is look at him," Thompson replied. "He's not exactly the poster child for a fitness center."

Ann nodded in agreement. "But he did it at a time when everyone was focused on Shelby's funeral," she said.

"Precisely." Thompson was in full professor mode at this point. "Whatever the reason, right now it's a page two story."

"Makes sense," Ann said, following Thompson's logic. "I still don't understand why you're bringing up Mack and us getting back into the game."

It was time for Thompson to drop the big bomb. "Wilson's resignation leaves Governor Latimer with an appointment to the open Senate seat." He paused. "She wants to appoint me."

"You?" Ann asked. "Why not Josh?"

"I asked the same thing," Thompson replied. "The Governor thinks he's too young. And she's probably right. Plus he might beat her in a primary."

Ann paused. "You?" she repeated.

"Yeah, me."

Thompson could feel himself start to sweat a bit as Ann peered at him. He was totally surprised when she started giggling. It started as a gasp, but then quickly accelerated to a full belly laugh. Ann placed her hand over her mouth, trying not to snort. "What's so damn funny?" Thompson asked.

As Ann stifled her laughter, she waved her hand at Thompson. "I'm sorry," she replied. "I can't do this anymore with a straight face."

"Do what?"

"Bust your chops," Ann replied.

Thompson was totally confused. "Huh?"

Ann smiled. "Griff already called and told me all about it."

Thompson was not happy. "Griff called," he repeated.

"Yeah," Ann said. "So did Josh. It was his idea for me to Chump Charlie you a bit."

Thompson shook his head. "I never did like that boy."

Ann pulled herself from the bed and walked over to Thompson. She put her arms around his neck. "Don't be mad at them."

"Why not," Thompson said rigidly.

"Because they were both right," she said.

"About what?"

"About how you'd try to sell me — they said the professor in you would come out and you'd run straight at it with me – no bullshit along the way," Ann said. She paused. "But I didn't expect the roses. Nice touch."

Thompson put his arms around Ann's waist. "I thought so," he replied. "Well, you've obviously spent some time pondering it. What do you think?"

Ann broke the embrace and walked away. To Thompson, the pause seemed like an eternity, until she turned back. "This is really, really hard for me to say, but I think you ought to do it."

Thompson was shocked by the statement. "Really?" he asked rhetorically. "I thought you'd be a tough sell."

"I was," Ann replied. "Until Griff made a good point."

"What point?"

"Everybody in the game puts themselves in the position to be 'the guy,'" Ann said. "If you turn down the opportunity when it's offered, you disappear. You're irrelevant."

"Now I'm the one who is confused," Thompson said.

"You're still relevant," Ann replied. "Maybe you're relevant now more than ever. You walked away. You showed them all you didn't need it."

"Don't be so sure," Thompson said lowering his head. "I've missed it."

"Missed it and desiring to get back to what you're good at is far different than needing it," Ann insisted. "Now you can go back for a couple years or so and speak your mind and people will pay attention. Then when you're done, you can walk away again."

Thompson walked over to Ann and kissed her. "You're really for this?"

"I believe in you, baby," Ann replied, her voice breaking a bit. "I always have. Believing is what drew me to you all those years ago." She kissed Thompson lightly. "I'll always believe in you."

Thompson kissed Ann back – deeply – passionately. Slowly, Ann pulled him towards the bed. As they walked, Ann began unbuttoning her husband's shirt. When they got to the bed, she pulled her own nightgown over her head, leaving her naked body totally exposed. Their passion was so intense they never heard the story being reported by CNN on the television at the end of their bed indicating sources were investigating one of the Vice President's aides in his death.

Chapter 7

John Dosser shifted his weight nervously from side to side as he waited for President Jake Rohman to acknowledge his presence. Tall and lanky, with tufts of curly salt and pepper hair wandering in every direction, Rohman was known for being a bit aloof at times. Dosser knew him for decades and was accustomed to his bouts of odd behavior, but today the President seemed even more alone in his thoughts than usual.

The pair were friends and political allies from years back. Initially Dosser had not identified Rohman as the man who would take him to the White House. He thought many more along the way far more capable, but politics is a strange business and Dosser kept his net cast wide. The more Rohman rose, the more Dosser pledged his allegiance. If only for his own benefit, he was loyal. Or, at least, he exuded loyalty. Which is why he presumed the President summoned him to the Oval Office this morning. It was a no brainer.

The President requested the meeting, Dosser presumed, to talk about whom to nominate as Vice President Shelby's replacement in office and on the ticket. Dosser expected an engaging review of the President's "to-do" list for vetting names. In fact, he fully expected the President to select him to head the team assigned to narrow the list for Shelby's replacement.

But when Dosser entered the room, Rohman was standing and quietly staring out the back window of the Oval Office. It shook Dosser when his friend did not even acknowledge his presence. He seemed oblivious to the fact Dosser was even in the office.

In an attempt to make himself feel more comfortable, Dosser looked around the famous room. The Oval Office is smaller and more intimate than it looks on television.

Body shifts failed to gain Rohman's attention, and the silence started to feel uncomfortable. So Dosser spoke. "Mr. President," he said softly.

Rohman looked over his shoulder almost surprised to find Dosser in the room.

"If this is a bad time, Mr. President," Dosser said. "I can come back later."

The President turned and Dosser could see the glint of a tear in his eye. "No," Rohman said. "Now is fine."

Dosser and the President had already spoken on several occasions about the death of Paul Shelby, but it was either on the phone or with others in the room. This was the first time they were together privately. To Dosser, Rohman looked haunted by the events in Los Angeles. He watched as the man he helped elect walked – almost aimlessly – around the desk and directed him to sit on one of the couches in the middle of the room with an absent wave of his arm. Dosser moved to the couch, waiting for the President to sit in an accompanying chair before sitting himself.

"These are the times defining a presidency, Jon," Rohman started. "Every president experiences one. Kennedy's was the Cuban Missile Crisis."

"Some more than others," Dosser chimed in. "Kennedy was also Commander-in-Chief for the Bay of Pigs."

Rohman shrugged his shoulders in acknowledgement, but clearly did not appreciate the interruption. "I understand the importance of this particular point in time," he continued. "No administration's lost a Vice President like this – killed in office. How I handle the nomination of Shelby's replacement will define this term and set the stage for the next."

Dosser was not quite sure where Rohman was headed, but decided to play along. He had already prepared a short-list of potential successors to recommend. "I totally agree, Mr. President."

"This is a pivotal moment," Rohman said, gently tapping his fist into his palm assertively. "Everything must be planned and our moves precise. Otherwise it all could spin wildly in the wrong direction."

Thinking now Rohman was referring to him, Dosser sat up straight on the couch and squared his jaw. "Absolutely," he replied. "You know I'm ready to do whatever it takes, Mr. President."

"Good," Rohman replied nodding. "Then I hope you'll understand why I've asked Ambassador Crump to head up the team."

Dosser felt the blood drain from his face. "Of course, sir," he replied, feeling the wind knocked out of him – like he was punched in the stomach. Bill Crump was a retired businessman from Mississippi, who once served a stint as the US Ambassador to Norway. He was well liked, but Dosser considered him politically inept – too folksy. Nevertheless Dosser nodded and he tried not to show his emotions. As much as he tried to hide it, Rohman could sense what was happening.

The President leaned over and put his hand on Dosser's knee. "Jon," he said sincerely. "We've known each other for a long time. So I can speak frankly with you. I don't blame you for what happened in LA."

So that's what this is about, Dosser thought to himself, struggling to retain his composure. *He does blame me. He's looking for a scapegoat. He's laying this at my feet.*

"But you were there," the President continued. "And the guy who allowed Paul to walk the rope line can't head up the team to pick his replacement."

Rage built up inside of Dosser and he wanted to scream at the President of the United States, a man he helped get to the White House. Dosser spent a lifetime getting himself to this position – being the power behind the throne. Now it felt like he was being pushed aside. Still he tried to keep his face blank. He tried to keep his composure. "I understand, Mr. President," he said calmly, although with a slight quiver in his voice. "I think Ambassador Crump is the right choice."

"Perfect," Rohman replied. "I'd like for you to coordinate with him on the names you vetted during the campaign."

Despite knowing he was being cut out of the process, Dosser nodded approvingly. He was, in fact, angry at himself for not being better prepared. He had not anticipated this sudden change of events. There were no cards up his sleeve. "I'd be glad to Mr. President," he said. "I'll get my files together immediately and set up a meeting with the Ambassador."

"Thank you, Jon," the President replied. "I appreciate your being so understanding."

Dosser nodded acknowledgment to the President, but felt the need to change the direction of the conversation. If it continued down the current path, he feared losing his cool. "Any word on the Wilson seat?"

"Governor Latimer called me this morning," Rohman replied.

"Was she sober?" Dosser attempted to add some levity to the situation.

Rohman chuckled. "I think so," he said smiling. "It was too early – even for her."

"Who's the new Senator from Kentucky ... her?" Dosser actually suspected she would appoint herself to the open Senate seat.

"Richard Thompson."

"Wow," Dosser replied stunned. "How did he get the nod?"

"He's Michael Griffith's old college roommate," Rohman replied calmly.

"Well that explains a lot," Dosser said. "I should have known Griff would want to keep it in the family."

The President suddenly stood indicating their meeting was complete. "Thank you, Mr. President," Dosser stuttered at the abrupt ending. As the men shook hands, he asked, "So, where's the investigation?"

Rohman shook his head negatively. "Every agency in the government is feeding me information. But I'm not sure we're any further along than we were on day one," he said.

"I'm sorry," Dosser replied.

"Me, too," Rohman said in a tone indicating his growing frustration with the lack of anything certain in the investigation.

"The leads are not developing fast enough for me," Rohman said with exasperation in his voice. "It's a cluster-fuck of major league proportions."

"CSI Effect," Dosser replied.

"Pardon me?" Rohman asked.

"The CSI Effect, sir," Dosser smiled at his little dig at the President. "Thanks to television shows like CSI, everyone expects cases to be wrapped up within an hour."

The President frowned, but Dosser did not particularly care. He made his point.

"What about David Unger?" Dosser asked. He was then unpleasantly shocked for the second time in their meeting

The President shook his head. "They kicked him this morning."

Chapter 8

When the US government hired French architect Pierre Charles L'Enfant to plan a street design for what is now known as the District of Columbia, it is hard to imagine what was going through his head as he laid out the maze of streets and traffic circles making up Washington. Conspiracy theorists believe you can find Masonic symbols in the design, while some Christian zealots believe the streets form a satanic pentagram placing the White House in the center and channeling Beelzebub's earthly presence through the Oval Office. DuPont Circle is one of three traffic circles intersected by six streets, adding a 666 label to their Lucifer claim.

Historical lore is George Washington tasked L'Enfant to design the grid to allow military encampments at the circles, protecting the government from any advancing enemy infantry – a theory advanced by the frustration any driver experiences trying to navigate the streets of the nation's capital during rush hour.

More than likely, the circles were simply designed to be the centers of planned neighborhoods, around which people would start businesses and build homes. Of this theory, no area of DC is more an example than DuPont Circle. A vibrant and flourishing neighborhood exists around the park dedicated to Civil War hero Rear Admiral Samuel Francis DuPont.

It was mid-morning in DC as David Unger stumbled through DuPont Circle, hoping the walk would clear his head. He had been asleep for the better part of 24 hours. The marble fountain in the middle of the square was recently cleaned and the water turned on for the spring. He sat on a bench and stared at the three goddess-like figures representing the sea, the stars, and the wind – a gift of the DuPont family who thought the original bronze statue of Samuel DuPont an insufficient memorial to their ancestor. The sound of the water soothed Unger's mind, but could not drown out the living hell his life had become over the last several days.

Vice President Paul Shelby was dead, and Unger had been in custody a good portion of the time following the killing. Largely deprived of sleep while being asked seemingly the same questions over and over again by Secret Service detectives, he lost all conception of time. His body literally ached from fatigue and even after his release and a long sleep his head was still pounding. He needed more than a walk to clear his head. He needed coffee. He got up from his bench, headed up New Jersey Avenue toward his favorite coffee shop across the street from his apartment at The Cairo.

Along Q Street, Unger noticed his reflection in the window of one of the brown stone embassies, confirming he looked as bad as he felt. His clothes were wrinkled, his hair messed, and the bags under his eyes were so dark it looked like someone had punched him. He felt so bad, maybe someone had actually decked him and he just did not remember.

Outside the coffee shop, Unger looked at a copy of the *Washington Post* in a news rack simply to check the date. Headlines about the continuing investigation into the death of Vice President Shelby forced him to dig into his pocket for change. He sat down on one of the metal chairs outside the café. Tossing open the paper, he scoured the stories. Pictures from the funeral and promises from the President about getting to the bottom of the assassination filled the pages.

Once Unger finished reading the lead story, he quickly scanned the rest of the paper. Since he was in custody while the story developed, Unger was short on exact details. The stories in the *Post* started filling in gaps.

While Unger was in transit between Los Angeles and Washington, Shelby went through his regular routine. Everything was running on schedule and uneventfully until the Vice President decided to walk the rope line before the event. Slow motion YouTube videos showed the Vice President pulling a pen from his pocket, placing the cap between his teeth, and then having the top portion of his head blown off by a small incendiary explosion. Conspiracy theories abounded.

Unaware as he was of the details of the Vice President's murder, his own interrogation was tedious. The initial questions about his knowledge of explosives and trigger devices were mystifying. Of course, once Agent Scott Proctor told him the way Shelby died, the previous hours of questioning made sense. Now, reading stories about the assassination, he began to think through the thousands of questions, desperately trying to remember exactly how he answered.

Unger thought about the place the explosion took place – along the rope line. It did not make sense to him. The place was so public.

Of course, what made less sense to Unger was the other line of questioning he dealt with while in custody – questions about Unger's personal relationship with Shelby. He was not sure how questions about what they did in their 'private time' on the schedule mattered – nor did questions about who he dated in high school and college.

Despite understanding his Miranda rights, Unger refused to have an attorney present during his questioning. He knew he was innocent in the Vice President's death and he certainly had nothing to hide. At the time, he believed the White House would assist him in clearing up his daily schedule with Shelby. He thought "lawyering-up" would only make his superiors at the White House suspicious. Still, despite his refusal of an attorney, when Unger was finally released, he was warned not to report to the White House until further notice.

Unger's bad news did not stop with banishment from the White House. When he finally got home to his apartment at The Cairo, it was a wreck. Armed with a search warrant, federal agents ripped it to shreds. The search for evidence left him minus his desktop computer and with a tornado-style mess to clean up. The contents of every drawer were dumped on the floor. Every article of clothing was inspected and tossed onto the same pile. Even the refrigerator's contents were removed, examined and left on the kitchen counters to spoil. The place smelled awful, so awful he wanted to throw up.

Despite the clutter and smell, for the first day following his release David Unger just slept. He last shut his eyes on his commercial flight from Los Angeles. The events were taking their toll on him. He was physically and mentally exhausted. When he finally did return home, he marched past the mess, took two sleeping pills and fell into bed. Unger just closed his eyes, hoping against hope when he awakened, the whole atrocity would just be a bad dream.

It was not.

When Unger awoke, the mess was still in his home and still in his life. The new information Unger ascertained as he ventured out onto DuPont Circle in search of caffeine was not making things better.

Unger tossed the newspaper into a trash can, stood up and entered the coffee shop. Having spent just enough time off the road to get to know the baristas at the store, Unger greeted the cashier by name. "Hey, Molly," he said.

"Hey," she replied, the usual smile gone from her pierced lips.

Trying to act like nothing was amiss, Unger continued. "Been out of town for a while," he said nodding, hands in pockets. "Good to be home though."

Molly was having none of it. "What do ya need?" she asked in a tone of voice indicating she was not far from adding the word 'asshole' to her query.

Nervously shifting his weight from side-to-side, Unger said, "Large vanilla latte, skim milk with an extra shot of espresso."

As Molly went about making Unger's drink, all further attempts at conversation with the young tattooed woman failed. Large vanilla latte in hand, Unger sat down at a table and pulled out his smart phone. He barely registered the missed calls from his grandparents. He was not up to talking to them yet.

Unger was not particularly surprised when his attempt to log onto the White House server was met with a system error message. When Unger was told he was banned from the White House, he assumed he was going to be shut out from his official email account. The attempt was more of a confirmation.

Unger started to log onto his personal email account when he heard his name emanating from the television in the coffee shop. He looked up to see a photo of him and Vice President Shelby on the screen.

"As we reported exclusively last night, sources close to the investigation into the death of Vice President Paul Shelby have informed CNN that agents are focusing on this man, in charge of Shelby's advance detail, David Unger." His heart skipped a beat as the screen flashed his grainy college year book photo. Hand visibly shaking, Unger slowly lowered his drink to the table.

"Authorities are apparently looking into Unger's mental stability and are focusing on some papers he wrote in college. Unger, a recent hire at the White House, was released from custody yesterday by authorities who nevertheless are keeping him at the top of their list of suspects."

Unger's could not look away. It was all too surreal.

"Since we initially reported this story, we have learned David Unger is from North Dakota and currently lives in the DuPont Circle section of Washington."

Instantly, Unger felt the stares of those in the café. Cold, angry accusing eyes were all focused on him as the man who looked remarkably like the man from DuPont Circle on the television screen. One person snapped a picture on her cell phone and immediately began texting it to her friends.

Unger grabbed his coffee, stood up and exited the coffee shop. His heart racing, it suddenly seemed as if everyone on the street was looking at him. Avoiding all eye contact, he quickly crossed the street. The walk back to his home seemed to take longer than normal. Unger felt the stares from all angles.

While walking, Unger dialed the personal cell phone of his boss, Chief of Staff Jon Dosser. "Mr. Dosser," he said in a harried tone. "This is David Unger."

"David?" Dosser replied. "Where the hell are you?"

"Headed home," Unger said. "I just saw the news story. Holy cow, sir. I had nothing to do with the death of the Vice President."

There was silence on the other end. "You gotta believe me, sir." He was relieved to hear the reply.

"I do, son," Dosser replied. "But I can't talk to you anymore about it. The Secret Service locked your office down. I think you need to go home and find a lawyer."

"But ..." Unger protested.

"But nothing," Dosser replied.

"If I get a lawyer everyone will think I'm guilty," Unger said as he looked around for whoever might be listening. He lowered his voice. "I didn't do anything."

"Look, David," Dosser said. "I know it's hard to wrap your arms around this whole thing, but you've got to get your head together."

Unger began to tear up at the thought. "My head together," he exclaimed. Dosser obviously was not listening. "About what? I don't know anything. I didn't do anything."

"Maybe," Dosser whispered. "But your name is out there and until another name comes to light, you're the one in the public eye."

"I'm ..." Unger tried to speak, but words did not come out.

"This shit is serious, David. I can't say anything else and you shouldn't either."

The phone went dead. Unger's head was spinning. He tried to figure out his next move. Instead of taking Dosser's advice and calling an attorney, Unger decided to call Scott Proctor at the Secret Service. Proctor had interrogated him endlessly before releasing him, but maybe he could plead his case to Proctor again. As he hustled back to his building, he placed the call. When Unger got no response, he decided against leaving a message. Instead, he texted Proctor and asked him to call.

Wanting to avoid all human contact, Unger walked past the elevators and headed up the stairs to the seventh floor where his small, exposed-brick studio apartment was located. He was surprised to find his door slightly ajar. Unger slowly pried the door open with the palm of his hand. He walked around the corner to notice a short, stubby man in a dark suit, white shirt, and red tie sitting at his kitchen table. His face was puffy, with jet black hair, slicked back with gel.

Unger immediately took him for one of the authorities who had torn his home apart, "Jesus Christ," Unger said angrily as he set his coffee down in front of the stranger. "I still haven't cleaned up the mess you made the first time you were here."

Little Stubby offered no response and stared emotionlessly at Unger.

Although Unger waived his right to an attorney during the interrogation, he was pissed about the intrusion and the mess they left in his apartment the last time. "I hope you have a warrant," he warned.

An evil grin spread across the man's face at the naïve statement by Unger. "I ain't from the government," Little Stubby replied, standing up as he spoke. "And I ain't got no warrant."

Heart beating quickly, Unger took in several details at once. He gasped, noticing the blue latex gloves and the huge bulge under Little Stubby's jacket that could only be a gun. Fear and adrenaline shook his body as he turned quickly and moved back towards the door. His retreat took him straight into a massive body. Unlike the other man, this guy was the exact opposite – tall and thick.

Dressed in a maroon running suit, Tall and Thick had olive skin and a buzz haircut. He wore a bunch of chains around his neck – several of which were adorned with medallions on them. Unger ran into the man with a grunt.

When the two collided, Unger must have caught him slightly off guard because Tall and Thick momentarily lost his balance and stumbled backwards. His right foot landed on one of the piles of clothes left in the middle of the room by the FBI. "You little sonofabitch," Tall and Thick growled as he went tumbling backwards into the table where Unger's television was located. The television and the man both went crashing to the ground.

Unger spun around and ducked toward the front door of his apartment. He closed the door behind him and then kicked it back open into Little Stubby's face, knocking him backwards on top of Tall and Thick. Heart racing even faster, Unger sprinted down the hall to the stairwells.

The stairwells located on either end of The Cairo always looked to Unger like something out of a cliché horror movie. When he walked them for exercise, he always imagined a grade-B character actor's body hurled down its center crevice to a bloody death on the tile floor below. Now, as he raced down the stairs, he hoped the body would not be his. He realized he had about a floor and a half lead when he heard the door open on the seventh floor above him as his unknown pursuers made chase.

Using his arm like a slingshot on the banister, Unger willed his body down the stairs at a pace he never imagined possible. Still the descent seemed to take twice as long as the slow walk he took up them only moments earlier, counting as he went – fourth floor, third, second. All the while, he was hearing two sets of feet pounding to catch up with him from above.

The stairwell door flew open as Unger burst into the stylish lobby. He shot out the front door with equal force. He took the five front stone steps in one long stride, fell onto the sidewalk, rolled twice and came up running across Q Street. A car screeched to a stop and a cab driver blew his horn as Unger cut in front of his bright yellow vehicle. Unger took in deep breaths as he ran as fast as he could into the coffee shop. With each step, Unger waited for a gunshot to end his life. As he entered the building, he looked back and saw Little Stubby losing ground on the steps with Tall and Thick just exiting the building.

Little Stubby bounced off the hood of a taxi and rolled across the quarter panel. He hit the pavement hard.

"Get your ass up," Tall and Thick snapped as he ran past Little Stubby.

In the coffee shop, Unger side swiped a customer, ran past Molly the barista, and hit the back door with a full head of steam. A fire alarm sounded as he threw open the door marked "Emergency Exit." A fence surrounding a bordering baseball field left him with two options – either circle back to his left or turn right and head toward DuPont Circle. He instinctively chose the right and cut up a second alley paralleling the ball field's left foul line. A short street appeared and he cut to his right.

With the alarm blaring, Tall and Thick rushed full speed into the store and collided head-on with the woman Unger spun around only moments before. The crash sent both of them sprawling onto the floor in a heap of bodies and hot espresso. Tall and Thick let out a string of curses as the woman began to scream.

Molly the barista grabbed her cell phone to call the police when Little Stubby ran into the store. She dropped the phone to the floor when Little Stubby pointed his gun at her. He picked up his partner and they both hustled out into the alley. Seeing no sign of Unger along the ball field fence, Little Stubby shouted they should split up. Each ran in an opposite direction.

Tall and Thick ran right and then headed down the alley parallel to the outfield of the ball park. When he got to the short street, he saw an older man tossing trash bags into a dumpster. "You see anyone run out this way?" Tall and Thick asked.

The man looked disinterested as he pointed towards the main drag. "That way," he said. "Took a left up there."

"He's headed up to DuPont Circle," Tall and Thick yelled to Little Stubby as they both ran up their respective ends of the alley and turned towards DuPont Circle in a full trot.

Chapter 9

Leo Argo nearly collapsed through the door of the townhouse he shared with CIA Director Jane Kline. He had been running almost nonstop since first getting the telephone call about Vice President Paul Shelby's assassination. He flew to Los Angeles in a military jet within an hour of the incident with nothing more than his emergency travel bag under his arm, working nonstop since then. Sleeping on the fly, Argo was under pressure from the Director of the FBI to produce results quickly. The declaration by the Secret Service that the Vice President's advance man was the primary suspect was enough for Director Cicero to order Argo home.

The Old Town Alexandria townhouse looked like an oasis to Argo. He shared the comfortable digs with Jane Kline and their black Labrador retriever named Hoover. Kline and Argo met while Kline was still an operative working in Romania. When Kline lost her leg in a bomb attack taking the life of former CIA Director Ellsworth Steele, Argo was the one who helped her recover physically and emotionally. They became roommates thereafter.

When Argo walked through the door of their townhouse, both Kline and Hoover were there to greet him.

"Hey, baby," Kline said as she placed her cane against the wall and hugged Argo around the neck. She kissed him and then drew back. "You look like hell."

"Thanks for noticing," Argo laughed, looking at his puffy, bloodshot eyes in the entry hall mirror. "Unfortunately, you're right. I do look like hell." He paused for effect. "I think you should leave me."

"You're not the first rugged cowboy I've ever dined with," Kline replied.

"I'm not?" Argo said, feigning disappointment.

"No," Kline teased. "But, stick around. Who knows? You might just get lucky tonight."

Argo narrowed his eyes. "Were you this easy with the other cowboys?" he asked.

"Yeah," Kline laughed. "I have a fetish for big disheveled Cubans who look like they haven't slept in days. I can't get enough of them."

"So I shouldn't feel special," Argo replied. He released his hug on Kline and bent down. Their big Labrador bumped Argo's knees, nearly knocking him over. "At least Hoover isn't so judgmental about my looks." Argo tussled with the dog and then asked "And why not?" When the dog did not reply, Argo supplied the answer in baby talk. "Cause him's a big sweetie. Him doesn't judge me."

Kline shook her head. "I'm in long-term relationship with a man who issues statements in third person on behalf of his dog."

"Well, who else will speak up for Hoover?" Argo asked. And again in a baby voice he said, "Certainly not the mean lady who thinks I look like Fidel's disheveled half-brother."

Kline laughed. "You're a moron," she said. Kline grabbed her cane and hobbled toward the kitchen. "When you're finished removing yourself from the cross, I just brewed up a fresh pot of coffee for you."

"Sorry boy," Argo said, rubbing Hoover behind the ears. "I gotta go. I need the caffeine." Argo stood up and followed Kline to find her pouring two cups of coffee. Hoover followed them both and flopped onto the tile floor. A small television on the kitchen counter was tuned to a cable channel playing soft jazz. Crooner Landau Eugene Murphy, Jr. was singing "Fly Me to the Moon."

"Cheers," Kline said, handing a mug to Argo. "I'm glad you're home."

"Me too," Argo replied, clinking his glass against Kline's. He sniffed the aroma before taking a sip. "God, it's good to be home. I'm beat. So how was your day yesterday?"

"Chinese cyber terrorism and Russian war ships in Havana," Kline responded before enjoying a taste of coffee for herself.

"So standard meat and potatoes," Argo laughed.

"Pretty much," Kline said. "You know, we're getting too old for this shit."

"You've been thinking about a liveaboard in the Keys again?" Argo asked. Their last vacation was spent on a 43 foot house boat in Marathon – a point of discussion more than once since they returned.

"It was a one-floor plan with no steps," Kline replied jokingly.

Argo pondered the ten days they spent fishing, swimming and drinking wine. "It would be nice to enjoy time alone without your staff briefing you three times a day on what was happening in some remote corner of the world."

Kline walked to the refrigerator and took out some cream cheese. "Speaking of staff briefings, my crew briefed me before I came home last night," she said. "The Service released your man Unger yesterday, but they still think he's your main culprit."

"I know," Argo replied with doubt shading his voice.

"You don't sound convinced." Kline cut off a slice of cheese and handed it to Argo.

Argo took the cream cheese and spread some across a bagel before popping a portion in his mouth. "I'm not," he said. "I argued with one of the Secret Service guys about it before I left LA."

"You?" Kline said mockingly. "Leo Argo – argumentative? I find it so hard to believe."

"Crazy as it sounds," Argo said. "But it happened."

"So what does your gut tell you," asked Kline. "Your instincts are as good as anyone downtown."

"Well," Argo took another sip of coffee. "There is a shitload of circumstantial evidence pointing to Unger, but apparently not enough to hold him. If he's guilty, why release him?"

"And your gut tells you he's not the guy?"

"It's not my gut," Argo replied. "This Unger guy may well be the killer."

"But ..." Kline begged the question.

"But everybody is so anxious to name him as the killer," Argo said. "It's bad politics to have an anonymous killer running around out there, especially one responsible for killing a national leader. So they gotta get a name and they gotta get it now."

"Something to be said for action," Kline said, playing a bit of the devil's advocate. "We don't want the people in a panic."

Argo held up his hand. "No party line, Jane," he said. "Not today anyway. I'm seriously concerned we're overlooking something in the name of political expediency. I mean, do you think it was Unger, or at the very least someone who used Unger?"

Kline kissed Argo lightly. "Bright line," she smiled. "You just crossed it."

"Aw, come on …"

"No pillow talk," Kline insisted. "Those are the rules we both agreed to when you moved in."

Argo nodded. "You're right," he said. "I'm just not buying the motive."

"Which is the obsessed gay admirer thing?" Kline offered.

"Yeah," Argo replied. "You don't seem shocked."

"Baby," Kline said. "I've traveled the world as a CIA operative. We bought elected officials in other countries with something as simple as a blow job from a hooker in the men's room. Nothing shocks me anymore."

"But, if jilted love is the motive," Argo continued "there were so many other opportunities for an easy kill. Why go through the problems and uncertainty with a public hit in LA?"

"Good question," Kline replied. "But, then again, he had access and a possible motive. Maybe he's your guy."

"Maybe," Argo nodded. "It's just too flimsy for me. I'd like to see some forensics before we wrap a bow on it." As Argo took the final sip from his mug and held it out to Kline for a refill, his cell phone rang. He pulled it out and looked at the number. It was the Director's private line.

FBI Director Rob Cicero was a broad-shouldered hulk of a man who once played college football for Notre Dame. His bald head would wrinkle up and turn red when agitated. When Argo answered, Cicero dispensed with any pleasantries. "Go to secure and call me back."

Argo dialed the number scrambling secure calls, placed his PIN into the system and then Cicero's number, who picked it up before the first ring ended. "What the hell is going on Leo?" barked Cicero.

Argo was caught off guard by the Director's demeanor. "I'm not sure what you mean, sir."

"Are you near a television?" the Director continued.

"Yes, sir." Argo motioned to Kline to hand him the remote control for the kitchen television.

"Well, turn on CNN," Cicero directed.

Argo grabbed the remote, changed the channel and turned up the volume. "Breaking News" was flashing across the top of the screen and "Shelby's Killer On The Run" was ribboned across the bottom. The video displayed the Secret Service talking to several local DC officers in front of the building where David Unger lived.

"What in the hell is happening down in DuPont Circle?" Cicero asked, continuing his interrogation.

"I just got home, sir," Argo replied. "And I have no idea what's going on at this scene on television."

"I know you've been on the road a lot the last week, Leo," Cicero offered, trying to calm his voice. "But I need you downtown right now. Get down there and find out what in the blazes is going on."

"Yes, sir," Argo replied and clicked off his phone. He did not have to say anything to Kline. It was hard to tell which pair of eyes showed more disappointment. "I gotta go," Argo sighed.

"It's part of the job," Kline said as she kissed him.

Argo responded by grabbing Kline's ass. "Rain check?"

"You sound awfully confident," Kline smiled.

"Next time I'm home for more than a quick cup of coffee, you'd better saddle up for this cowboy."

Chapter 10

Walk around the first floor of Kentucky's state capitol building in Frankfort and eventually you will likely find the bust of Col. Harlan Sanders, the holder of eleven secret herbs and spices and founder of Kentucky Fried Chicken. The building is a grand structure made of granite and limestone housing all three branches of state government. Completed in 1910, the interior of the building uses a combination of gray, white and dark green marble to create an elegant expanse. In the center of the building's rotunda is a statue of Kentucky native, President Abraham Lincoln. Kentucky was a neutral state during the Civil War, and just over Lincoln's shoulder is a statue of another Kentucky native – Jefferson Davis, President of the Confederacy. As if by design, keeping an eye on both of them is a statue of the Great Compromiser from Kentucky, Senator Henry Clay. Small and intimate, the rotunda is the perfect place for public announcements.

This day the rotunda was packed with people and the capitol abuzz with excitement. The voices of reporters, party faithful and state employees were all amplified by the echo off the marble walls. Earlier in the morning, news sources announced that Kentucky's senior Senator, Mack Wilson, resigned from office. If the announcement of Wilson's sudden departure from the US Senate was causing a stir in Frankfort, the news Governor Robin Latimer was immediately ready to announce Wilson's replacement was causing a media whirlwind. Every news outlet in the state was jockeying for camera and microphone position to have the best shot for their newscast.

Their iPhone video cameras in hand, a group of print journalists covering the state political beat hovered near the entrance to the

Governor's office, hoping to get the first shots of whomever walked out when Latimer opened her door.

"Anybody got any idea on who it is?" asked Joe Barth from Louisville, his graying goatee bouncing with excitement.

"I'm sure as heck not going to tell you," replied William Hammer from a rival newspaper in Lexington. The bald veteran reporter was straight-laced and one of the few around the state house who was never heard to utter a curse word.

A female reporter from Northern Kentucky, Sally Von Schultz laughed. "So you don't know either, do you Bill?"

Hammer smiled sheepishly as his cheeks reddened. "No," he laughed. "The Latimer folks kept this one close."

"Think she'll appoint herself?" Barth asked.

"No," Von Schultz was the first to respond. "You gotta believe she's drooling to be in the United States Senate, but appointing herself is too risky. If she moved herself to the top of the list, she may not even survive a primary."

"You think Barkman is on the list of potential appointees?" Hammer tossed out to the other two.

"Too young," Von Schultz said.

"Too popular," Barth interjected with authority.

"You sure?" Hammer nodded his head in the direction of the stairs leading up from the basement, where Josh Barkman bounded up the steps two at a time. The reporters rushed to the stairs and swarmed the young, bushy-haired Congressman as he reached the top.

Josh Barkman was a baby-faced rookie, fresh out of college when he entered politics as a staffer for Richard Thompson's first run for United States Congress. Barkman certainly matured in the years since his first race, yet the second-term Congressman's cherubic appearance made him seem younger. After a time as Thompson's Chief of Staff on the Hill, Barkman spent a couple years in Europe working for the US government in various roles. When Thompson announced he would not seek reelection as Kentucky's Fourth District Congressman, Barkman moved to Kentucky and won the seat. Single, handsome and possessing a mischievous, boyish charm, Barkman was listed in an inside-Washington publication as one of the nation's "most eligible bachelors."

"Congressman Barkman," Von Schultz said excitedly, trying to get the first question in. "What brings you to Frankfort? Is Governor Latimer appointing you to the open Senate seat?"

"I'm in Frankfort because the House will not reconvene until next week," Barkman said matter-of-factly. "We're still in our official days of mourning due to the death of Vice President Shelby. And 'no,' Sally – Governor Latimer is not appointing me to the US Senate."

"Then why are you here?" asked Hammer.

"The same reason you are, Bill," Barkman said as someone reached through the gaggle of reporters and shook the Congressman's hand. Barkman nodded an acknowledgement at the person as he continued to speak. "I want to see who will be representing me in the United States Senate."

Barth squared his phone camera before he asked his question. "Did Governor Latimer seek your counsel regarding the appointment?" asked Barth.

"She did," Barkman replied. He smiled softly. "And before you ask the follow up question, the answer is 'no.' I do not care to share with you the details of my discussions with Governor Latimer. How's that for a YouTube moment?"

Just as Barth started to respond, a commotion began around the governor's office. The reporters around Congressman Barkman dropped their questioning and scurried quickly to the entrance to Governor Latimer's door as she appeared with four other people.

"I'll be a son of a biscuit eater," said Hammer as he was the first to spot the Thompson family – Richard, Ann and their two kids. Successfully kept from the spotlight while in office, the Thompson children were now college students.

Barkman walked up behind the reporter and placed his hand on Hammer's shoulder. "Now, Bill," he warned jokingly. "Watch your language. Biscuit eater is pretty strong for you."

Hammer felt the hand and looked around. "No wonder you're here," he smiled over his shoulder. "I should have figured this out, but Thompson never really crossed my mind."

Governor Latimer made her way to Barkman. "Congressman," she said wryly. "Whatever on earth are you doing here today?"

"There was a hearing on clean coal technology in the state house today and thought I'd drop by to learn a thing or two. While I was in the building, I thought I'd come over and rub the boot of Abraham Lincoln for good luck," Barkman laughed. "It looks like you've got a press conference going on or something."

"Or something," Latimer said as she continued pushing her way through the crowd.

When Ann approached Barkman, she hugged him warmly. Ann and Richard Thompson thought of Barkman as if he was one of their own sons. Ann, in particular, was very close to him. "Thanks for being here, Josh," Ann said. "It really means a lot to us."

"Are you kidding me?" Barkman replied. "I wouldn't have missed this for the world."

Cameras were all focused on Thompson as he shook hands with his mentee. "Congressman," Thompson said respectfully as he pumped Barkman's hand.

"Boss," Barkman stumbled on his words. "Sorry, some habits die hard. I mean, Senator."

All of them walked to the podium holding the Great Seal of the Commonwealth of Kentucky. Once the crowd of party faithful saw who accompanied the Governor, there was an audible gasp, followed by murmurs and then polite applause. Since leaving office, Thompson showed little interest in public life. He stayed away from party events and, at times, openly criticized the party. He was not exactly coming back into the game riding the same wave of popularity he felt when he left office.

Governor Latimer quieted the crowd and pulled a prepared text from a lower shelf on the podium. "Ladies and Gentlemen of the Commonwealth – as you all well know, Mack Wilson tendered his resignation to our seat in the United States Senate. I join with all

Kentuckians in thanking Senator Wilson for his many years of dedicated service to our nation and to the Commonwealth. But the job of governing must go on in these difficult times. While we are all still mourning the loss of Vice President Paul Shelby, we must be ready to address the important issues pending before the Senate when they reconvene next week."

Ann reached over and grabbed Thompson's hand.

"Leaving me with the tough decision of whom to appoint to fill Senator Wilson's seat in the United States Senate. I considered several names, but I kept coming back to one." Governor Latimer paused and looked towards Thompson. "And as you can see, he is with us today – former Fourth District Congressman, Richard Thompson."

Polite applause followed as Thompson nodded an acknowledgement.

Latimer's Chief of Staff handed her a piece of paper and a pen. "By executing this Executive Order, I am asking the President of the Senate to immediately seat Richard Thompson as the Junior Senator from Kentucky." To another round of light applause, Governor Latimer signed the Executive Order, turned and then handed the ceremonial pen to Ann.

Thompson kissed Ann. "Damn," he whispered in her ear sarcastically. "Can't ya just feel the love in the room?"

Ann turned her head and whispered back, "No one said this was going to be easy." She nodded towards the kids. "We believe."

Thompson and Ann then took a moment to hug their children before shaking hands with the Governor and everyone on the stage, including Congressman Barkman. "Regular lunch on Tuesdays?" he asked jokingly as he shook his mentor's hand.

"Don't get used to it," Thompson replied. "I don't plan to be there long."

"Right," Barkman said skeptically.

Thompson turned, walked to the podium and nodded an appreciative acknowledgement first to the Governor and then to the Congressman. He took a deep breath. "Thank you, Governor Latimer," Thompson said as he pulled a single piece of paper from his coat pocket containing the comments Michael Griffith helped him prepare. Thompson and Latimer agreed it would be best if Griffith did not attend the announcement and he was hidden back in the Governor's Mansion watching from Latimer's private study.

Thompson began his short talk with the obligatory thank you comments to everyone from Governor Latimer to his wife and kids, which caused his voice to crack slightly. The text was short and to the point, attempting to assure everyone he harbored no intention to seek the nomination for the seat in the next election. When he finished his prepared text, he calmly refolded the speech and carefully placed it back in his coat pocket. "Before I turn it over to the press for a few questions," Thompson said. "I have a few things from the heart I'd like to say to the people of Kentucky."

Back in the Governor's Mansion, Griffith leaned forward. They rehearsed a few questions from the press, but Thompson failed to mention anything about impromptu remarks. Griffith always became nervous when his candidates strayed from the script and, despite their long-standing friendship, Thompson's deviation was no exception. Griffith shook his head, knowing he should have expected this. "The boy always finds a way to go off script," he mumbled to himself.

"When I left public office," Thompson said, "so many people supported my decision with their thoughts and prayers. Still, a few looked at my decision with great skepticism – thinking of it as just a political stunt. 'He'll jump back into the game' they said."

Thompson paused and pursed his lips. "I can assure you the honor of representing the good people of the Commonwealth in the United States Senate will be purely temporary. When I said I will not seek the nomination of my party for the position in the next election, you can take it to the bank."

"Instead," Thompson continued, "I am doing this to prove a point made by our Founders who suggested the Congress should be made up of citizen legislators, who leave their homes and put their own interests aside to act for the good of the people. When they are done, they return to their jobs, families, and communities."

"And besides," he continued. "If I tried to run again, my wife would beat the heck out of me and my kids would hold me down while she did it." Laughter echoed off the walls of the rotunda.

Back at the Governor's Mansion, Griffith smiled approvingly at the off-the-cuff comments. "Don't tell me you don't miss it," he said out loud to no one. "You miss it like Fredo Corleone missed free hookers."

"Now, Governor Latimer, if you'll join me back at the podium," Thompson said pointing at the throng of reporters in front of them. "I have the distinct impression some of these folks have a few questions they'd like to ask us." As Latimer approached, reporters began shouting questions with the intense fervor of a White House briefing.

Sitting back in his chair watching the scene unfold on television, Michael Griffith smiled. "He's back," he mumbled to himself. As soon as he realized he was by himself, he slapped his knee. "Hot spit, Richard Thompson is back."

Chapter 11

Senator Mack Wilson's massive frame cut a wide swath wherever he went. His booming, authoritative voice could grab the attention of the highest official testifying before his Foreign Affairs Committee. He was a popular figure with his colleagues on both sides of the aisle, spouting ideological party lines in public while brokering deals with the other side over alcohol inspired marathons of gin rummy in his private office.

Today, however, his bravado, stature and political gravitas were absent. Instead of being in his office on the Hill, he was in holed up in a sparsely furnished apartment in Cleveland Park – so close to the National Zoo he could hear the lions roar at feeding time. He was in hiding and scared.

Wilson picked up the remote control for his television and turned the volume down on the C-SPAN broadcast of Governor Latimer's press conference. He looked pale and tired. "I can't believe she gave my seat to such a goofy SOB," he mumbled. "Look," Wilson said, pointing at the image of Richard Thompson on the television screen. "He's a disgrace to the institution."

Jon Dosser looked emotionlessly at the screen. "A bit harsh, don't ya think?" he replied in a monotone.

"He's wearing an earring," boomed Wilson.

"So what?" Dosser replied, attempting to calm Wilson. "We've got more important items on our plate."

"My legacy is gone," Wilson boomed. "He's my replacement."

Dosser's voice remained steady. He put up with Wilson's tirades over many years and was bored with them. "He always was one of those flaky 'true believer' types. Your legacy is not important right now. We need to concentrate on the deal and on keeping you alive."

Wilson pounded his pudgy fist on the end table. "He'll get nothing accomplished up here," he said.

"You're assuming he's coming here to try to get something done," Dosser laughed. "Perhaps he wants just the opposite. Maybe he wants to prove the system is broken. People like him always want to show the world they are smarter than everyone else by pointing out the flaws in the system."

Wilson grunted an unconvinced acknowledgement. "How the hell did we get here, Jon?" he said. "A week ago I was a senior Senator and Chairman of the Foreign Relations Committee. Today I'm secretly living in a small apartment with used furniture."

"It could be worse," Dosser replied.

Wilson looked around the small, dirty apartment he was using literally as a hide-out. "I'm a Jimi Hendrix poster away from being back in college," Wilson said angrily as he looked out the window in disgust. His mood shifted as he answered pitifully, "I panicked, didn't I, Jon?"

Dosser knew the answer, but chose not to engage Wilson at this time. "I'm not sure, Mr. Chairman."

Wilson hung his head. "Don't call me Mr. Chairman anymore," he instructed. "I'm out. Remember?"

Dosser felt no interest in soothing Wilson's massive ego, but he needed him to remain calm. "Aren't you always supposed to address someone by the highest title they've held?"

"Yeah," Wilson nodded. "But I don't feel very important right now. Honorable Jackass is my new title."

Dosser walked up behind Wilson and placed his hand on his shoulder. For a fleeting moment, he honestly considered strangling him. "We'll get through this, Mack," Dosser said in an attempt to assuage Wilson.

"Easy for you to say, Jon," Wilson said as he patted Dosser's hand. "You're not in the crosshairs."

"I'm not so sure," Dosser replied.

"They don't know your involvement," Wilson said.

"Yet," Dosser said. "It's only a matter of time."

"I'm not in any position to tell anyone," Wilson said reassuringly.

Dosser patted Wilson on the shoulder. "I trust you, Mack," he lied.

Wilson looked over his shoulder. "I'm going crazy here, Jon."

"Well, you can't go out for a night on the town right now," Dosser replied. "We need you to stay low key."

"Think you could get me a bottle of scotch or something," Wilson asked, raising his eyebrows to indicate 'something' was not ice for the drinks. "I need a little companionship for the evening."

"I'll see what I can do," Dosser said, turning so Wilson could not see him roll his eyes.

"Here," Wilson said as he reached in his pocket and handed Dosser a card. "This is my escort service. You'll need to pay her for me and bring her here." When he saw Dosser's frown, he continued. "It's not like I can run down to the ATM right now."

Dosser took the card. "Sure," he said. "I'll send her over tonight."

"Damn." Wilson hung his head. "How did I get here?"

Dosser nodded back at the television in an attempt to redirect Wilson's attention and self-pity. "He's a caretaker," he said. "You heard him say he wasn't going to seek the nomination."

"And you think he's telling the truth?" Wilson asked.

"Sure," Dosser said. "If he tries to run, Latimer will cut his balls off."

"Yeah," Wilson laughed at the thought. Even while wallowing in his own self-pity, he could see the humor. "She wanted to appoint herself so badly." Wilson held his thumb and forefinger about an inch apart. "She was this close. You know it drove her nuts to give it to someone else. She could taste it."

Dosser nodded his agreement.

"She cut a deal," Wilson continued, referring to Latimer's appointment of Thompson. "Michael Griffith is behind it. Hell, Griff probably already got Thompson to sign Latimer's nomination petition."

"Calm down."

"Calm down, my ass," Wilson bellowed. "I can see him walking around the governor's office in those dirty jeans and cowboy boots – quoting lines from *The Godfather.* I hate the sonofabitch."

Wilson got up from his chair and walked over to the small galley kitchen in the apartment. "Thompson is another story," he said. "His idealism could be a thorn in the side of the administration for the next election," Wilson reached into the refrigerator for a soft drink.

"You've got to let it go, Mr. Chairman" Dosser replied keeping his eyes on the television rather than Wilson. "We've got far more important things to deal with right now."

Wilson took a drink of his diet soda. "I know, I know," he said. "I shouldn't have quit. I panicked."

"No shit," Dosser was now ready to agree with Wilson's statement.

"But you said yourself," Wilson continued. "Shelby's assassination was a message to me. You said so, Jon."

"And I meant it," Dosser replied. "I just never thought you'd quit before we talked again."

"If they got to Shelby, they could sure as hell can get to me," Wilson said.

"What's done is done," Dosser said. "Direct your attention to figuring a way out of this. If you can get this thing resolved quickly enough, I will talk to the President about naming you as Shelby's replacement." He did not want to tell him about Ambassador Crump being named to head up the search. He would have to plan when to drop that little bombshell.

Wilson's eyes lit up. "You think he'd consider it?"

"You were already vetted," Dosser said. "I mean, I handled your file personally. Remember?"

"Yeah."

Dosser turned to Wilson, thinking out loud as he moved. "We can spin it as you wanted to show your commitment to the President by getting out of the Senate before the process began."

Wilson was buying into the plan. "It might work," he said.

"But you've got to figure out a way to square it with the Russians," Dosser pointed a finger at Wilson. "Maybe we could use Thompson to run interference."

"Thompson's flaky enough to oppose the pipeline," Wilson said. "But he'll have no real influence on the outcome."

"The key is dragging it out," Dosser concluded.

"Exactly," Wilson replied as he began to pace back and forth. "Let's get a back channel to the Russians about how my support for the pipeline was forced by Shelby. I was all in, but he forced me to play both sides." He paused. "If it works, you can have Paul's share of the money."

That is what Dosser wanted to hear. He sat down on the couch. "I can tell them we're putting you in the number two slot to increase the environmental regulations for the pipeline. The right influence could push construction back decades."

"They've got to agree," Wilson replied. "Gas supply to Eastern Europe is the key for them. If North American oil stays out of Europe, they win the next Cold War without even trying."

Dosser nodded, contemplating the action. "This plan requires three things, sir."

"What three things are those?" Wilson said as he sat down next to Dosser.

"First, we have to get all the files out of your office and off your computer," Dosser said. "When you panicked and walked away you left too many fingerprints at the office."

Wilson nodded and thought for a minute. "Reach out to MacNamara," he said.

"Your press secretary?" Dosser asked.

"Yeah," Wilson nodded. "He's a real prick. Offer him something at the White House, but tell him he needs to do some house cleaning first. We need those files."

"Got it," Dosser replied. "It should be easy. We'll have plenty of slots for guys like him. Secondly, we have to make sure David Unger takes the fall for the assassination."

"Won't he tell a different story?" Wilson asked.

"Of course he will," Dosser replied. "Which is the reason we need to make sure he never gets the chance to talk. I've got some guys on it."

"What's the third thing?" Wilson asked. "You said there were three things for the plan to work."

"Yeah," Dosser said. "This may be the hardest one." Dosser stood up and headed for the door.

"What?"

"We've got to keep you alive long enough to pull it off."

Chapter 12

Outside The Cairo, FBI Agent Leo Argo looked up at the two grinning gargoyles guarding the building's entrance from high above. "What are you smiling at?" he mumbled as he ducked under yellow tape guarding his second crime scene in as many days. He barely made it back to his town house from LA when he got the call to suit up and head downtown to DC.

Back on his home turf, Argo did not have to flash his badge to get through the maze of agents blocking the street and guarding the check points. They all knew him and cleared a path. He left his car in the middle of the barricaded street and was met at the entrance by Scott Proctor of the Secret Service. The pair exchanged pleasantries as they walked up to the lobby. "You know this is the tallest building in DC?" Proctor said.

"Yeah?" Argo replied.

Proctor pointed skyward. "They built this one so tall, everyone thought someone would try to build one taller. So they imposed a height limit on all new buildings."

"Thanks, Frank Lloyd," Argo huffed, tired and unimpressed by Proctor's knowledge of Washington's building codes. Actually, he was unimpressed by Proctor in general. It was more than simple inter-agency friction. Argo always thought Proctor was a little too aggressive at protecting interests of the residents of the White House – like he had a personal interest in their future.

The pair did not speak again until the elevator doors were closed. "What we got here?" Argo asked.

Proctor pushed the button to the seventh floor. "Disturbance call to the home of one David Unger."

"Shelby's advance man." Argo replied. "Didn't you guys just spring him?"

"Yeah," said Proctor.

"And didn't you tail him?"

"Of course we did," Proctor said as the elevator bell dinged their arrival on the designated floor. "He went out for a walk this morning. First time he left his place since we cut him loose. Our guys watched from a car about a block away. Five minutes after Unger gets back from his walk, he came running out the front door with two males in hot pursuit."

"And I assume your guys lost all three of them," Argo said as he got off the elevator.

"Don't sound so damn pompous, Leo," Proctor shot back. "They ran into the coffee shop across the street. We followed, but all of them disappeared."

Argo walked past a uniformed officer guarding the front door and checked out Unger's apartment. "This place is a fucking pig sty," he said, looking around at the mess made by the initial search of the apartment. Shaking his head, Argo stepped over a pile of clothes and walked around the small flat, making a quick assessment of the scene.

"Your guys work," Proctor replied, referring to the mess made by the FBI during their search done while Unger was in custody. "Nice job."

"I'll make sure to send your compliments along the chain of command," Argo responded. He walked around the living room looking at the various piles of crap dumped unceremoniously around the floor. "I bet we didn't break the television," Argo mused as he gazed blankly at the Washington Monument from the apartment window, and contemplated what must have taken place. The apartment was small and it did not take him long to survey the entire premises.

When Argo's tour was complete, Proctor spoke. "We're assuming the guys chasing Unger were waiting for him when he got back from the coffee shop. The people down the hall heard some yelling and then people running down the stairwell."

"So he runs out of the building and back into the crowd?" Argo asked.

"Apparently," Proctor acknowledged.

"And we're sure the first guy through the door at the coffee shop was Unger?"

"Absolutely," replied Proctor. "The girl who runs the place knows him by name and said he'd just bought a coffee about ten minutes earlier."

"How about the two chasing him?" Argo asked.

"She'd never seen them before," Proctor said.

Argo nodded and made another pass around the apartment. He started to walk back out the door when something shiny on the floor caught his eye. He headed straight to the busted television and crouched down to get a better look. "Get me an evidence bag," he instructed.

Proctor walked over to a kit by the door, retrieved a bag and handed it to Argo "What the hell is this?" Proctor asked.

Argo took a pen from his pocket and nudged the item into the zip lock bag. "A boxing glove," Argo replied.

"A boxing glove?"

Argo stood up and held up the bag containing the charm. "Not just a boxing glove," Argo replied holding up the bag. "A Golden Glove – given to champions in junior amateur boxing. I won a couple myself back in the day." He eyed the glove closely. "I never read anywhere in the file David Unger was a boxer."

"Me neither." Proctor replied.

"Doesn't our intel say the exact opposite," Argo continued. "In fact, isn't Unger kind of on the nerdy side?"

"Oh, absolutely."

"Not a jock."

"No."

"Then this Golden Glove belongs to someone else."

Chapter 13

Little Stubby slowly dialed the number he had been avoiding. He hated to be the bearer of bad news – especially when it was being delivered on account of his own mistake. Tall and Thick watched nervously from a short distance away while his partner counted the rings, hoping against hope the person on the other end would just fail to answer. No such luck. The phone picked up on the third ring. Little Stubby turned his back on Tall and Thick and walked away as he anticipated the worst. And, in case he placed the blame on his partner, he did not want the big man to hear.

"Yeah," the voice responded.

Little Stubby paused to take a deep breath. "We fucked up," he announced.

"Not what I want to hear."

There was no good way for Little Stubby to present the news. "He got away," he said with a sigh.

"Please tell me this call is not happening" The voice was flat – emotionless. "Please tell me this is your bad attempt at a joke."

"It's no joke," Little Stubby scratched the back of his head.

"How in the name of hell could this happen?"

Little Stubby did not realize the question was rhetorical and started to tell the story. "Well, the place was a mess from the FBI raid and …"

"Shut up," the voice replied disgustedly.

Little Stubby tried to explain. "Well, you see you asked how this happened and I was trying to tell you …"

"I don't need to know details. All I need to know is you were hired to off some scrawny-ass kid and make it look like a suicide."

"I know, but ..."

"But nothing," the voice boomed. There was a pause as the person on the other end of the phone attempted to calm down. "I sent you to do a job and you failed."

"We haven't failed yet," Little Stubby said. "We can still get him."

"How?" the voice asked. "Unger is probably a hundred miles from here by now."

"I don't think so," Little Stubby replied. "He couldn't have gone too far. He was on foot and the place is crawling with cops. His face is all over television. My guess is he's hiding out somewhere.

"Where are you now? Are you still in the DuPont area?"

"Yeah." Little Stubby lied. "We're covering the street. The little punk shows as much as a pimple on his ass and he's ours."

"Good. Don't call me back with another fuck up. I need this kid gone." There were no other pleasantries or goodbyes. The line simply went dead.

Little Stubby walked back towards Tall and Thick. "We gotta find this kid before the cops," he said.

"How?"

Little Stubby shrugged his shoulders. "I don't know," he said. "But if we don't, we're dead men."

Chapter 14

When the last patron left the Blue Steel Café, Jared Willis locked the front door to the establishment. He still wore his chef's apron when he reached up and flipped the multi-colored rainbow sign on the front door window from the "Open" to the "Closed" side. He pulled down the blind on the door window.

A smallish man in his late forties, Willis was the well-known owner and chef at a popular bar about a block off DuPont Circle. Originally from the Northwest, he lived most of his adult life in DC. Having first come to the nation's political epicenter to work on Capitol Hill, he worked at bars in the evening to make ends meet. Eventually his passion for owning a business of his own overtook his passion for politics and he opened a bar near Capitol Hill that, like so many little bars on Capitol Hill, failed.

It was not until he met a wealthy gay man from the inner-power circle of DC he found people willing to invest in a more profitable venture. The Blue Steel Café became a staple in DuPont Circle thereafter.

Willis was in the alley earlier in the day tossing some garbage into the dumpster when a young man came tearing out of the fire exit of a neighboring coffee shop with a wild look on his face. Seeing fear in the young man's eyes and sensing his terror, Willis simply nodded towards steps and a basement door below his bar. Without hesitation David Unger entered Willis' bar and life.

The business day now over, Willis bypassed his normal routine of counting the drawer and preparing the nightly bank deposit. Instead he headed to the kitchen and opened the door to the establishment's walk-in refrigerator.

When Willis swung open the large door, there sat the nation's most wanted man – David Unger. Wearing a J. Crew heavy winter jacket Willis brought him from the bar's lost and found bin, Unger looked up with a sad, desperate expression on his face.

Looking at Unger sitting on a case of long-neck beers, Willis smiled. In fact, had Willis not comprehended the dire nature of Unger's situation, he might have burst into raucous laughter at the sight. "How ya holding up?" Willis asked sincerely, suppressing his odd sense of humor.

"Colder than blue blazes, man," Unger replied. His teeth literally clattered as he spoke. "I think I lost my left big toe about two hours ago."

"Come on out," Willis said.

Unger looked unsure.

"It's okay," Willis said. "We're closed for the night."

"Thank God," Unger replied. He did not need much encouragement and he hurried past Willis into the kitchen, rubbing his arms to get circulation flowing. "I'm freezing."

"Be glad it's not a weekend or you might be holed up in here for another day," Willis replied. "Tonight was a bit slow, so I ran everybody out and closed up early."

Unger's eyes shot around the room. The interior was long with an elaborate mahogany bar on one side taking up the entire length of the building. An open loft near the back overlooked the main floor.

Seeing Unger stare at the video screens hanging on the exposed brick walls and then the disco ball in the center of the room, Willis spoke up. "We move the tables out on Friday and Saturday nights for dancing."

"Dancing?" Unger sounded confused.

"It's a gay bar, son," Willis responded. "My customers like to dance."

Unger was not quite sure how to respond. He knew DuPont Circle was known for its establishments catering to the LBGT community. Guys at the White House teased him about living in DuPont. But since he did not frequent bars generally, let alone gay bars, he did not care. As he looked around with curiosity, his predicament came back to him. "And you're sure no one else is here," Unger asked.

"Yeah," Willis replied. "We're all shut down. I told the staff I'd clean up."

"And they didn't have a clue you were hiding me in the walk-in?"

Willis shook his head. "Nope. They all know the kitchen is pretty much off limits. Unless I give them a pass, they stay out of my domain."

"Thank you," Unger said. "I'm sorry you closed up early."

"Not a problem," Willis replied. "Drink orders were slowing down and the crowd was pretty thin anyway. Everybody looking for a pal for the night either found one or just went home alone to jack off."

Unger was a bit taken back by the frank statement, but quickly reassessed his quandary. While the Blue Steel Café was his first visit to a gay bar, he was not in a position to complain about the owner's bawdy attempt at humor.

"We never were properly introduced back in the alley this morning." Willis stuck out his hand. "I'm Jared Willis. I own this place – head chef and chief bottle washer."

Unger shook Willis' hand. "Yeah, thanks for saving my butt," he replied. "I'm ..." Unger hesitated. With his name being bantered around on the news, he paused and considered whether to give away his real name.

"You're David Unger," Willis replied.

Unger looked surprised Willis knew his name.

Willis laughed. "Dude," he said, "don't look so shocked. "Right now, everybody in DC knows who you are. Hell, probably everyone in the country knows your name."

Unger pursed his lips. "So, like I was saying, I'm David Unger."

"America's Most Wanted Man," Willis added, pointing to the door. "Or, at least, the most wanted man in DuPont Circle. Be thankful you're in my fridge. It's like an episode of *Cops* out there."

"Really?" Unger hoped his run from The Cairo went unnoticed.

"Right after you arrived," Willis said, "this place started crawling with police looking for you."

Unger blew out heavily as he shook his head at Willis. "I don't understand."

"What?"

"Why you didn't tell them I was here?" Unger asked nodding toward the street.

"I thought about it at first," Willis said. He took off his apron and walked behind the bar. "Drink? It's on the house."

"I don't drink," Unger replied. "But I sure could use some hot coffee."

Willis began to pour Unger a coffee and continued. "I was going to call the cops, but then I thought about the stories I was seeing about you on television." He finished pouring two cups. "I'm going to add some Irish whiskey to mine," he said. "You sure you won't join me."

"No," Unger replied as he reached for the cup. "Hot, black and strong is just fine."

"Just like I like my men," Willis said without missing a beat. "Anyway, when the news stories said they were looking at you as the prime suspect because of your 'close personal relationship' with Vice President Shelby, something didn't ring true with me." He passed the cup over to Unger, who took a sip and then cupped it in his palm to warm his hands.

"This is really good," Unger said savoring the taste as much as the warmth. Perplexed by the statement, he asked, "ring true?"

"Oh dear, you are corn-bred," Willis laughed. "Honey, unless my gaydar is way off, you're not an obsessed gay man stalking the late-Vice President."

Unger nearly spit up his coffee "Gay?"

Willis started cleaning up behind the bar. "Yeah," he replied. "What do you think 'close personal relationship' means?"

Unger pondered the question for a moment. "I hadn't thought about it," he said. "It means we were friends, I guess."

"Or lovers," Willis said matter of factly. "In the community, we know 'close personal relationship' is a straight person's way of saying queer."

Unger was suddenly confused on so many levels. "The community?"

"The gay people of the city," Willis said. "The community."

Unger looked at his drink and then up at Willis. "But I'm not gay."

"Precisely," Willis nodded. "Which is why before I contemplated calling the police, I called a very good friend of mine to gather a little dirt on you."

"Dirt?" Unger asked.

Willis shrugged his shoulders. "A good friend of mine – one of the investors in this café – is very well connected in the highest levels of government. I told him my situation and he made a few calls to people in the community who know you. None of them were buying the 'gay stalker' storyline."

It took a moment for the statement to sink in. Unger stood up and walked around and then looked at Willis as if the revelation hit him like a lightning bolt. "Oh my God," he declared. "Everyone thinks I'm queer." Understanding the nature of the insult he just hurled, he lamely added, "No offense."

Willis smiled softly. "So you have a conscience," he said pausing. "Considering your circumstances – no offense taken. Just remember, it's this queer who saved your ass from those two goons this morning and who's keeping you safe right now."

"I'm sorry," Unger was sincere in his apology. He sat back down at the bar and placed his head in his hands.

"Anyway, you're not in police custody right now, because my friend thought it best to hide you for a few days." Willis put his hand on Unger's shoulder in a comforting manner.

"I'm just going to turn myself in," Unger concluded.

"Bad move," Willis replied. "There will be a time to surrender. Right now, give my friend a few days to figure out the appropriate time."

"This is a nightmare." Unger exclaimed. "It's beyond comprehension."

Willis grabbed Unger's coffee and topped it off. "Well, my new friend," he said, "in the words of Lee Harvey Oswald – Mr. Unger, you are someone's patsy. It looks like someone is trying to frame you."

"This can't be happening." Unger exhaled heavily as he spoke.

"Those two men this morning," Willis asked. "Have you ever seen them before?"

"Never," Unger replied. "They were at my apartment when I came back from getting coffee."

"Well, they're not from this neighborhood," Willis said. "And they aren't cops."

Unger made the same assumption, but asked, "How do you know?"

"They hung around the block for about an hour or so," Willis said waving his hand in the direction of the front door. "They even came in and asked if I saw you again. But then the streets started crawling with cops and they disappeared."

"So there are a lot of cops out there?" Unger repeated.

"You better believe it," Willis said. "They are all over the place. They kept coming in all night hassling my customers and showing your picture to everyone in the place." He pointed at Unger, "You, my friend, are the nation's most wanted queer."

"You sure are frank," Unger replied.

"I grew up gay out west," Willis said. "I've earned it."

"Really?" Unger was surprised at the revelation. "You're from the west? Where?"

"Wyoming," Willis replied. "Just outside Jackson Hole. Please, no jokes."

Unger smiled. "I'm from North Dakota," he said. "We're practically neighbors."

Unger drank up the rest of his coffee in one contemplative gulp. "So what do I do now?" he asked.

"The streets were bustling after your little alley dash," Willis said. "There is no way David Unger can walk out of here tonight."

"Darn," was all Unger could muster.

"Yeah," Willis replied. "One step on the street and, within a block, you're in custody."

Unger shook his head. "So what do I do?"

"Well," Willis replied. "David Unger is the most wanted man in DC."

"You've made the point."

"So, we've got to get rid of David Unger."

Chapter 15

"Good evening, Madame Director." The President stuck out his hand to welcome CIA Director Jane Kline.

Kline returned the firm handshake. "Mr. President," she replied.

"How's the wheel feel?" Rohman pointed to Kline's prosthetic leg.

"Pretty good," Kline nodded politely. She did not like her injury being the center of a conversation, but it was hard to deny a comment coming from the leader of the free world. "I keep up a pretty active workout regime."

"So I've heard," Rohman laughed. "Why do you think I've never invited you to run with me at Camp David?"

Kline shrugged her shoulders. "I assumed it was because I don't run anymore."

"Hell no," Rohman boomed. "I'm afraid you'll still outrun me."

Despite finding no humor in Rohman's assertion whatsoever, she laughed. It's what you do when the President tells a joke – funny or grossly inappropriate. "Anyway, Mr. President, I suppose you want me to brief you on any foreign involvement we've tracked in the Shelby assassination."

"Actually, no," Rohman nodded.

"No?" Kline was puzzled.

"No, I've followed everyone's theory on Shelby," Rohman snarled, shaking his head in disgust. "No one knows a damn thing yet."

"It's still very early," Kline replied.

"You're starting to sound like the FBI," Rohman said. He knew of Kline's relationship with Leo Argo, but did not apologize for the pointed reference.

Kline was unamused and decided to change the subject. "So, if I'm not here about Shelby, what do you need from me?"

"What I need, Madame Director," the President said, "is for you to step out of your comfort zone a little for me."

Kline chuckled at the thought. Prior to being Director of the Central Intelligence Agency, she was an operative conducting Company business in places most people could not find on a map and doing things unthinkable in a civilized society. She scratched her head. "Pretty narrow territory," she replied smiling. "I'm pretty comfortable doing whatever you ask."

"I know," President Rohman nodded. "But I think I have the one task you'll hate."

The President had Kline's attention. She leaned forward. "So what's so far out of my zone you have to call me to the Oval Office to break it to me?"

The President smiled a big toothy grin. "Lobbying."

Kline shook her head. Without even waiting for the ask, she declined. "No way."

"Jane, I know you hate the political side," the President said reassuringly. "But this one is right in your wheel house."

"Nothing on the political side is in my wheel house," Kline argued. She shook her head disapprovingly. "I have no idea what you need, but I can assure you I'm not the right person for the job."

"This isn't a request, Jane," the President said sternly. "It's one only you can pull off and it's part of the overall foreign strategy we've discussed. It's right up your alley."

"Understood." Kline pursed her lips in consternation. "So what's the assignment?"

Chapter 16

Andy MacNamara stumbled around the mosh pit in front of the stage at the Fillmore in Silver Spring as the Dropkick Murphy's blasted out a punk version of the Irish folk classic, "The Wild Rover." His glassy blue eyes, and the manner in which he was hoisting his Guinness in toast to the song, indicated he consumed one too many pints. Tall, thin, and sporting short, receding red hair, he stumbled around, bouncing to-and-fro off those around him. It was hard to tell if the movements were those of a drunk or a punk-inspired, slam dancer. To those around him, it probably did not matter.

When someone wanted to be hoisted into the air to crowd-surf, MacNamara would be right there, pushing the person forward and, whether it was a girl or a guy, copping a free feel in the process. The image hardly squared with that of a young man who, until recently, was the press secretary to the Chairman of the Senate Foreign Relations Committee. But then again, DC's avante-guard nightlife possessed a peculiar way of hiding people's daily professions.

Hailing from a suburb of Boston, MacNamara was accustomed to blending into the crowds who frequented shows by the Dropkick Murphys. He was a regular to their shows back in Bean Town and his favorite pub there was McGreevy's Third Base Pub in Back Bay, owned in part by a couple of the Murphy's themselves.

MacNamara drank hard the entire day leading up to the concert, a tradition amongst true Dropkick fans. But, his alcoholic overindulgence was not fueled by thoughts of Irish punk, but by rage. MacNamara had been employed by Kentucky Senator Mack Wilson.

MacNamara was pissed Wilson quit – his anger resonating in a drunken, mosh-pit slam dance.

At one point he wandered from the center of the action to a restroom along the exterior wall of the concert hall. While in line, MacNamara noticed a staffer from another Senate office. "What's up?" MacNamara mumbled.

"Hey, man," the guy said over a combination of shouts and piped-in music filling the small, rank smelling urinal. "I didn't know you were a Dropkicker."

MacNamara looked straight ahead, hoping the mark in the wall he was staring at would somehow keep him from falling down or passing out. "I'm from Boston, dude," MacNamara replied. "Unless Areosmith is in town, ain't nothin' else for a Bostonian to listen to."

"I'm hip," the man replied.

"So kiss me, I'm shitfaced," MacNamara sang off-tune.

"Sorry to hear about the Boss stepping down. What happened?"

"I've got no bloody clue," MacNamara slurred. "Wilson just up and quit. I never spoke to him. He left me to handle all the press calls."

"No shit," the man responded in disbelief.

"Worked my ass off for the fat bastard," MacNamara said. "And he repays me by dumping his resignation in my lap."

"Cold, dude," the man said, steadying himself by placing his free hand against the wall. "What are you going to do? You got options?"

"Yeah," MacNamara spewed. "I got options. The chairmen of the Fortune 100 are beating a path to my door step."

The other man laughed. "Seriously, what are you going to do?"

"Im going to work for some old dude the Governor appointed."

"Welcome to the world of politics."

"Tell me about it," MacNamara replied as he zipped up his pants and turned to leave. "I started with a ticket on the fastest thoroughbred in the field, and now I'm hoping to watch some old broken-down nag cross the finish line."

MacNamara turned and tried to steady himself before stumbling out the door.

Chapter 17

David Unger looked into the mirror in the Blue Steel Café's unisex bathroom and could hardly believe his eyes. Had he not known it to be true, he would not have believed the image staring back at him was – well – himself.

Willis cut off all but an inch or so of his droopy black hair and used peroxide to dye the rest white. A little dab of gel spiked his hair up in the middle. Willis also pierced Unger's left ear three times using ice cubes and a sewing needle, and then inserted three black stud earrings into the fresh holes. His eyebrows remained black, but Willis used an electric razor to thin them and cut a notch in the left one.

Unger thought of the photo on the cable news network at the coffee shop. "This just may work," he whispered to himself.

"Put these on," Willis instructed as he handed Unger a pair of white plastic horn-rimmed glasses. "They're cheater glasses I use for reading. They shouldn't bother you too much and they'll add to the look."

Unger put the glasses on and gazed again into the mirror, turning his head to the left and right to admire Willis' handiwork. "And you think we can walk out of here tonight like this?" he asked.

"Tonight?" Willis replied shaking his head. "No way, Junior."

Unger was stunned by the response. He turned quickly to Willis. "What do you mean, no?" he asked. "Did you make me up to look like Billy Idol with glasses just for your own personal amusement?"

Willis chuckled at the reference. "No," Willis replied. "Of course, I do always joke about turning straight guys gay. Maybe if I send your picture in to *The Advocate*, they'll give me a toaster," he said referring to DC's alternative lifestyle newspaper.

"Color me 'not amused,'" Unger sneered.

"Calm down," Willis replied. "The hair is just part of the transformation."

"There's more?" Unger asked.

"I may have dyed your hair, but you still look straight," Willis said, looking Unger up and down. "You may get past the cops on the street, but the queers in the neighborhood would pick you out in a minute."

"I still look straight?" Unger responded. "I didn't know straight came with a particular look."

Willis laughed. "The clothes, girlfriend," he said.

Unger looked down at his baggy jeans and Lynyrd Skynyrd tee shirt. "What's wrong with my clothes?"

"No self-respecting gay man would be caught dead in your outfit," said Willis while shaking his head. "Lynyrd Skynyrd? Really?"

"Then what am I going to do?" Unger asked. "I can't stay here forever."

I'll bring in some clothes for you to wear. In a couple of days, with practice, you'll walk out into the lunch traffic unrecognized and not as the man accused of killing the Vice President."

"You think it'll work?" Unger asked scratching his newly blond head.

"It better," Willis replied. "Or we're both going to jail."

Unger paused to think about the implications. "Okay," he said. "We've got a plan to get out of here. But what do I do when I'm out?"

"Then," Willis nodded. "You go see Charlie."

Chapter 18

Joe Bradley scurried down the hallway of the top floor of the Hart Senate Office Building. Anal retentive to a point at which a doctor might diagnose him as obsessive-compulsive, being late was not in his nature. Nicknamed "The Fat Man" at his law firm, Bradley's short stocky frame, ill-fitting clothes and scruffy beard gave him a disheveled appearance causing many wrongly to discount his Mensa level intellect.

Thompson met The Fat Man following his stint on Capitol Hill as a legislative staffer. The pair fought many legal battles together before Thompson's election to Congress. When the switch came, The Fat Man stayed at his law firm, but true to his reputation, learned all he could about politics. He remained by Thompson's side through each reelect and was key in the decision to leave the political arena.

The Fat Man threw his shoulder into the door of Senator Thompson's private suite and hustled past a dozen or so cubicles containing young men and women acting busy for the new boss. He knocked lightly and then burst into Thompson's office. "Sorry I'm late," he apologized between breaths.

Thompson spun away from the computer screen where he was checking out the morning news stories. He looked at his watch. "You're not late," Thompson replied. "We've got another ten minutes before the staff meeting."

"For me," The Fat Man huffed, "being just ten minutes early is being five minutes late."

"What took you so long?" Thompson asked.

"Did you see the line outside to get through security?"

"No."

"Of course you didn't," The Fat Man responded. "They gave you your 'I'm a Big Shot' lapel pin yesterday."

Thompson smiled and rubbed the lapel pin announcing to everyone around the United States Capitol he was a Senator. "Jealous?" he asked.

"After standing in line for half an hour just to get into the building," The Fat Man said. "Yes. I'm real jealous." He put his day planner on a black leather chair in front of Thompson's desk, bent over and placed his hands on his knees, drawing in air.

"And apparently winded," Thompson added.

"Thanks for noticing," The Fat Man said sarcastically while straightening up. "I still can't believe I let you talk me into this."

The "this" The Fat Man was referring, was taking a leave of absence from the law firm to become Thompson's Chief of Staff in the US Senate. When Thompson agreed to accept Latimer's appointment to the Senate, he decided to keep Wilson's entire staff in place. What he failed to consider was many of the staff would not want to work for a time-limited Senator with no seniority. Several of Wilson's top staff left for jobs with more senior Senators or K Street. When Thompson first visited the office, about half of the desks were empty.

Michael Griffith accompanied Thompson on his first unofficial visit and both agreed Thompson needed someone trusted at the helm. He kept using Godfather terminology to suggest names for a consigliore. In the end, The Fat Man was the obvious choice.

Initially, The Fat Man declined, noting his lack of Hill experience as a reason to stay in his comfortable surroundings. But as Thompson and Griffith worked on him, his mood changed. Within a few hours after the idea was first raised to him, The Fat Man began to understand, with Thompson's obscure agenda, he needed someone watching his backside. The Fat Man decided he could leave his desk in Kentucky for a temporary assignment beyond his silk-stocking, legal comfort zone.

Griffith was so pleased with the decision he offered The Fat Man a bed in his apartment for the duration of his stay in DC. However, once The Fat Man flew up to DC, got his bearings and saw the mess that is Griffith's bachelor pad, he opted for an extended stay hotel in Northern Virginia. He failed to add time for the security line to get into the Hart Building into his commute time. He would correct that tomorrow.

"Yes, I did talk you into this," Thompson said triumphantly. "And, we've got a big day ahead of us. Let's get it in gear."

"Got it under control," The Fat Man said. "You'll be spending some time getting to know your staff, or what's left of it – two more quit yesterday."

"Great," Thompson grimaced. "Pretty soon it will be you and me."

The Fat Man ignored the comment and continued. "Then around noon, Ann and the kids get here for the swearing in. Did you get a chance to look at the notebook I made for you?"

"Yeah," Thompson replied. "Nice work. I'll give it another look before they all come in."

Thompson reminisced while thumbing through the biographies of young men and women from various parts of the country attempting to find their fame and fortune in the nation's center of power. *Just fame, I guess*, Thompson thought to himself. *There is no fortune to be found at a staffer's desk on the Hill.* The first bio he stopped on was his soon-to-be first Legislative Director, Sharon Straight, suggested for promotion by The Fat Man. Straight was in a lower spot when the previous LD resigned to take a position with a committee staff. She was still relatively fresh, but The Fat Man talked to her and he thought her up to the task. Thompson ran his finger down the bio and noticed she was a graduate of Eastern Kentucky University, his and Griffith's alma matter. "Go Big E," he mumbled.

Andy MacNamara, only in his 30's but already a Hill veteran, was Thompson's Press Secretary from Boston, Massachusetts. *I need to stroke him a bit,* Thompson thought to himself reviewing MacNamara's impressive credentials. *He's not happy about his lot in life today. I need to change his attitude.*

Thompson flipped a couple more pages before he stopped on the bio for the scheduler, Marianne Devlin, a crusty old red-haired gal from Mississippi. Upon entering the office, she handed Thompson a lanyard style plastic sleeve filled with note cards explaining precisely how she would track his daily comings and goings. *I can't wait until The Fat Man tells her he wants it electronic instead of on paper.* Thompson chuckled at the thought.

"Ready when you are, Boss," The Fat Man said. "I've got everyone assembled in the conference room and an intern from next door is answering our phones."

"You warned them I am a hard ass, right?

"Just like you said."

It was show time. Thompson spent his lifetime seemingly performing in front of people – teachers, bosses, juries and voters. This meeting was more important to him than most, however. Thompson wanted to connect with his new staff, and let them each know their job was safe, while at the same time starting to build up some loyalty to him in the process. With the exception of The Fat Man, everyone in the room was a Wilson staffer. He needed to build some credibility and the first staff meeting was the perfect place to start.

Thompson walked into the room and acted very businesslike as he scanned the faces sitting around the conference table or standing behind it against the back wall. When he entered the room, all talking immediately ceased.

"Okay," he said as if getting right to business. "I've reviewed everyone's bio and noticed there is quite a bit of information missing for me to decide who stays and who goes."

Panicked eyes shifted around the room.

Thompson sat down and opened up the binder. "Everyone please give me your name, where you're from and the last concert you attended." It was a trick Thompson used when conducting voir dire to choose potential jurors for a trial. The question itself usually relaxed the jury panel, and Thompson always felt like knowing a person's taste in music gave him a little insight into their personality. "We'll start with you." Thompson pointed at Sharon Straight.

"Sharon Straight from Lexington and my last concert was to see ..." Her voice trailed off. "God, I can't remember."

"It's okay," Thompson said. "We'll wait."

"I can't think of who I saw last," Straight stammered. "But, I've got tickets to see Jimmy Buffett this summer out at Wolf Trap."

"Sell them," Thompson instructed.

"Pardon me?"

"I said sell them," Thompson repeated. "I can't have a Parrot Head as my new Legislative Director."

"But I'm not ..."

"You are now," interjected The Fat Man.

A huge grin broke out on Straight's face as other staffers began patting her on the back in congratulations. "Thank you, Senator."

"We'll discuss salary later today," The Fat Man said. "And don't put the Buffett tickets on eBay just yet. I'm sure I can convince the Senator to let you slide this one time."

"Whatever," Thompson said as he switched his gaze to Devlin.

"Marianne Devlin," she said with a strong southern drawl.

"Mississippi, right?' Thompson asked.

"Down to my toes," Devlin replied boldly.

"State or Ole Miss," Thompson asked.

"Why Ole Miss, of course," Devlin said in a manner indicating any other answer would be unthinkable. "And last week I went to the Kennedy Center to hear Tony Bennett."

"Ah," Thompson smiled. "You know, Johnny Carson used to call Bennett the singer's singer." He quickly looked around the room. "And anyone who asks who Carson is will be docked a day's pay."

With the mood lightened, the Press Secretary jumped in without even asking. "Andy MacNamara from Boston," he said, his accent also giving away his home region. "And the last band I saw in concert was Meat Loaf."

"You, sir, are a liar," Thompson declared, looking straight at MacNamara. The joviality suddenly ceased. No one was quite sure if their new boss was serious or kidding. They looked nervously back and forth between the pair.

"You have proof?" MacNamara was testing Thompson in their first meeting.

Thompson liked the balls the young man was showing and jumped on the challenge. "First, you're too young."

MacNamara did not hesitate. "My dad was a fan," he said. "I grew up listening to oldies like Meat Loaf."

"Ouch," mumbled The Fat Man to the age reference.

Not deterred, Thompson continued. "Secondly, Meat Loaf is a person, not a band," he said. "You referred to 'band' not 'him.'"

"The two are intertwined," MacNamara said undeterred. "Meat Loaf is a band and a person – a rock and roll contronym, as it were."

"Finally, I am going to assume you looked up my favorite bands on my Facebook page."

"Maybe," MacNamara said, smiling.

Thompson sighed. "Mr. MacNamara, I was going to fire you following this meeting," he said. "But your ability to go to great lengths to suck up to me earned you a special place in my heart. I shall hold off on my decision to ax you until tomorrow."

The Fat Man jumped in. "And anyone who can guess the movie reference the Senator just made gets a dollar."

"Princess Bride," whispered a young woman standing against the wall.

The Fat Man stood up, pulled out his wallet and walked to the young woman. He handed her a dollar. "I've got my eye on you," he said, repeatedly pointing two fingers at his own eyes and then hers. "You're going places."

"Seriously though," Thompson said through the nervous laughter in the room, "Mr. MacNamara, you're from Boston. I'm guessing you went to see the Drop Kick Murphy's last night at the Fillmore in Silver Spring. Am I right?"

MacNamara was impressed and nodded affirmatively. "On the money."

The rest of the staff went around the room introducing themselves to their new boss. Each time someone mentioned their last concert, Thompson would toss in some related musical reference or sing a line or two from a song only a fan of the group would recognize.

Once the ice-breaker was over, Thompson stood up. "Down to brass tacks," he said. Slowly he looked around the room. "I know I'm not what you signed up for."

Thompson pushed his chair into the table and started into his professor posturing. "I worked on the Hill once and I know each of you want to work for somebody relevant and important. I'm neither. I'm some washed up former Congressman from Kentucky appointed to keep an eye on a Senate seat until the next election. I understand you're rightfully disappointed."

Thompson walked to the front of the conference room and opened the door. "Anyone who wants to leave can head out now and I'll write you a glowing letter of recommendation."

No one moved. "Don't worry about walking out now in front of your friends," Thompson smiled. "I only did it for effect. My offer is open for the rest of the week."

Thompson closed the door and walked back to the table. "But for those who choose to stay I promise two things." Thompson held up his index finger. "First, if a candidate from our side wins the election for the seat, I'll recommend everyone sticking with me for a job with the new Senator. And if we, as we are so often prone to do, lose the seat, I'll make personal calls until everyone finds a job."

Heads were nodding in appreciation.

Thompson held up two fingers. "Secondly, I intend to be more than some demanding Member you're here to support. I'm here to see you succeed. If you stay, you'll be required to meet with me monthly to discuss your future goals and we'll work together on how to get you there. Ask Congressman Barkman—when you join the Family, you're in for life. I'll do what I can to help."

Thompson sat back down and pulled out the lanyard filled with note cards. He looked at Devlin. "According to my schedule," he said, shuffling the cards, "at 2:00 pm today, I'll be sworn in as a

Senator." He put the cards back in his jacket pocket. "There will be a lot of folks from back home wandering around the office to see my new digs. Please do not bury your head in your desk. My family and I are going to enjoy the festivities, and it is part of your job requirements to do the same. Our office will close early for the reception over at the Dubliner."

Thompson looked at The Fat Man. "Joey, you got anything to add?"

"Don't enjoy the Guinness too much," The Fat Man added. "Sharon, the Senator will be in a committee hearing tomorrow at 10:00 a.m. I want him briefed on the witnesses with some good questions to ask. Also, get whoever is covering tomorrow's votes in here to let him know what's on the floor."

"And I'd like a run down on everything Wilson was working on," Thompson added. "From case work to legislation – I want to know everything. I don't want to leave any loose strings left hanging."

Heads nodded as staffers busily scribbled notes, but snapped up when The Fat Man made an odd statement. "And there is a new requirement in order for staff to get a paycheck," he said. "In order to be paid, everyone must text me a photo of them being somewhere new to them in DC."

Thompson smiled at the puzzled young faces. "My wife and I both worked on the Hill when we were your age," he said. "We moved home with a long list of things we wished we would have done. I want to make sure your list is as short as possible."

"How about you, Senator," Devlin interjected. "Where are you going?"

"Good question, Marianne," Thompson replied smiling. "I never went to Roosevelt Island, where I will be heading before my first check is due."

"Just making sure we're all playing by the same rules," Devlin added.

"Good," said Thompson. "I appreciate everyone's work. Any questions?"

"Yeah," MacNamara said with a sneer. "I got one. What was your last concert?

Thompson smiled. "Last night," he said. "I saw the Drop Kick Murphys, too." Thompson paused.

"Really?" MacNamara replied.

"Really, Mr. MacNamara." Thompson winked. "You should probably pay more attention to who's standing next to you in the bathroom. The next old nag you complain about could end up being your boss."

Chapter 19

Clad in a pair of tight black peg-legged pants, a black and white striped, ribbed t shirt and rainbow flip-flops, David Unger sat nervously at the front bar of the Blue Steel Café sipping on a tonic water Willis provided for him. They thought it best for the transformed Unger to hang around the bar for a day or two in order to get used to his new identity. Willis also wanted to make sure his regular clientele did not recognize Unger from the photographs appearing on television and in the papers. When a bearded businessman hit on Unger and left his phone number on a small card provided by the owner for such introductions, Willis figured he succeeded at readying Unger for movement outside the bar.

Willis watched as Unger repeatedly stirred the ice cubes in his glass with a swizzle stick. He walked up and placed his hand gently on Unger's in an attempt to calm him down. "Nervous?" Willis asked.

"As much as one of your regular customers at Catholic confession," Unger mumbled. He pulled his hand from the glass and held it out in front of him.

Willis laughed at the reference. "Ah," he said. "You have a sense of humor, too. There may be some hope for you yet." He looked at Unger's hand. It was shaking ever so slightly – less than before, but still visible.

"Yeah," Unger said in a quiet voice. "When I'm in jail maybe I can do stand-up on Saturday's Open Microphone Night. Good evening folks, I'm the straight gay guy who killed the Vice President. I'll be here all week." Unger waved his hand like he was acknowledging a crowd. "Hell, I'll be here for the rest of my life."

Willis shook his head and smiled at the line. "After the way I've helped," Willis replied, "maybe we can be cellmates."

"I'll put in a good word for you at the prison kitchen," Unger said.

Willis and Unger waited as a customer paid his tab and walked out the front door. Willis leaned forward and spoke in nearly a whisper. "Give me your wallet," he instructed sticking out his hand.

Looking more than a little surprised at the demand, Unger reached into his pants pocket and handed over his wallet. Thinking Willis wanted payment for his effort, Unger said, "There's not much in it, but you can have it all for what you've done."

Shocked by the comment, Willis tilted his head and looked at Unger with a disgusted gaze. He understood Unger was under a lot of pressure, but the reference was insulting and for a moment he had trouble letting it roll off his back. He took a deep breath, opened the cash register and counted out three hundred dollars in tens and twenties. "You'll need this," he said as he stuffed the money in Unger's wallet.

More than embarrassed, Unger realized how rude the comment about payment must have sounded to Willis. "I'm sorry," Unger apologized "I didn't mean to sound ungrateful."

"Not a problem," Willis said as he emptied the wallet of every identification and credit card bearing Unger's name. "You can't use these anymore. They'll be tracking your accounts." Willis cut up the contents of the wallet before tossing everything into a garbage can under the bar. He handed the empty wallet back across the bar. "I'll get rid of these for you," he said.

"Got it," Unger said as he retrieved his wallet and slipped it into the back pocket of his tight pants. "I'm a man without an identity."

"For a while," Willis replied. "Pretty much so."

"When you hit the street," Willis instructed. "Just walk casually to the Metro. There are not as many cops around looking for you as the other day. I think they presumed you escaped the neighborhood. Still, don't make direct eye contact with them, but don't look away either. Just look nonchalantly ahead. Try to act as disinterested as any other zombie on their way to the subway."

"What if someone talks to me?" Unger asked.

"Head nods work best," Willis said. "If it doesn't work, try some gay humor."

"Gay humor?"

Willis chuckled. "Yeah," he said. "Like, what's the hardest part of learning to roller blade?"

"I don't know, what?"

"Telling your parents you're gay."

Unger laughed out loud at the punch line.

Willis pulled a legal pad from a drawer by the cash register. He wrote down a name and an address. "Take the Red Line to Metro Center and then transfer to the Blue Line. Take the train to Capitol South. You'll come up right next to the Cannon House Office Building, so don't be surprised to see lots of cops. Head in the opposite direction a block towards the ballpark. There will be a small gray office building on the left side of the street – Suite 302 – Charlie will be waiting for you."

"Who is Charlie, anyway?" Unger said. "You mentioned him before."

"Charlie is a man who is very well connected in this city," Willis replied. "He's a dear friend and a good customer. I talked to him in detail about your situation. Like me, he doesn't believe the story planted about you in the press."

Unger thought about it for a minute. "I assume Charlie is gay, too."

"Absolutely," Willis replied.

Unger shook his head. "Is everyone in this town gay?" Unger asked with mock exasperation.

"No," Willis laughed. "But you'd be surprised at how many LGBTs there are in and around government. Charlie's advised more Administrations than anyone would want to admit. Around DuPont we call him the Queen Mum."

"Really?" Unger was astonished and scratched his head at the revelation. "I just never …"

"Honey," Willis cut him off. "There are more tortured queens in the Halls of Congress than there were in the Tower of London."

Unger was starting to like Willis' bizarre sense of humor. "You're funny," he chuckled.

"Look," Willis said. "In most power towns, there's a group of gay men and women who are in the center of the action. Some people refer to it as the Lavender Mafia. In other circles it's called the Velvet Glove."

"I've read stories about the influence of the gay community in New York and LA," Unger said. "But I never thought about there being such a strong presence in DC."

"We've wandered the streets of DC longer than most party regulars," Willis said. "And we'll still be here long after each administration heads home."

Unger readied himself to leave when he was suddenly confused about the oddity of his situation. "How do you know I'm not going to take the money and run?" he asked.

"Maybe you will," Willis replied. "But you can't run too far on three fins. They'll catch you pretty quickly. I think you want to be vindicated. And the police aren't going to do it for you. You need us – the community – to clear your name. Charlie's the key."

Unger stood up, folded the paper and stuffed it into his pants pocket. "I can't say thank you enough," he said, sticking out his hand.

Willis ignored the offer of a handshake and instead hugged Unger. "You seem like a good man. I hope you'll get out of this."

Unger turned, walked out the door and felt the warmth of the sunshine on his face for the first time since being chased into the alley behind the Blue Steel Café. The noon-time lunch crowd began to wander out of their offices and shops onto the sidewalks of DuPont Circle. As instructed, Unger stared blankly ahead as he gathered his bearings for the Metro stop. From the corner of his vision, he could sense where the police were standing, none of whom seemed to be interested in him. His confidence increased with each step.

As Unger crossed the street towards the DuPont Circle Metro Station, he looked down Q Street in the direction of The Cairo. Yellow crime scene tape dangled from the front steps and flapped in the breeze from the wrought iron hand rail. Despite his curious desire to walk past the place, he continued to walk towards the subway. Except for glancing at an occasional yard sign demanding "DC Statehood NOW," Unger looked straight ahead.

Once at the station, Unger boarded the long escalator to the subway platform below. The unspoken DC escalator etiquette requires people who desire to ride the stairs to the bottom step to the right, allowing those in a hurry to walk past on the left. A man in spandex shorts with a bicycle slung over his shoulder thwarted those in a hurry by blocking the left walking lane. The rubber handrails of the old escalator make a squeaking noise sounding like an off-tune saxophone solo. Despite the slowdown and collapse of people, no one looked twice at Unger.

He felt increasingly comfortable. He reached the machine dispensing subway passes and studied the map to determine how much he needed to pay for a ticket to the Capitol South stop as Willis directed.

"Hey," said a voice from over Unger's shoulder. When Unger glanced around, he saw a buff man about his age peering at the same subway map. The man was dressed in cargo shorts and a muscle tee barely hiding the pink triangle tattoo on his right breast, the young man smiled at Unger. Unger remembered Willis' advice and simply nodded a response.

"Where you headed?" the man asked.

The moment of truth was at hand. Unger turned around and, before he could say a word, burst into laughter. A pair of roller blades were slung over the stranger's left shoulder.

Chapter 20

One by one, the lunch crowd at the Blue Steel Café had finished up their meals and slowly made their way out of the little bar and back onto the streets around DuPont Circle. Jared Willis let all but one of his staff take off for the remainder of the afternoon. The waiter was out front tending the bar, while Willis was cleaning up around the kitchen and lazily beginning prep for the evening dinner crowd.

Willis took a towel off one of the stainless steel tables and ran hot water over it before patting the cloth over his face. Wiping the oil from his skin, he quickly concluded he was exhausted. A couple days ago, David Unger scrambled into his life, Willis was tired from lack of sleep. He looked up when the bartender, Lowell, wandered into the room. "Pretty good crowd today," Willis said. "Tips okay?"

"It ain't over yet, honey," Lowell said, dramatically sweeping his hand over his forehead.

"What's up?" Willis asked.

"Two stragglers for lunch," Lowell announced.

"Shit," Willis sighed. He was sleepy from the excitement and was hoping to catch a quick nap before the dinner crowd arrived. "Things could be worse than cooking for two more," he mumbled as he scratched his head. "What do they want to eat?"

Lowell put his hands on his hips. "They wouldn't tell me, baby doll," he said. "They want to talk to the chef about how you prepare the sea bass."

"Jesus," Willis shook his head. "All I need today are a couple of last minute walk-ins who watch too damn many cooking shows on television." Willis pulled his apron back on over his head and straightened the front before striding out to the dining room. He nearly stopped in his tracks when he saw Tall and Thick and Little Stubby sitting at a booth near the window. He tried not to look shaken up as he walked to the table.

"Gentlemen," he said as he clasped his hands together. "You were interested in how I prepare the sea bass."

"Not really," Little Stubby said. He smiled slyly as he spoke. "I assume you remember us from the other day?"

Willis shook his head. "No, not really."

"Aw come on, Bobby Flay," Tall and Thick snapped. "I asked if you'd seen some dude run down the alley, and you pointed us in the right direction. Remember?"

"Oh yeah," Willis replied trying to act as if his memory was suddenly refreshed. "Now I remember you two. Hey, did you ever catch the guy you were running after?"

"Naw," Little Stubby interjected. "He got away from us. Even after you gave us such good directions, he got away from us. He was a quick little guy to disappear so fast."

"Must have," Willis replied. "So if you don't want the sea bass, tell me what I can do for you gentlemen? I need to get ready for my dinner crowd."

"Nothing to eat for us," Little Stubby said. "Just get us a couple of draft beers."

"Two draft beers coming right up."

Willis started to turn when Tall and Thick reached into his shirt pocket and handed over the pieces of a cut up credit card. "In fact," Tall and Thick added, "let's start a tab."

"Yeah," Little Stubby replied. "Let's start a tab." He nodded at the shredded credit card. "Put the beers on this card."

Willis looked down, not needing to piece the card back together to know it was David Unger's.

"Really, Bobby Flay," Tall and Thick said. "You should cut those things up better before you toss them in the garbage. You never know what kind of criminals may be diving through your dumpster." He got up and headed to the front door, clicked the lock and looked back at Willis smiling. "Now let's talk about which direction David Unger ran when he hit your alley."

The day shift waiter who told Willis about the late lunch customers was standing behind the bar watching the entire scene unfold. Lowell picked up the telephone and waved it in the direction of the two men. "I'm calling the police," he said in a snotty tone.

Little Stubby pulled out a Sig Sauer with a silencer on the end and fired one shot. The bullet hit Lowell in the right cheek, just below the eye. The gun barely made a sound. Lowell's head snapped back causing his entire body to spin violently. The bullet exited the back of his head and exploded into a bottle of Absolut vodka behind the bar. Lowell's body slammed into the rear bar upending more bottles, before falling to the floor with a thud. Top shelf booze and blood streamed down the mirror behind the bar.

"What the fuck?" screamed Willis as he watched Lowell die right in front of him. He tried to think of his next move, but was literally frozen by fear. His eyes shot around the room before they locked on Little Stubby.

Little Stubby grinned evilly. "Good," he said in recognition of the eye contact. "I see I have your attention."

Willis was visibly shaking. "Oh my God, you killed Lowell," he stammered through clattering teeth. "What the fuck? What do you want from me?"

Little Stubby spoke in a slow, measured monotone. "Where is the man who we were chasing in the alley?" he asked.

"I don't know," Willis replied, all the while noticing the other man in the room moved his large frame between Willis and the back door.

"Oh, are we really going to have to go there?" Little Stubby asked, shaking his head in mock disbelief. "I was hoping it wouldn't come to this."

As Willis began to stammer, Tall and Thick grabbed a small vase filled with flowers off a table and smashed it on the back of Willis' head. Willis crumpled to his knees. As Little Stubby laughed, Willis felt the blood run down the side of his face. He touched the blood and held his hand in front of his face to inspect the cherry red liquid.

"We can do this the hard way, or the easy way," Little Stubby said, the pistol aimed at Willis as he spoke. "Now where did David Unger really go when he ran down the alley?"

Chapter 21

The Cairo was within walking distance of the White House, so David Unger did not use the subway very often during his short DC tenure. The few times he traveled on the Metro, he did so with a similar disinterest to which he now observed on other passengers' sullen faces. Shortly after his train pulled out, he was spooked by a woman looking at him. As the light of dim fluorescent tubes located on the tunnel walls danced across her face, he realized she did not really see him, but through him. If he was the Pope in full dress, this woman would not have noticed.

At Metro Center, as Unger leaned against a concrete barricade waiting for the blinking platform lights to announce an oncoming train, he concluded all those around him were clueless. They were in the great mixing bowl of humanity. Each person on the platform was nearly oblivious to the others' existence. It was an odd experience for Unger, who at the moment was more observant of his surroundings than at any point in his young life.

During the ride along the Washington Metro's Blue Line, Unger noticed the seats –once blue, orange and yellow were now mustard, rust and a shade of blue as yet unidentified on the color spectrum. When the conductor announced over a scratchy speaker food and drink were prohibited in the subway, Unger cringed at the thought of what else might have caused the innumerable dark stains on the train's carpeted floor.

David Unger spied a copy of the morning newspaper resting on one of the seats. He scooted onto the otherwise vacant bench. As the train's conductor rattled off the name of the stop in a muffled tone which could just have just as well been the repeat of a food order over a fast food drive-through speaker, he picked up the paper. A color picture of the front steps leading up to The Cairo stared back at him under the headline "Shelby's Advance Man At Large."

Spooked yet again by a story featuring him as the subject, his eyes darted around the inside of the subway car. It was not a peak time on the line and most of the other passengers either listened to music with their eyes closed or looked blankly ahead as people do in public places when they are intentionally trying to avoid all eye contact. A man sat three rows in front of him preaching the Gospel to an imaginary congregation. A woman with a surgical mask over her nose and mouth clutched her purse. Unger scrunched up his shoulders and held the paper up a little in front of him in order to hide his face.

The story recounted most of what Jared Willis told Unger. Reading further, he noticed one substantial change in the reporting. Previous articles hinted at an affection Unger may have felt for the Vice President. Those references seemed to be stronger in this article and, while not stating it directly, seemed to paint Unger as some sort of crazed sexual stalker. For half a second he imagined what the people back home were thinking.

When the speaker announced "Capitol South," Unger snapped to and tossed the newspaper back onto the seat, and jumped from the train to the dark tile floor station platform as soon as the doors opened. The trip up the long escalator allowed Unger's eyes to adjust to the bright sunlight at the top. He was familiar with the neighborhood near the Library of Congress from a previous trip. When he came out of the tunnel, he turned right and headed towards the address given to him by Willis. Because of the stop's proximity to the United States Capitol, the street was crawling with police officers, as Willis predicted. Unger kept pace with others on the sidewalk in an effort to blend in.

Entering the small lobby of the non-descript four-story building on First Street, Unger sought out the office directory. His finger scurried down the list of associations and professionals occupying the building until he found the name he was looking for. Comparing the suite numbers with the one listed on the piece of paper Willis gave him, he spied the name of Charles Patterson, a solo practice lawyer.

Running his fingers through his newly shortened hair, Unger took a deep breath. He had asked Willis about trying to disappear, because the thought repeatedly circulated through his head ever since they changed his appearance. Running away was still an option, albeit one Unger concluded once started would never stop. He climbed the internal steps of the building to the third floor and knocked on the door to Suite 302.

"Come in," came a deep voice from the other side of the door.

Unger nervously walked through the door and into a small office. A thin man with grey hair, appearing to be in his early sixties walked in, his hand extended. The jacket of his dark blue pinstripe suit hung neatly over the back of a chair and leather braided suspenders striped down the front of his French cuffed shirt. "Hi," he said, a warm smile engulfing his round face. "I'm Charlie Patterson."

"Pleased to meet you." Unger returned the firm handshake, noticing the man's cuff links – black cobalt, bearing the seal of the President of the United States. The cobalt cuff links were reserved for each President's closest friends. "I'm David ..."

"David," Patterson interjected quickly. "For the time being, you're just David. I really don't want to know any last names."

Unger started to speak, but Patterson cut him off. "You see, at this point, if I know anything more about you, I may be required by the ethics of my profession to turn you over to the authorities."

"Okay," Unger nodded while fidgeting back and forth, shifting his weight from foot to foot.

"So, at this point," Patterson said. "You're David – a customer of my friend Jared Willis who may need some legal advice."

Unger suddenly understood. The explanation seemed logical and actually caused Unger to have a bit of trust in Patterson. "Got it," he said nodding.

Patterson made his way to his desk and pointed his right hand in the direction of the red leather tufted chairs. "Have a seat, David," he said. "And try to relax."

"It shows pretty badly, huh?" Unger averted his eyes from Patterson and looked down at the expensive Oriental rug under his chair.

"Yeah," Patterson replied. Patterson knew Unger's face from television and the papers, and he looked the young man up and down. He chuckled, noticing the manner in which Willis dressed Unger and changed his physical features. "You know," Patterson continued. "This entire town is looking for some local man who allegedly stalked and killed Vice President Shelby."

"So I hear," Unger replied. He was not quite sure where the conversation was heading. So he offered little in return.

"I've seen this kid everyone is looking for on the news," Patterson said. He cocked his head back and forth a time or two, again judging Unger's look. "He looks nothing like you."

Unger smiled and looked back up at Patterson. "Your friend Jared Willis has quite a flair for fashion," he said.

"So he does," Patterson replied. He pursed his lips. "And so, as long as the authorities are looking for the man I saw on television this morning, I think you – David – can walk the streets of DC fairly undetected."

"Good," Unger sighed with relief.

"But anonymity won't last forever," Patterson continued. "At some point, they will start using some of their advanced identity recognition technology to alter the pictures I've seen on television. Who knows, this Unger fellow may look like you with darker, longer hair. It could make it quite uncomfortable for someone with the same facial features as you."

Unger took in the information and simply nodded his acknowledgement.

Patterson got up from his desk and came around to sit in the other chair next to Unger's. "But, I'm troubled by this whole investigation," he said.

"How so," said Unger, playing along with Patterson's coy manner.

"Well," Patterson replied. "I'm not sure they're looking for the right man. This Unger fellow just doesn't seem to fit the profile of a killer – or at least the killer they're looking for."

"And you've come to such a conclusion, because …?" Unger allowed his voice to trail off in order to let Patterson complete his thought.

"Good question," said Patterson, nonchalantly readjusting a stack of Congressional seal coasters on the table between the two chairs. "The basis for the case against this Unger fellow seems to rest on a foundation that the culprit – Mr. Unger – is some sort of psychopathic gay stalker."

"And?" Unger replied attempting to further extend Patterson's train of thought.

"And," Patterson replied authoritatively. "I am pretty certain the Vice President's advance man is not gay, let alone a stalker."

"He's not." Unger tried to make the utterance come out as a question but it rolled off his tongue as an affirmation.

"No," Patterson said shaking his head. He looked at Unger's attire. "Unger may be a bit unique in his personal traits, but from what I have heard he's not gay." The silence was only a few moments, but to Unger it seemed to hang in the air for a lifetime. "And I'll tell you one more thing," Patterson continued, breaking the silence.

"What?" Unger asked looking up.

"He's not a psychopath either…"

"Do you truly believe he's okay?" Unger asked.

"Yes," Patterson said, leaning forward and placing a reassuring hand on Unger's knee. "I truly believe you, David Unger."

Patterson speaking his name as a point of reassurance was totally lost on Unger. "Thank you," Unger said, making eye contact with Patterson before placing his head in his hands. "Thank God someone believes I'm innocent."

Undaunted by Unger failing to catch the full-name reference, Patterson continued. "Someone set you up, son," he concluded.

"Who?" asked Unger. "Who would want to set me up?"

"Don't take it personaly," Patterson replied. He got up from the chair and walked back to his desk. "This isn't about you. It was about Vice President Shelby. Unfortunately, whoever is really behind the assassination needs you dead."

"Dead?" Unger looked up with sad eyes.

"Dead men tell no tales," Patterson said matter-of-factly. "If you're out of the picture, they can blame whatever they want on you. With you alive, there are varying accounts. They need you dead."

"I can't fight this," Unger blurted out. "Everyone already thinks I'm the guy."

Patterson nodded in agreement. "Precisely," he said. "This is why I need you to disappear, but just for a day or two. I need to figure out what is going on here. I need to clear your name."

"Why?" asked a confused Unger.

"Because you didn't do it?" Patterson replied.

"No, different question," Unger corrected.

"What then?" Patterson shook his head.

"Why do you care?" Unger questioned in a puzzled tone.

Patterson smiled. "I'd like to say I want to see justice done for you and whoever really killed the Vice President, but my motivation is a bit different," he said. "Personally, I never really liked Paul Shelby. He was an untrustworthy, power-hungry twit. All his aw-shucks, Midwestern stuff was just a political ploy."

"Then why?" Unger repeated the query.

Patterson sat down again next to Unger and looked squarely at him. "You seem like a nice kid," he said softly. "But in most circumstances, you'd be on your own."

"Then why?"

"Because if they blame this on some sort of gay stalker plot, it will set gay rights back two decades." Patterson let the comment sink in. "I've worked a lifetime to establish the right to live my life as I please. I don't want to go backwards. Call getting your name cleared my own personal Stonewall."

Unger did not understand the reference to the 1969 riots in Greenwich Village that led to the gay liberation movement, but nodded nevertheless.

Patterson scribbled an address down on a yellow legal pad, tore off the piece of paper and handed it to Unger. "Go here."

Unger looked at the address. He knew the neighborhood. "What is this place?"

"The Hawk's Cove – a bar in North West," Patterson said. "It's not a leather bar or anything, so you should fit in well enough. Go there and just sit at the rail. At 9:30 a gentleman named Tommy will come up and want to buy you a drink. Go with him. He'll keep you under wraps for a couple of days while I try to figure this thing out. And Jared will want to know you're safe. I'll text him where you're going to be."

"Thanks," Unger said as he folded up the piece of paper and tucked it into his front pants pocket.

"Now please excuse me," Patterson pointed to the door. "One of my old, dear friends, Richard Thompson, was appointed to the United States Senate. He was sworn in today and his celebration started about ten minutes ago. I need to head over to the Dubliner to welcome him and his wife back to Washington."

Chapter 22

"I met my love by the gas works wall,
Dreamed a dream by the old canal,
I kissed my girl by the factory wall,
Dirty old town,
Dirty old town."

The guitar player strummed out a classic Pogues tune as Senator Richard Thompson and his wife Ann entered the Dubliner. About a hundred people who were jammed into the front bar of one of America's best known Irish pubs burst into spontaneous applause. Ann squeezed her husband's hand and the wide smile across his face was not one of those phony smiles some politicians develop for public gatherings to convey trustworthiness. Thompson's smile was true and genuine. Of all his old haunts, the Dubliner was where he actually relaxed.

When Richard and Ann Thompson first met on Capitol Hill, he worked as a staffer for a Kentucky Congressman and she worked for a Florida Congresswoman. He fell hard, totally smitten by her girl-next-door good looks and sparkling charm. In the beginning, Ann was totally unimpressed by the well-intentioned but socially awkward Thompson. Yet, through a date brokered by Michael Griffith – who advised the campaigns for both of their bosses – Ann agreed to go out with Thompson. They quickly became an item, nearly inseparable on the DC reception circuit.

The pair met before Congress revised its internal ethics rules, and each night on the Hill was filled with lavish receptions hosted by the National Association of Everybody where the shrimp were large and the liquor was top-shelf. It was also during a time before Congress applied wage and hour laws to itself. Most staffers worked long hours for low wages just for the experience of working on the Hill. The food served at the nightly receptions became the staple of staffers who relied on them for survival. A hearty handshake and feigned interest in a conversation about whatever issue the host organization lobbied for was a small price to pay for oysters Rockefeller, rounds of beef, and a bourbon Manhattan on the rocks.

Following a good grazing at the nightly reception du-jour, Ann, Thompson – and usually Griffith – could be found at the Dubliner, which is only a block or so from the United States Senate. A fan of Irish folk music, Thompson loved to sit near the small stage and sing along with the classic tunes the musicians would play. A mandolin player who made up for his lack of talent by playing with gusto, Thompson occasionally joined the duo on stage to perform "Dirty Old Town."

When Thompson agreed to accept the appointment of Governor Robin Latimer to become the junior Senator from Kentucky, he and Ann decided to forgo the confines of some Senate subcommittee room for the swearing-in reception in favor of the front bar at the Dubliner. It was an unconventional choice of venue, but then again, those who knew Thompson well understood he was going to be an unconventional Senator. The carefree nature of those who frequented the bar on a regular basis matched the Thompsons' collective demeanor since leaving Washington. The regulars at the bar were more interested in the Leinster rugby score than the fact a United States Senator was entering the room.

Earlier, Thompson's swearing-in on the floor of the United States Senate came off without a hitch. Unlike most initiated into the most prestigious fraternity in the world, his comments were brief. Like most, either elected or appointed, Thompson thanked his family, friends and people from his state. However, in his short comments Thompson did something unique: he delivered a message to his community college government class back in Kentucky. Reciting a musical reference as he often did in class, Thompson looked directly into the Senate's cameras and said: "To my students I abandoned in mid-semester back in Kentucky, I apologize for the sudden diversion in my lecture notes, but sometimes destiny makes a call requiring you to answer. Your substitute professor today gave you a lecture about dissent and when to object to authority."

Thompson paused, smiled and then added, "In the words of the great philosopher, Warren Zevon, you're my witness. I'm you're mutineer."

When Ann and Thompson arrived at the Dubliner, the party was already in full gear. Gavin Coleman, son of the bar's founder Daniel, met them at the door. "I never thought I'd see you two here again," he said, warmly embracing Ann. "*Céad míle fáilte*," he continued as he shook Thompson's hand.

"And a hundred thousand welcomes to you, too, my friend," Thompson replied as he surveyed the room of staff, friends and political supporters from both DC and back home. "It's been way too long."

"Not so long that we forgot," Coleman said pointing to the stage. "Dad made sure we got a mandolin tuned up for you. You know, just in case you wanted to play."

Thompson smiled his approval. "I'd never miss the opportunity to stroke an ax."

"Richard, really?" Ann interjected. "You're going to play? Tonight? Here?"

"Absolutely," Thompson said, winking at Coleman. "Your father would be offended if I didn't, right?"

"Aye," nodded Coleman. "Can't let the old man down now, can we?"

The Fat Man walked up to the trio. "Good crowd," he said.

Ann grabbed The Fat Man's hand. "Thanks Joey," she said smiling. "We really appreciate what you're doing. How are you enjoying the new role?"

"Pretty interesting," The Fat Man replied. "I only got lost twice in the tunnels of the Senate today."

"So, anyone here I really need to impress?" Thompson asked mockingly.

"Governor Latimer is here," The Fat Man replied. "But she's pretty liquored up on Irish whiskey."

"Great," mumbled Ann. "Keep her away from the press."

"I've already got MacNamara working on it," The Fat Man replied. "If I can keep him sober, he'll be able to handle it."

"He likes the rye a bit, does he?" interjected Coleman.

The Fat Man made a gesture with his index finger and thumb. "A wee bit," he replied.

"Anybody else?" Ann asked.

"Josh is here and telling everybody he's going to resign from Congress to be your Chief of Staff."

"Did you tell him the job is already taken?" Thompson quickly replied.

"Aw, he's just kidding around," The Fat Man said, only partially believing his own words.

As Thompson looked nonchalantly over The Fat Man's shoulder – a move he learned from his days as a staffer to spy who may have wandered into the room – he noticed Michael Griffith standing just beyond the grasp of Governor Latimer. Their eyes locked. Griffith did not say a word. He did not need to. He orchestrated the entire day. A nod from his best friend was all Griffith needed to satisfy his ego.

Thompson kissed his wife. "I've got to go to work," he said.

"I know," Ann sighed. "Just don't forget we're having dinner tonight with Jane and Leo," she instructed, reminding Thompson of their evening engagement with CIA Director Jane Kline and FBI Agent Leo Argo.

"You're on your own on this one," The Fat Man interjected. "Leo is coming by in a few minutes to pick me up. I'll meet you there."

Thompson looked at Ann and pointed at his watch. "Keep us on time then, babe," Thompson instructed as he dove into the crowd shaking hands and posing for pictures.

"How do you do it?" Coleman asked Ann, as Thompson made his way through the crowd.

"Do what?" Ann replied.

"This," Coleman said, waving his hand in the direction of the crowd. "All this madness. People are always pulling at him. Do you ever have a private moment?"

"Believe it or not," Ann said with a smile, "when we left, he missed it."

"Really?" Coleman replied. "He doesn't seem like the kind of guy to miss the spotlight. I thought he was different."

"They all love the spotlight," Ann replied. Pointing to Thompson she continued. "He'd never admit to it, but he missed it. They are all driven by it to one degree or another. And he is different. He cares about what to do with the spotlight while it's on him."

"Speaking of the spotlight," Coleman said, pointing to the stage as Thompson stepped up and strapped a mandolin over his shoulder. "It looks like the Senator is about ready to grab it."

Just as Richard Thompson began playing the intro to "The Irish Rover," Charlie Patterson walked into the Dubliner. An old friend of the Thompson's, Ann's eyes lit up when Patterson kissed her cheek. "My goodness," she said. "If this isn't old home week."

"I'll ignore the 'old' reference," Patterson grinned.

Ann flipped her hand at the gray in Patterson's temples. "Be proud, Charlie," she said. "You've earned them."

"I guess," Patterson replied. "But I'm still trying to figure out the connection between gray hair and my ability to get through the day without a proper nap. I assume there is a scientific connection somewhere."

Ann laughed and shook her head. "I have a hard time believing you've lost a step. You still appear not to have a care in the world."

"Oh, if you only knew," Patterson replied. "If you only knew."

Chapter 23

"Feel honored," Leo Argo said steering his black Crown Victoria sedan down a side street in Arlington, Virginia. "I usually complain about working with a partner."

"This wasn't exactly my idea," The Fat Man responded. "You were the one who offered to pick me up on our way to dinner. I didn't know you'd be taking me on a perp watch along the way."

Argo laughed. "Perp watch?" he asked. "Man, you're watching too many crime shows on television."

"What can I say?" The Fat Man replied. "My wife is addicted." He pointed to an open parking space about a half block away. "There's one up there."

"I see it," Argo replied as he put on his turn signal and began to slow the car. "Did you explain to her we're not as pretty as the people on those shows?"

"Naw," The Fat Man replied looking down at his belly. "I really don't have a problem with her closing her eyes and seeing Mark Harmon."

"You're sick," Argo said as he angled the Crown Vic into the parking place.

"You should try it," The Fat Man suggested. "You think Jane wants to come home to you every night? What should you care if she sees someone else with her eyes closed?"

Argo shook his head. "Alright, we've gone too far now. I don't want to know about your sex life and I sure as hell don't want to tell you about mine."

"To each his own," The Fat Man said as he shrugged his shoulder. "So tell me again why we're taking the long way to your townhouse?"

"Just a hunch in a case I'm working on," Argo said as he shut off the engine. "I've visited boxing gyms in DC all day. This is the last one on my list and it's on our way home."

"No it isn't," The Fat Man corrected.

"Just humor me," Argo responded.

"Whatever," The Fat Man said as he huffed to pull his pear shaped body from the car.

"What the hell are you doing?" Argo looked across the hood of the car as The Fat Man adjusted his tie and straightened his suit jacket.

"Coming with you," The Fat Man was heading across the street before Argo could object.

"Fine," Argo rolled his eyes as he responded. "Just try not to get into trouble."

The Arlington Boxing Club was located in a small, old warehouse just off Lee Highway. The outside may have looked like an abandoned building, but when Argo walked through the door—the sights, sounds and smell of the facility immediately took him back to his youth. A Golden Glove champion in Miami as a kid, the scene made Argo think of the days he spent hanging around the 5th Street Gym on South Beach.

"It stinks in here," The Fat Man whispered to Argo while watching the flurry of activity around him. One man was working a speed bag causing the whole place to reverberate with a noise reminding The Fat Man of rapid machine gun fire. Two men in headgear sparred in one of the three rings located around the concrete floor.

"It smells like when I was young," Argo replied.

"You must have been a stinky kid," The Fat Man laughed.

"Can I help you?" a voice said from behind the pair. A lanky African-American with gray hair approached and stuck out his hand. "I'm Mike. This is my place."

"My name's Leo." Argo returned the handshake. "And this is my pal Joey."

The Fat Man and Mike exchanged head nods. "Hey," The Fat Man said.

"I've driven past this place a thousand times and always wanted to drop in," Argo replied, looking around with admiration as he spoke. "This is the real deal."

"Trainin' folks here for better than thirty years," Mike said proudly. "You box?"

"Not since Tyson carried his own spit bucket," Argo laughed. "But I used to train on South Beach."

"No shit," Mike replied respectfully. "5th Street?"

Argo smiled. "You betcha."

The Fat Man looked puzzled at the instant bond occurring between the two men. "What's on 5th Street?" he asked.

"The Fifth Street Gym," Mike replied. "The best in the world trained there with Angelo Dundee. It's where Ali trained for his fights with Sonny Liston."

"I saw Sugar Ray work out there," Argo boasted.

"Robinson?" asked The Fat Man.

Mike and Argo burst into laughter. "Leonard," said Argo. "I watched Sugar Ray Leonard hit the bag. I may look old, but I'm not old enough for Sugar Ray Robinson."

"Well, Leo," Mike said. "It ain't 5th Street and this ain't Miami, but it's the best training facility in this area."

"I can see you're tops," Argo replied, nodding his head in approval. "I assume you train kids in Golden Glove."

Mike smiled. "Of course, I do," he said. "All the martial arts, cage fightin' shit took a lot of kids away from the program, but I've trained quite a few champions over the years."

"Really?" Argo continued. "Tell me about your program."

While Argo talked with Mike about the gym's Golden Glove program, The Fat Man wandered around to get a close-up view of the various boxers and their training regimen. In one part of the room closest to the locker rooms, a tall, thick man wandered out to begin his workout. He was followed by a man best described as short and stubby. Tall and Thick walked up to a bag and began throwing punch after punch. Little Stubby held the bag and stared at the man who was talking with the gym's owner near the front door.

"What ya' lookin' at?" Tall and Thick grunted at Little Stubby, sweat starting to drip from his brow.

"Those two guys," Little Stubby replied, looking first at Argo and then at The Fat Man.

Tall and Thick threw a punch and then looked around to sneak a peek. "The one guy was on television the other night," he said.

"Yeah," Little Stubby replied, peering at Argo. "Except he was wearing his FBI fraternity letters at the time."

Tall and Thick snuck another glance. "Who's the other dude? The fat one?"

"I don't know," Little Stubby said, observing The Fat Man's portly frame. "But he sure as hell doesn't look like he's FBI."

"What do you think they're doing here?" Tall and Thick hit the bag hard with a right, then a left.

Little Stubby held the bag against his chest and absorbed the force of the punches. "I don't know, but it can't be good."

The Fat Man approached the two men and stared, marveling at the strength Tall and Thick exerted with each punch into the bag.

The Fat Man's stares drew Tall and Thick's attention. He quit hitting the bag and took a step towards The Fat Man. "What the fuck you want, fat boy?" he snarled.

Taken aback by the rudeness of the boxer, The Fat Man tried to smooth it over. "Sorry to interrupt your workout," he said apologetically. "I've never walked around a gym like this before."

Tall and Thick looked at The Fat Man's physique. "No shit," he exclaimed. "I thought you were Macho Camacho."

"Who?"

"Get the fuck out of here," Little Stubby barked.

Argo and Mike watched the dust up starting and immediately came to the aid of The Fat Man. "These boys are my guests," Mike said. "You leave 'em alone."

"I don't care who they are," Tall and Thick said. "Just keep this little fat fuck away from me."

"Cool it, man," Little Stubby warned.

"Yeah, man," Mike said. "You're way out of line."

"Just get Pedro and Macho Camacho away from me," Tall and Thick said as he turned his back away.

The comment by Tall and Thick pushed Argo too far. He took a step forward. "What did you say?"

The Fat Man tried to intervene. "Let's just leave," he interjected.

Tall and Thick straightened up his back and looked at Argo. "You heard me, beaner," he said clearly enough to properly convey the insult.

"Beaner?" Argo said incredulously, the veins starting to stick out on his reddening neck. "You realize I'm Cuban, right?"

"Mexican. Cuban. Whatever," Tall and Thick stepped towards Argo and laughed. "I'm sorry if I insulted you, Fidel," he taunted.

Argo snapped, put his fists up in a defensive position and lunged towards Tall and Thick. Mike stepped in between them and pushed Argo backwards. "Calm down, man," Mike instructed. He looked at Little Stubby. "You ain't even from around here. You two are suspended for a month. Get the hell out of here."

Argo stepped back and looked at Mike. "No need to suspend them, Mike," Argo said, looking at Tall and Thick the entire time. He broke Mike's clasp around his arms. "You got any extra gear back in the locker room?" he asked.

"Yeah," Mike responded.

"Let them stay," Argo snarled. "I need a workout."

"What?" Tall and Thick said smiling. "The old man wants to lace them up?"

"Unless you're afraid," Argo hissed. It was not Argo's style to trash, but he was suddenly looking for a fight.

"Bring it on, Fidel," Tall and Thick replied with a little less bravado than his previous taunts.

When Mike, Argo and The Fat Man retreated to the locker room, Little Stubby snapped his head around to Tall and Thick. "Are you nuts?" he asked.

"Not at all," Tall and Thick replied.

"Then what the hell are you doing?" Little Stubby barked.

"While I'm in the process of kicking the old man's ass," Tall and Thick said. "go out and tag his car. He wants this kid as badly as we do. Let him do the hard work and lead us to him."

In the locker room, Argo changed from his suit to a pair of baggy shorts, t-shirt and tennis shoes Mike lent him. "You've not fought in the squared circle for some time, have you?" Mike asked.

"It's been a while," Argo admitted. "But some things you don't forget."

"I'm not sure this is a good idea," The Fat Man added, pacing nervously around the room. Then, as if to affirm his statement, he added, "This is definitely a bad idea."

"Calm down, Joe," Argo instructed before grabbing a pair of red boxing gloves off a hook on the wall and tossing them to The Fat Man. "Help me put these one," he said. "This is going to be fun."

"Fun?" The Fat Man asked, sliding a glove onto Argo's hand. "I know fun. Space Mountain at Disney World is fun. This is definitely not fun."

"Lighten up, Joe," Argo said in an assuring voice, pounding one glove against the other.

"Just be careful out there," The Fat Man said. "Okay?"

Argo just winked at The Fat Man before putting on his head gear. The Fat Man snapped it in place. "I mean it."

Tall and Thick was waiting in a corner of the ring with his head gear on and a mouthpiece already in when Argo climbed between the ropes. The Fat Man headed to Argo's corner while Mike entered the ring to be a referee. "Three rounds, gentlemen," Mike said. "I'll keep time on my watch. Break on my instructions, or I'll stop everything." Several fighters in the room stopped their workouts and were gathering around the ring to watch. Mike pointed at them. "The boys will be the judges. One knockdown and it's over. If no one goes down, their scoring determines the winner."

When Mike announced the start of round one, Argo bounced up on the balls of his feet and paced carefully to the center of the ring. He threw a right lead catching Tall and Thick on the side of his head.

When the punch landed, a couple of the men watching let out approving groans.

Tall and Thick shook the punch off like nothing. He smiled at Argo and lunged a left. Argo ducked the punch and threw another right lead landing about the same place on Tall and Thick's temple.

"Damn," one of the fighters shouted. "Go Old School!"

Tall and Thick was clearly irritated by the two head shots and by the ribbing from the other fighters. He walked in and threw a roundhouse punch that met its mark under Argo's eye, causing the big Cuban to flinch. The two men then locked arms until Mike broke the clinch. On the break, Tall and Thick threw a punch landing on Argo's lip, drawing a bit of blood.

"No hittin' on the break, boy," Mike shouted.

Now it was Argo's turn to offer a sardonic smile. As he did so, he wiped his glove across his lip and examined the blood. Unfazed, Argo walked in and threw yet another right lead, but this time followed with a left combination. Tall and Thick swung wildly. Argo ducked the punch and landed a solid blow to the ribs.

By the time Mike called "time" for the end of the round, both men were sweating. Tall and Thick seemed to be breathing just as heavy as Argo. The Fat Man tossed a stool into the ring and Argo flopped onto it. He handed Argo a water bottle and started rubbing Argo's shoulders.

"What are you doing?" Argo asked looking backwards.

The Fat Man bobbed back and forth as he rubbed. "Giving you a rub down," he said.

"Why?" Argo snarled.

"Because it's what Mickey did for Rocky between rounds," The Fat Man said.

"Well, I ain't Sylvester Stallone and you're not Burgess Meredith," Argo replied. "It's creepy. Knock it off."

After checking on Tall and Thick first, Mike came to Argo's corner. "How ya feelin,' son?"

"I'm fine," Argo said. "My job keeps me in pretty good shape."

"Well, you're getting to him," Mike said softly. He leaned in, pretending to look at Argo's eyes. "Keep throwin' the right leads. It's pissin' him off, big time. Get him angry enough and he'll mess up and leave himself open."

While The Fat Man was a huge sports fan, he did not know boxing. The reference confused him. "What's special about right leads?" he asked.

"He can see them coming from a mile away and they take a while to land," Argo replied. "When I do land one, I'm letting him know how slow he is and how little respect I have for him. In boxing parlance, it's an insult – trash talking without words."

"Cool," The Fat Man replied, pouring some water into Argo's mouth. "Do more of it."

Argo swished the water around in his mouth and then spit in a bucket. "It's an old trick I was taught as a kid at the gym in Miami," Argo said as he stood up. "Ali used it against Foreman in the Rumble in the Jungle," he continued, before putting his mouthpiece back in and clapping his gloves together.

The Fat Man quickly got the Ali reference. "Argo, boom ba yay," he said loudly, echoing the chant the crowd cheered in Zaire in 1974 urging Ali to literally kill George Foreman.

The second round started pretty much the same as the first, with Argo landing right leads, ducking the wild punches of Tall and Thick, and then countering with solid body punches. Each time Argo landed a right lead, Tall and Thick would get angrier and his counters wilder. The fact the local fighters watching were clearly rooting for Argo did not help his rising temper.

About midway through the second round, Argo hit Tall and Thick with yet another right lead. Tall and Thick literally growled as he lunged at Argo, who threw his hardest punch yet. It landed on Tall and Thick's jaw. Argo chased him to the corner, driving him backwards with strong body punches. Tall and Thick hit the turnbuckle, and he tried to slide to Argo's left. When he did, Argo popped him hard with a punch to the side of the head. Tall and Thick went down to one knee.

Mike jumped in and waved his arms above his head. The fighters watching cheered Argo and jeered Tall and Thick.

"I slipped," Tall and Thick argued, pulling himself up against the ropes.

Little Stubby pushed Tall and Thick back to the corner and shook his head. "Just shut the fuck up, man."

Chapter 24

Newly minted Senator Richard Thompson slowly strolled around the first floor of Jane Kline's roomy townhouse, with Kline's dog, Hoover, following closely behind. Ann disappeared into the kitchen to chat with Kline while she opened a bottle of wine. Either in the spirit of friendliness or an abundance of caution, Hoover chose to stay with Thompson.

Looking around at the mix of styles in the living room, Thompson concluded the eclectic collection of furnishings – although nicely blended – defied labeling. "Early contemporary American deco," Thompson mumbled to Hoover as they walked. The dog seemed unimpressed with Thompson's attempt at humor.

In the foyer, Thompson studied the photos hanging on the wall. It seems every person who spends time in Washington maintains a "brag wall" filled with pictures taken with the famous people they met along the way. As the Director of the Central Intelligence Agency, Kline was with the President on a regular basis. With a photographer constantly at the President's side, Thompson was actually surprised to see only one photo of Kline with President Rohman – one taken with Leo Argo and the First Lady at the While House Christmas party.

Rather than a multitude of pictures of national and world leaders, Kline's "brag wall" was filled with pictures of fish she caught over the years. Having learned the sport from her late-father, Director Kline was an avid fisherman – an interest she shared with Thompson. Photos showed her on boats and in rivers and lakes around the world. Thompson smiled when he noticed one of the pictures on the wall was one he snapped on an expedition they took together on the Cumberland River in Kentucky. Kline was proudly holding a 22 inch rainbow trout.

Kline and Ann entered the foyer side by side. A drink in one hand and a cane in the other, Kline said "Senator" formally, and handed Thompson a glass of bourbon. "Pappy's, my friend."

"Pappy's?" Thompson exclaimed, holding the glass to the light while examining Kentucky's most exclusive export.

"Twenty-two years old," she added smiling.

"How the heck did you find twenty-two year old Pappy's in DC?"

"I'm head of the CIA," Kline replied. "We found Che Guevara in a ravine in the backwoods of Bolivia. Finding Pappy's in DC was a snap, Senator."

"Senator?" Ann declared. She handed Kline's glass of wine to her as she spoke. "Jane, you and Leo are our friends. Please just call him Richard."

Kline smiled in appreciation of Ann's offer. "Friends or not – in this town, he's Senator Thompson," she replied. She pointed to the picture from their fishing trip. "Maybe when we're on the river again, you can go back to being Richard."

Thompson tipped his glass to Kline before taking a sip. "Well, if we're going to be formal, then thank you Madam Director." He followed the first sip with a quick second and turned back to the brag wall. "I love the picture of you on the Cumberland. You put it up on my account?"

"Hell no," Kline replied. "A big rainbow on a dry fly from a shore cast." Kline laughed. "A fish with shoulders. I don't care if the President of Russia snapped the picture, I was putting it on the wall. I should have mounted it and hung it over the fireplace."

"Then we couldn't have eaten it," Thompson reminded Kline.

"I swear I don't understand what you two see in this sport," Ann said, shaking her head as she spoke.

"Which is why you and Leo stayed back in the lodge the day we went out," Thompson added, looking closely again at the photo. "It was a beautiful fish."

"Speaking of Leo," Ann followed the lead of Thompson's previous comment, "where is he? Wasn't he picking up Joe?"

"Yeah," Kline said, looking at her wrist watch. Her scowl indicated she was unhappy at his tardiness. "My beloved Leo is apparently running a bit behind. But running on FBI time is the order of the day lately."

"The investigation into the assassination of Vice President Shelby taking up all of his time, I take it?" Thompson asked. He could see Kline's frustration and trying to offer a change of subject in order to save Argo from Kline's irritation.

"Comes with the turf," Kline said, nodding an affirmative response to his question. "But I did think he'd be on time tonight."

"No big deal," Thompson said. He pointed his drink in the direction of the living room. "We've got no place to go – other than a comfy looking couch."

Kline appreciated Thompson's relaxed demeanor. She turned to lead them to the living room. "Most of your new colleagues don't treat me with as much patience," she said as she walked.

"Most of his colleagues are horses' asses with overinflated egos," Ann snapped. Her sharp tone suggested she was not kidding in stating her opinion of the other ninety-nine who filled the floor of the United States Senate.

"As you can tell," Thompson said, shaking his head in mock disbelief, "nothing changes in my life. One of the crosses I bear is my lovely wife still has a problem expressing her true feelings," he sighed.

"In the line of work we've chosen for ourselves," Kline replied as she sat down in an overstuffed white leather chair, "isn't it kind of refreshing?"

Thompson and Ann sat down on the sofa. "Yeah," Thompson laughed, resting his drink on a coaster. "She's real refreshing – until you become the object of her scorn."

"You have such a rough life," Ann teased as she slapped Thompson on his knee. Ann looked at Kline jokingly. "But then again, you're the head of the CIA, so I guess you already know the details of his life."

"Yes," Kline declared smiling. "I check on his life each morning – right after I set the weather patterns and determine the international price of gold for the day."

"Let's not go there," Thompson said, waggling his index finger at Kline. "I was appointed to the subcommittee authorizing the Export-Import Bank. Some of my colleagues would be thrilled if I confirmed you're really the one in charge of everything."

"I do it from a bunker in the basement," Kline added.

Thompson shook his head. "Stop it," he reiterated in jest. "You're killing me."

"Seriously then," Kline said changing her tone. "You got the sub with jurisdiction over the Ex-Im?"

"Yeah," Thompson replied. He received his committee and subcommittee assignments shortly after being sworn in. "I'm on the Subcommittee on National Security, International Trade and Finance – only five people on the committee. I may actually get to ask questions at hearings."

"Well, doesn't the subcommittee cover more than just the Export-Import Bank?" Kline asked. "There are a lot of deals coming through."

"I've just started the research," Thompson replied nonchalantly. "I'm really not sure what's on our plate."

"The pipeline." Kline cringed as she blurted out the words. The President's instructions for lobbying Thompson on the pipeline were firm. Senator Wilson was opposed the Administration's position and they needed Thompson on board. But she was bad at politics and knew it. Her rough edges showed.

"Really?" Thompson said. He had not done much research on the subcommittee's jurisdictional issues yet, and he was genuinely surprised. He puffed his lips out and jogged his head from side to side. "I didn't know."

"Concurrent jurisdiction," Kline continued her assault into the issue. "It's in your lap. Well, yours and probably ten other subcommittees in the Senate."

The term "concurrent jurisdiction" was not normally tossed around in polite dinner conversation. Thompson realized what was happening and smiled softly. "Have we just ventured from pleasure to business?" he asked.

Kline slyly cocked her head a bit. Thompson was letting her up and she appreciated the effort. "Maybe," she said. "The President would like to know if you're talking with Wilson on the pipeline."

Knowing Thompson and Kline were about to have a detailed discussion about policy, Ann decided to excuse herself from the conversation. "I'm going to go in the kitchen and slice up some cheese. Leo and Joe should be getting back any time now."

Thompson watched his wife walk out of the room. He was slightly troubled by the change in the direction of conversation with Kline. He thought the dinner invitation was extended out of friendship. The venture into politics threw him a curve. He decided to respond in a coy manner. When Ann was out of ear shot, he said, "Everybody back home seems to like Senator Wilson."

Kline felt the sting of the response and averted her eyes. Pausing for a moment, she decided to speak frankly. "I'm sorry, Richard."

It was not lost on Thompson that Kline referred to him by his first name. "It's okay," he replied accepting her apology.

"Mack Wilson opposed us on the pipeline," Kline continued. "It doesn't make sense, but he was on the other side. I didn't invite you here for this reason, but the President asked me to discuss your position on the issue. It's an important national security issue for the administration. Oil from North America makes Europe less dependent on the Russians."

"Alright, Jane," Thompson replied. He felt Kline's discomfort. Still, he did not want to answer the question directly – yet. "Let me first give you my take on Mack Wilson. He's a gifted politician who is incredibly shrewd and a virtual master at the game." He paused for emphasis. "But he is untrustworthy as hell."

"You sound like you speak from experience," Kline added.

"I do," Thompson replied. "Congressman Barkman and Senator Wilson were butting heads on a federal project back in Kentucky last year. There was some road fund money available in an appropriation bill and each of them wanted the pork to go to a different bridge. Wilson called me to intervene. I refused, saying I was out of the game."

Kline took a sip from her wine. "I assume Wilson wasn't too happy with your neutrality."

"If he was angry," Thompson said, shaking his head, "he sure didn't let on. Thanked me and I quickly forgot about it."

"So, I assume it's not the end of the story?" Kline replied.

"Not by a long shot," Thompson said. "Ever hear of Billy Straub?"

"Yeah," Kline nodded. "He used to cover the White House for the *Washington Post*."

"Used to," Thompson repeated. "He's a freelancer now. He writes some real heavy investigative stuff – a real muckraker."

"I assume he'd take it as a compliment," Kline said.

"Absolutely," Thompson said. "Straub calls me and starts asking about a federal grant I helped get for a local health agency nearly a decade ago. And he starts questioning me about being on their board before and after I was in Congress."

"Interesting timing," Kline said.

"To say the least," Thompson replied. "So I answered all of his questions and argued with him a bit over the premise of the story. I even gave him some sources to call."

"The nice guy you are and all," Kline said.

"I never fought with the press," Thompson assured Kline. "I always appreciated their job."

"Better attitude than me," Kline laughed.

"Anyway, I'm sitting at home a day or two later, and Straub calls me back." Thompson leaned back on the couch. "He called to apologize. He called my sources and confirmed the appropriation was for a homeless clinic."

"Really?"

"Apparently," Thompson said. "Straub's source told him the appropriation was for some mega-health care institution. When he discovered it was for a homeless clinic, he was pissed. He called to apologize."

"There's something you don't see too often," Kline said. "I don't think I have ever received a call from a reporter apologizing."

"He did more than apologize," Thompson added. "He gave me his source."

"Don't tell me," Kline smiled. "Wilson?"

"Yup," Thompson said. "Hand delivered by his Chief of Staff."

"Amazing." Kline shook her head.

"No, it isn't," Thompson corrected. "Wilson was the typical Member on a power trip. Between you and me, the sonofabitch would run over his grandmother for a vote."

"Great," Kline said sarcastically.

"He's not just sneaky," Thompson added. "I never trusted his intentions. If he's opposed to the pipeline, his reasons may not jive with national security policy."

Kline suddenly understood where Thompson was heading.

"If you and the President need to make a case for the pipeline," Thompson continued as he tipped his glass, "make it. I'll listen."

Kline returned the toast and took a sip of wine. "Wilson seems to thrive on conspiracies," Kline pointed out. "Is it really a part of his persona, or does he just throw all of it out there as raw meat for the ideologues?"

"A little of both, probably," Thompson replied. He considered that very question several times over the years. "I used to think it was all just a dance he did for the wing nuts."

"And you've changed your mind?" Kline questioned.

"Not entirely," Thompson said. "At least not yet. I still think his primary motivation is playing to a constituency. But we've found dozens of banker's boxes in the office, filled with files and documents about his various international conspiracies. Joe's going through them quickly with staff and there seem to be a few with legs."

"Interesting," Kline mumbled.

"He's going to go over them with our new Legislative Director," Thompson said. "Who knows? There might actually be something in there worth pursuing. But I'm not ready to audit the Federal Reserve quite yet."

Suddenly Hoover jumped up and started barking. "What is it baby? Someone out there?" The words were barely out of her mouth when they heard the garage door to the townhouse opening. "Speaking of Joe, I think he's pulling up with my so-called better half." Kline looked at her watch and grumbled, "Better late than never." Kline got up and headed to the kitchen. Thompson followed.

Hoover's paws tapped on the tile floor and he barked when the door from the garage to the kitchen swung open. The Fat Man entered first. "Joe!" Kline said, hugging The Fat Man. "It's so great to see you."

"You too, Jane," The Fat Man said. "I'm still allowed to call you Jane, right?"

"Please do," Kline smiled at The Fat Man's concern over protocol. "I'd be offended if you called me anything else."

When Argo entered the room, Kline stared at his reddened left eye. She grabbed him by the chin and looked closely at the moderate swelling. "Jesus Christ, Leo," Kline asked. "What the hell happened to your eye?"

Argo used tongs to toss a few ice cubes from a bucket into a paper napkin. He placed the napkin on his cheek. "I slipped on a bar of soap," he said laughingly. "Who's ready for me to grill up some pork chops?"

Chapter 25

Leo Argo stood on the cedar deck in back of his Old Towne Alexandria townhome poking a long fork into the pork chops sizzling on the open grill with one hand while rolling a cold glass of white wine across the small knot under his left eye with the other. He now wore a pair of khaki cargo shorts and a black FBI t shirt. Over the t shirt, he sported an unbuttoned grey flannel baseball jersey with the words Sugar Kings embroidered in red across the front. He also wore a red, white, and blue apron, fashioned in a triangle to resemble the Cuban flag.

Thompson stood on one side of the deck, occasionally sipping his second Pappy's of the evening, and noticing that with the right angle, he had a decent view of the Potomac River. His curiosity about the lump under Leo's eye was eating at him, but he decided The Fat Man would tell him later. The Fat Man himself sat back on a bench built into the deck railing. His shaggy grey hair and scruffy beard poked out from underneath a Cincinnati Reds baseball cap. Over his white dress shirt and tie, he also wore a Sugar King's team baseball jersey – identical to the one Argo was wearing.

Argo put down his glass of wine and adjusted his apron. "I still can't believe you found this apron and these jerseys," Argo said. Once they arrived at the townhouse, The Fat Man presented Argo with the gifts he found during one of his many on-line eBay searches. Argo put it on with great enthusiasm, and he had kept looking at it ever since. "My old man would have loved this apron," he said. "He was born just outside of Havana."

"You're welcome," The Fat Man replied.

Argo pointed the fork at The Fat Man's jersey. "You know, he saw the Sugar Kings play ball before he came to America on one of the early Freedom Flights." Pulling at the jersey, Argo added, "You really gotta know your baseball to know about the Havana Sugar Kings."

"Are you kidding me?" Thompson replied, humored by the remark. "Joey knows each stat of every person in the game since the New York Knickerbockers took the field."

The Fat Man was basking in the praise of the gifts he procured for his friend Argo. They met when Thompson first ran for Congress and remained friends ever since. The Fat Man looked at Thompson. "You have no idea who the Sugar Kings are, do you?"

"No," Thompson replied, smiling because The Fat Man was starting to get excited the way he usually did when talking about his favorite sport. "But I have the distinct impression you're about to tell me."

"AAA farm club of the Cincinnati Reds in the 50's," Argo interjected as he flipped pork chops.

"No shit?" Thompson replied. "I never knew there were minor league clubs in Cuba."

The Fat Man jumped in. "The Sugar Kings played in the old Florida International League."

Thompson shook his head. "I don't remember that league," he said.

"Well, the league kind of ceased being international around 1960," The Fat Man continued. "It became just the Florida League when the borders were shut down. A couple of MLB teams kept minor league clubs in Cuba."

"I never knew," Thompson said shaking his head. He always marveled at The Fat Man's knowledge of America's pastime.

The Fat Man took a sip from his bottled water and tried to think of a way to relate the team to Thompson. His eyes brightened. "Remember Leo Cardenas?" he asked.

Thompson did not follow baseball as closely as The Fat Man, but he certainly remembered the names of the Reds players from his youth. "Mr. Automatic," Thompson replied. "Called him, Chico, didn't they?"

"Yup," The Fat Man nodded.

"Maybe one of the best fielding shortstops ever," Thompson said.

The Fat Man smiled fondly remembering the journeyman who spent several seasons with the Cincinnati Reds. "There's hope for you yet," he said. "Anyway, Cardenas came up through the system with the Sugar Kings."

"I never knew Leo started in Cuba," Thompson said. He pondered the comment for a moment and then added. "No one knows such obscure facts, except you."

"I did," Argo said as he raised his hand. "Chico was one of the last players to make it out of Cuba before all the shit hit the fan and Castro locked down the borders."

The Fat Man was pleased Argo also knew about Cardenas. "Did you know Cardenas was shot while he played for the Sugar Kings?"

"Shot?" Thompson asked quizzically, drawing out the single word question as he spoke. "Like with a gun?"

"Yeah," Argo jumped in. "Fidel had a big celebration of the revolution at the ball park. He got everyone all excited and they pulled out guns and started shooting them in the air. Somehow, Chico got popped."

Thompson took a drink and then pointed at Argo. "You're scaring me now, you know as much about this as him."

"Man, the Sugar Kings are one of the reasons so many Cubans are Reds fans," Argo paused and added. "Well, the Kings and Tony Perez." Argo cut off a small piece of a pork chop and tossed it to Hoover who gobbled it down quickly.

"Big Doggie is the best," The Fat Man said. Perez was his favorite all-time baseball player. The customized vanity license plates on his two cars were "C D BOL" and "HT D BOL" in honor of Perez's oft-quoted broken-English interview comment, "I see the ball, I hit the ball." The cars always had to be parked side-by-side in the driveway so passersby along the street could read the message.

"As a kid growing up in Miami, we always followed the Red Legs," Argo said. "Hell, when we'd play street ball, we'd fight over who got to be Perez."

"Judging by the eye," Thompson laughed, "I assume you were the Big Dog more often than not."

Argo just smiled and took a sip from his wine. He looked over at The Fat Man and winked.

As the trio looked around awkwardly at each other following Thompson's eye comment, the sliding glass door to the deck opened. Ann and Kline walked onto the deck with the others. "Alright boys," Ann said sternly. "Cut the chit-chat. The 'taters are done and we're hungry."

"Perfect timing, my dear," Thompson said, walking over to his wife and kissing her on the cheek. The Fat Man and Argo chuckled at the comment.

"Just in time for the Senator's favorite meal to be done," Argo said as he started picking up pork chops with a fork and placing them on a platter.

"You are going to take off the apron for dinner, aren't you?" Kline asked Argo.

Argo kissed Kline and then handed her the platter. "I'll take off the apron, but I'm leaving the jersey on."

"I have an idea you're going to be sleeping in it."

"TMI," Ann threw up her hand. "I really don't want to know Leo's sleeping attire."

* * *

The dinner conversation was flowing as freely as the food and drink when it was interrupted by the ring of Argo's cell phone. He pulled it out of his pants pocket and looked at the caller ID. Kline looked slightly irritated he had not put the phone on silent or vibrate.

Argo grimaced at the number calling him. "Excuse me, folks," he said politely. "Unfortunately, I have to take this." He looked at Kline. "Sorry."

The conversation restarted as soon as Argo left the table. He hit the talk button on his phone and made his way into the first floor study. He closed the door behind him for privacy. "Argo here," he said.

The voice on the other end was Secret Service Agent Scott Proctor. "Sorry to bother you at home, Leo," he said.

"Yeah," Argo replied as he looked through the glass door into the dining room. "It's really bad timing," he said.

"Well, this is pretty important," Proctor said.

"It damn well better be," Argo said. "Or I may be sleeping on the couch tonight. And I'm talking about your couch, not mine."

"Metro Police are investigating the murder of two men at a bar about a block from The Cairo," Proctor said.

"The building where Unger lives," Argo replied.

"Yeah," Proctor replied. "Apparently, it's a pretty grizzly crime scene. One man was shot, but the other one had the hell beaten out of him before he was shot."

"And?" Argo begged the question

"And you better get over there and take charge of the situation," Proctor said.

"I've got a US Senator at my house right now having dinner."

"Leo," Proctor said, "David Unger's fingerprints are all over the bar."

Chapter 26

David Unger stood outside the building housing Charlie Patterson's law office and looked at Patterson's instructions. The address was located just outside of Georgetown. His first instinct had been to head for the subway, but it was quitting time on the Hill and a steady stream of people filled the long escalator taking them to the platform of the Capitol South Metro stop. Unger had become fairly confident of his new persona on the subway ride over to Patterson's office when only a few people occupied the train. However, the influx of people made him consider taking an alternate mode of transportation to Georgetown. After all, these were not mid-day Zombies hopping on the subway. These were Hill Rats. His disguise might not hold up under the scrutiny of people whose lives revolved around the political rumors swirling within the Beltway.

Ruling out the subway, Unger's only transportation options were a cab or walking. As he watched cab after cab drive past, he became concerned most of the cabbies were foreigners. He did not want to end up with a driver who could be ratting him out to a taxi dispatcher in Farsi while he peered happily out the window.

So Unger decided to walk to Georgetown. It would take him an hour or better, but he realized most folks walking the streets of big cities try to avoid eye contact. Even more than subway travelers, walkers wear their disinterest in their fellow travelers like a badge of honor. Unger stuffed the piece of paper containing the address back into his pants pocket and headed up the street towards Constitution Avenue.

Remembering Willis' advice, he paced his steps to match the speed of his fellow foot travelers, trying to blend in and not draw attention. With the Capitol in sight, he stepped off the curb to cross the street. When a Capitol Hill Police Officer shouted at him, his heart skipped a beat and he froze in his steps. Instincts told him to run. As he looked up, the officer who was controlling the traffic light from across the street shouted a warning. "Wait for the light, pal!"

Unger looked down and smiled. "Sorry, officer," he replied. When the light changed he crossed without so much as a second glance from the officer.

As Unger headed west on Constitution Avenue, he pondered again the bizarre set of circumstances leading him to this point in his life. One moment he had the best job he could have ever hoped for out of college. Then, in the blink of an eye, he became the nation's most wanted fugitive, hiding in plain sight on the streets of DC.

Unger pondered the statement Willis made about being someone's patsy. As he walked, Unger tried to make a mental list of who might be setting him up. From his perspective the possibilities seemed endless.

Chapter 27

Night had fallen by the time Leo Argo drove past the Blue Steel Café. It was an old habit for Argo – drive past the address to survey the scene before parking. The review of the perimeter from the front seat of his car, and then taking the extra time for the walk back up the street to the spot where he was actually going, were all part of the way he worked a crime scene. Parking his car about a block away, he sighed as he exited the car. As he looked down the street, he shook his head in disgust at the buzz of activity. "I'm getting damn tired of yellow tape," he mumbled to himself as he stepped into the street.

Taking a moment to absorb the sights and sounds of the neighborhood, Argo looked up and down the street to get an overview of the nicely kept storefronts and townhouses. He leaned back against his car for a minute to observe the people walking by. They seemed to be showing nothing more than mere curiosity in the activities taking place a block away. *Just another day in the big city*, Argo thought to himself. He watched a couple walk by pushing a baby stroller, oblivious to what was happening in plain sight. He envied their ignorance.

Argo began to make his way slowly down the street. Scott Proctor spied him approaching and walked up the street to meet him. He stuck out his hand. "Sorry to break up the dinner party, man," Proctor said apologetically.

"Not a problem," Leo replied, returning the firm handshake. "Though Jane wasn't real happy about me cutting out early."

"Tell me about it," Proctor replied. "The old 'it's just part of the job' excuse gets stale after a while, doesn't it?"

"It isn't the hours," Argo replied, shaking his head as he spoke. "I just seem to be cutting and running a lot these days."

"I feel your pain, bro," Proctor said. "I remember the days when I used to curse working the night shift. Now I'm on-call. I'd kill to be tied to a shift."

Argo looked at the officers establishing the perimeter around the entrance to the Blue Steel Café. "The price we pay for all this fame and glory, I guess," he laughed.

Proctor looked around to make sure all the reporters were out of the range of his voice, and then he leaned into Argo. "Well, maybe we'll find this kid soon," he replied, pointing to the door of the Blue Steel Café. "Maybe something in there is what we're looking for. Let's find Unger and we can all go home for dinner," he said.

As they passed under a street light, Proctor got a glance at the bruise under Argo's eye. "What's with the shiner?" he asked.

Argo did not want to go into a lengthy explanation and used what was quickly becoming his standard comeback. "I ran into a door knob."

Proctor stopped, and Argo instinctively stopped as well. Argo turned to Proctor, blinked a couple of times, and said, "What?"

With a slight head nod that wordlessly sought permission, Proctor slowly reached out and turned Argo's head so he could get a better view of it in the light. "Seriously man," Proctor said. "Did Jane pop you for leaving early? I know she used to be an operative, but smacking you around – bad ass, dude."

Exasperated, Argo swatted Proctor's hand away from his face. Proctor was not going to leave it alone. "If you must know, I used to box a lot as a kid. I got back into the gym recently. I did a little sparring earlier today."

Sensing Argo clearly did not care to elaborate, Proctor decided to gig him a little before letting the subject drop. "But I guess I should see the other guy, right?" he asked.

"Yeah," Argo said nodding. "Something like that."

As they approached the entrance to the cafe, Argo glanced at the reporters standing just beyond the crime scene tape. It seemed to be all local reporters. He looked around, and he noticed there were no national or cable network trucks on the street. "I assume the vultures haven't figured it out yet?"

"Radio silent thus far," Proctor said as he nodded his head in the direction of the reporters. "These guys think we're investigating a routine drug-related robbery and murder."

"Good," Argo replied. "The longer we can keep them thinking this is a routine case, the better."

"I agree," Proctor said. "Press is just another layer of frustration for me. We just need to keep the implications of this as far away from the White House for as long as possible. Let the folks in Public Affairs decide how they want to handle it."

When Argo entered the bar area of the cafe, all activity stopped momentarily as the forensics investigators glanced up to see who had entered the room. As Argo looked around at the horrendous crime scene, all of them went quickly back to their business. It was like a well-choreographed ballet. Each technician executed his or her job within the confines of that individuals own strict procedures.

Deciding to start with the closest person to him, Argo walked further into the bar area. The technician, a chubby brunette standing behind the bar, made eye contact with him and nodded toward the floor. Argo walked around to the side of the bar and looked down at the floor behind it. There he saw the body of a man with a bullet hole in the front of his head. Argo studied the body for a moment and then glanced up at the dried blood on the mirror behind the bar.

"The bartender," the technician said matter-of-factly. "Single shot to the head. Poor bastard came to work today to make a buck and got whacked for his efforts."

"I assume we have no doubt here about the cause of death?" Argo asked the tech who was scouring the area around the liquor shelves for anything other than blood.

The tech looked back at Argo and raised her eyebrows at what she considered a stupid question. "Only questions here are who, what, and why," she replied.

"Recover the slug yet?" Argo asked as he knelt down to examine the lifeless body.

"Yeah," she replied. "One shot. It's already on its way to the Hoover Building for testing."

Argo looked at the back of the victim's head. "Pretty clean exit wound," he commented before standing back up.

"Our people downtown will determine for sure, but I'm guessing a nine millimeter," the technician declared. "I'm not finding much brain or bone back here. The result of a small slug – quick in, quick out, not much mess."

"Thanks," Argo said turning to exit from behind the bar. He headed to the middle of the cafe to take a look at the second body. A photographer was clicking pictures as he approached. "Who we got here?" Argo asked.

"The owner of the place," the photographer replied. He opened up his notebook to make sure he got the name right. "Jared Willis."

As the photographer clicked away, Argo studied the corpse on the floor. Unlike the other dead body, Argo assumed the cause of death for Jared Willis would be far less certain at this point. There was a bullet hole between his eyes, but the swelling on the man's face and dried blood on other places on his head indicated he had endured a serious beating before he was shot. Argo surmised the gun shot was fired following the man's actual demise – a simple insurance policy of death.

"Moved him yet?" Argo asked the photographer.

"Not yet," he replied. "But I got all I need. Do what you gotta do."

Argo walked over to one of the evidence boxes and grabbed a pair of blue latex gloves. He snapped them onto his hands and went back over to Willis' body. Gently lifting up the corpse's head, he saw it had the same type of exit wound he had observed on the other body. "I'm betting the same gun," he said to no one in particular.

Argo noticed a large laceration on the back of the man's head, then looked to a spot where yet another crime scene technician was picking up glass scattered on the floor. "You get any good fingerprints on the bigger pieces?" Argo asked.

"One or two," the tech replied, not looking up from her work. "But they look like they belonged to the waiter behind the bar."

Argo indicated his understanding. After a few other observations, he stood up, removed the gloves and tossed them into a garbage bag in the center of the room. He looked at a man who was digging a pair of large tweezers into the floor. "The bullet?" he asked.

"I'm pretty sure," the man replied.

"Small caliber?" Argo asked

The man retrieved the bullet and placed the slug into an evidence bag. "Yes, sir," he replied.

Argo glanced away as Proctor approached. "What did you find?" Argo asked.

"Something you need to see," Proctor replied, handing the bag to Argo, who held up the evidence and peered at the cut up plastic cards inside. "David Unger's driver's license and credit cards," Proctor declared. "They were scattered all over the floor."

As Agro closed his eyes and tried to take it all in, Proctor continued. "We've got two dead bodies, Unger's shredded credit cards and his finger prints are all over the place."

"Cell phone?" Argo inquired.

"Missing," Proctor replied.

Argo held up his hand. He had heard enough. "I'm calling my boss, and I suggest you do the same. This is over our pay scale at this point. I'm not doing shit without direction from the Attorney General or someone pretty high up at Justice," Argo said. "They can make the call on who gets the warrant on cell phone records."

"What do you suggest?" Proctor asked.

"I'm going to head downtown to make a call to the Director. I need a secure line." He pointed a finger at Proctor. "Our bosses can talk and figure out the next moves. I suspect sometime tomorrow the world will know there is a manhunt on for David Unger."

Proctor nodded his agreement. "When this becomes public, the shit is going to hit the fan. The White House isn't going to like it, not one bit. We've got to wrap this up."

When Argo turned and headed for the door, an agent came around the corner from the kitchen and saw him leaving. "Hey, Leo," the voice was loud and excited. "Don't head out just yet. I need you to look at something."

Proctor in tow, Argo walked to the back of the bar as the agent led them to a bathroom just off the kitchen. It was separate from the public bathrooms off the seating area. "What's up?" Argo asked.

The man pointed to a trash can beside the sink. "Rubber gloves, peroxide and black hair." He then pointed to the tile floor. "And more black hair down there."

Argo looked at the agent. "Do we know the owner?"

"Naw," the agent replied. "But I'll bet you a cup of joe it's David Unger."

"I'm not taking that bet," Argo said. He closed his eyes and said out loud what everyone else was thinking. "Looks like our boy changed his appearance before he headed out."

"Shit," Proctor exclaimed.

"Yup," Argo replied, frustrated for not thinking of it earlier. "We're looking for a different David Unger."

A few minutes later, Argo tossed open the front door of the Blue Steel Café and trudged back out onto the street toward his car. He already called the Hoover Building for a sit down with the artist responsible for drawing most wanted pictures. He needed to know immediately what David Unger might look like with short peroxide blond hair.

Argo ducked under the yellow crime scene tape and was heading towards his car when a young man broke away from the group of reporters and approached him in a trot. "Are you Leo Argo?" the man asked as he caught up.

"Yeah," Argo said as he turned.

"Gene Monks," the man replied. "I own the *Potomac River News*."

Argo shook his head. "Never heard of it," he replied sharply.

"I don't expect you have," Monks said, smiling softly. "The PRN is an alternative newspaper and on-line blog covering the LBGT community in DC."

"I don't do press, son," Argo said, continuing to his car. "If you're looking for a statement, you're barking up the wrong tree, my man. I've got nothing for you."

"I'm not looking for a quote," Monks said. Undeterred he continued to follow Argo. "I'm just kind of curious, you know. Most of those reporters back there cover the local crime beat."

"Nice catch," Argo said sarcastically. "Keep working on the Pulitzer Prize."

Monks was undaunted by the insult. "They don't know who you are. But I do."

"Congratulations," Argo replied as he reached into his pocket for his car keys. "I'll see if I can get you a guest spot on Jeopardy."

Ignoring the second snide remark, Monks did not let up. "And it makes me wonder why the FBI would be interested in a lowly crime scene in DuPont Circle."

"Off the record?" Argo asked, hoping to keep the aggressive reporter at bay.

"Sure," Monks agreed.

"We get called in for our forensic expertise all the time," Argo said. "For anything on the record, call Public Affairs." Argo reached into his pocket and pulled out a card with the contact information for the FBI's public affairs bureau. "Here's the number."

"Thanks," Monks said appreciatively, looking at the card. "Hey, would you do me a favor and ask them to give me a call." Before Argo could deny the request, Monks started scribbling on a piece of paper.

Argo shook his head at the determination of the man. "Sure," he replied. At this point Argo would say anything to get the guy off his back and be on his way.

Monks scribbled something on the paper and handed it to Argo, who stuffed it in his pants pocket before jumping into his car and abruptly driving off.

Chapter 28

David Unger shook his head while looking at his watch. His walk to the Hawk's Cove bar took about as long as expected, but he was still early. He hung out across the street for a few minutes and watched the clientele enter the establishment. It was an odd mix of men, ranging from those wearing business suits like he was used to at the White House, to men in tight peg leg jeans. He fit in on the Metro and the street, but this masquerade made him nervous. After all, he needed to appear gay in a room full of gay men.

Scratching his head at the implications, Unger took a deep breath. He had always been somewhat ambivalent in his feelings about a person's sexual orientation. Of course, he had little experience around gay men – at least none he knew of. Now as he impersonated being gay to save his own skin, he felt apprehensive. The problem was, he was not sure about the source of his uneasiness. On one hand, he felt self-conscience about random people on the street viewing him as something he was not. On the other hand, he felt a bit of guilt at feeling shame over judging the very people trying to help him. Still, he had no time for moral judgment of either himself or his protectors. His life was at stake. He crossed the street and headed to the bar.

Once inside, Unger quickly scanned the room. His entrance was, for all intents and purposes, uneventful. In an effort to further survey the room, he walked back to the restroom. Catching glimpses from the corner of his vision while he worked his way through the crowd, he observed his entrance went unnoticed. He was not sure if people saw him as particularly straight or gay – or just another patron in the bar.

Emboldened by his new-found sense of anonymity, Unger followed Charlie Patterson's instructions. On his way back from the restroom, he found an empty seat at the bar and sat down. Unger surveyed the men sitting around the bar and recognized all of them had either a beer or a mixed drink in front of them. Concluding that ordering a Diet Coke would make him stand out, Unger ordered a drink he enjoyed a few times in college – a rum and coke with a twist of lime.

"Got some identification?" the bartender queried.

Unger was taken by surprise at the request. Knowing he had left all his identification with Jared Willis back at the Blue Steel Café, he began to panic. "I … I …" was all he could say.

"Come on, kid," the bartender insisted. "No ID, no drink."

Unger's breathing quickened as he struggled for a strategic response. Nothing was forthcoming. He had visions of his entire ruse coming to a close over an errant drink order. He fiddled with his pockets.

Suddenly, out of nowhere, Unger felt an arm around his shoulder. He looked up and saw a large man in his late forties, with salt-and-pepper curly hair. "It's okay, Mikey," the man said in a deep voice with a slight Cajun accent. "He's with me. Put it on my tab."

"Okay, Tommy," the bartender replied as he reached back behind the bar for some rum. "What brand?"

"He'll have Mount Gay," Tommy ordered before Unger could respond.

The bartender grabbed a bottle and poured the rum into the glass. "Sorry, kid," the man said as he spritzed some Coke onto the rum. "I just don't need any shit from the locals over serving some underage twink." He shoved the drink in front of Unger. "But if Tommy says you're okay, then you're okay with me."

Unger nodded appreciatively at Tommy and took a reluctant sip from his cocktail. He was not sure what to make of the situation until Tommy leaned forward and put his arm around Unger in a move giving the appearance of intimacy. When Unger tried to pull back,

Tommy drew him close and whispered in his ear. "I'm a friend of Charlie's," he said.

Unger exhaled heavily and his shoulders relaxed a bit at the revelation. "Good to hear," he said.

"Act like we're together," Tommy said, nuzzling his lips against Unger's neck. "We've got a problem," he whispered in Unger's ear.

Unger's eyes shot sideways at Tommy. "A problem?" he asked softly.

"Yeah," Tommy replied. He saw the instant concern in the young man's eyes. "I said to act nonchalant. I've got a few things to tell you, but you can't freak out."

"Right," Unger replied, trying to act as comfortable as possible under the circumstances. "How bad is it?"

Tommy exaggerated his Cajun accent for emphasis. "A big 'ol problem – h-o-t, hot."

"What's wrong?" Unger focused on Tommy's eyes, trying to read his reaction.

"Don't wig out on me," Tommy instructed. "You can't flip out at what I'm about to tell you."

Unger's trepidation was growing. "I won't," he pleaded, trying to reassure Tommy by softening the tone of his voice. "Just please tell me what's going on."

Tommy leaned forward and again whispered in Unger's ear. "Our friend Jared Willis is dead."

Unger stiffened at the revelation. Tommy drew him closer. "I told you not to react. Put your arm around me," he said as he pulled him back in.

"But …" Unger's eyes filled with tears. Words failed to come. Still, he put his arm around Tommy as directed.

"Good," Tommy said, his voice soothing. "After you left his bar and headed to Charlie's office," Tommy continued to lean forward and talk softly into Unger's ear, "someone came to his place and killed him and one of his waiters."

Unger began to shake. He was devastated knowing the one person who reached out to him was dead and all because of him. "Who?" he asked.

"Boy," Tommy said trying to hold Unger reassuringly. "I've got no earthly idea. The only thing I know is there are a lot of people on the street looking for you."

"Okay," Unger mumbled, still reeling the news, he was having trouble putting words together.

"And the folks who visited Jared probably know you've changed your appearance. They probably know you're hiding in plain sight."

"Oh shit," Unger replied, his voice pitiful and weak. "I'm a dead man."

"We've got to assume they are in this bar right now."

Tommy's words hit Unger like a brick. He felt the blood draining from his face as he looked around the room. His eyes quickly scanned the four corners of the establishment. "I don't see anyone."

"Calm down," Tommy said. "I know most people at this place. I'm a regular here. The King of the Bears."

"I don't know what that means," Unger replied.

"Good," Tommy said, smiling at Unger's uncomfortable predicament. "But take a look over my left shoulder," he said. "Check out those two guys over there who walked in while you were in the head. I've never seen them in here before."

Unger scanned the crowd over Tommy's shoulder. He saw two men sitting at a corner table. One was tall and thick. The other was short and stubby. "Oh, my God," Unger mumbled. "They're here."

"Who?" Tommy replied. "Who's here?"

"The two guys who chased me into Jared's bar," Unger said in short breaths, averting his gaze downward in hopes he would not be recognized. "Those guys must have killed Jared while looking for me. This is all my fault."

Tommy grabbed Unger's chin and moved it upwards, making eye contact. "Alright," he said with intensity. "Look at me and calm down."

Unger did as instructed, his eyes wild and panicked, but focused on Tommy's.

"You're going to kiss me," Tommy said.

"What?" Unger was shocked at the instruction.

"You're going to kiss me," Tommy repeated forcefully. "Then we're going to walk out of here like we just hooked up and are headed back to my place. If we're lucky, they didn't recognize you. We'll figure out what to do after we get the hell out of here."

"I don't know," Unger replied hesitantly.

"Are you shitting me?" Tommy replied, softly incredulous. "Those guys want to kill you and you're worried about kissing a dude."

The argument seemed logical under the circumstances and Unger leaned forward. Tommy responded accordingly and their lips met. "You okay?" Tommy asked as he pulled back.

"Not as revolted as I thought I'd be," Unger replied.

"Great," Tommy said jokingly. "You're a good kisser, too." He put his arm around Unger and turned him towards the door, talking to other patrons of the bar as they moved. As they reached the front door, Tommy looked back. "Aw, fuck me raw," he said.

"What's wrong?" Unger replied.

"Your friends are following us."

Chapter 29

Argo drove east and suddenly found himself looking at the people walking around the streets. Prior to tonight, he had a mental picture of David Unger with his black hair falling lazily across his forehead. The trip to the Blue Steel Café changed his mental vision of his number one suspect in the death of Vice President Shelby. Argo hit the steering wheel firmly in frustration at his rookie mistake. With a pair of scissors and a squirt of peroxide, Unger changed his appearance. Argo underestimated his foe. He was pissed he wasted so much time looking for the wrong guy.

When Argo pulled into the secured parking garage of the Hoover Building, he swiped his access card across the reader and drove down the ramp. Argo closed his eyes in disgust as red warning lights announced his arrival.

Louis Ramerez, one of the attendants, walked over to Argo's car. Louis, a graying, 60ish Cuban refugee Argo helped find employment years earlier, said "Hey, Big Papi," with a big toothy grin.

"Hey, Lou," Argo replied, returning the friendly smile. As frustrated as he was knowing his car was about to be inspected, he genuinely liked Ramerez. *"Que pasa, amigo?"*

"Just livin' the dream," Louis replied, still smiling. "Where chu been tonight?"

"Down in DuPont at a crime scene," Argo replied. "Why?"

"Well, you sent the beepers off," Louis said. "Probably a false-positive, but I gotta take the car and get it checked out."

Argo turned off the car, stepped out and extended his hand to shake with Louis, who ignored the gesture and returned the handshake with a bear hug. "You'd think we'd get detectors that didn't go off every time we picked up some dust at a crime scene," Argo said.

"Don't tell me," Louis said, pointing to the back of the parking garage. "I've already got three lined up tonight for inspection. Chu gonna be here a while?"

"I hope not," Argo replied. "I've got to call the Director and then I'm out of here. If I'm lucky, Jane hasn't changed the locks on our townhouse."

Louis nodded his head in appreciation of his friend's family predicament. "I'll move you to the front 'den," he said. "I'll get chu home in time."

Argo patted Louis on the back. "You're the man, Louis."

"I try," Louis said smiling. "Chu tell Miss Jane I got chu home on time, but ..."

"I know, I know," Argo laughed. He had heard Louis say the same thing every time he saw him. "Her end of the bargain is to whack Fidel and Raoul."

"Fair deal in my book," Louis replied.

"You're killing me, Louis," Argo shouted, pushing the up call button for the elevator. Once on the elevator, he turned to see Louis starting his inspection of Argo's car by running a mirror under the chassis. He waved as he hit the button for the fifth floor.

When Argo bounded off the elevator at the area in front of his office, the room was active. It did not go unnoticed when Argo entered.

"You're up past your bedtime, old man," a young agent working the night shift shouted at Argo as he entered the collection of cubicles.

"Bite me," Argo responded. "This old top can still out work your young ass any day of the week."

Several agents laughed out loud and began to rib the younger agent for his comment.

"Keep it up and you'll never make it off night shift," Argo added while pointing his finger at the man. The laughter and ribbing continued.

Argo walked over to where the night receptionist was sitting. Allison Anderson was about Argo's age and had been working at the FBI as long as Argo could remember. "Hey, Ally," Argo greeted the busty bleach blond.

"Hey, Leo," Anderson replied. Looking sideways at Argo, she continued, "So what's with the eye?"

Argo winked at Anderson and made some hand gestures only slightly resembling the closing of a door. "I ran into a door knob," he smirked.

Anderson laughed out loud at an explanation so obviously a lie. "So a straight answer is out of the question?"

"Are you kidding me?" Argo replied. "I'd be better off telling Public Affairs than blabbing it to you and all your night shift flunkies."

Anderson flipped Argo the bird. "So, what are you doing out late with us lowly third-shifters?"

"I need you to set up a secure line to the Director, Ally," Argo replied, his demeanor suddenly business-like. "Call me in my office when you get him on the phone."

Anderson recognized the abrupt change in Argo's tone and became instantly serious. "You got it, Leo," she replied.

Argo went to his office and closed the door. He walked over to his desk and waited. It was only a moment before his phone rang. "Good evening, Mr. Director," Argo said as he picked up the phone.

"Good evening, Leo," Director Cicero replied. "I'm surprised to hear your voice tonight. I thought you and Director Kline were entertaining the new Senator from Kentucky."

"We were," Argo replied, as he leaned against his desk. "But Proctor over at Secret Service called with some breaking news about David Unger's whereabouts. I left early."

"Sorry the dinner plans didn't work out," Director Cicero replied. "But I hope you're calling to tell me you have Unger's head on a stick."

"Not exactly," Argo said wincing. He knew Cicero wanted results.

"I need something definitive," Cicero said. "What do you have on our boy?"

"There was a double murder down in DuPont this afternoon," Argo said. The long telephone cord seemed to chase him as he walked.

"You're getting to know the neighborhood," Cicero replied. "Unger lives in DuPont, doesn't he?"

"Yes, sir," Argo replied. "The murder was about a block and a half from Unger's place."

"And there is a connection?"

Argo pulled the chair out from behind his desk and sat down. "Well, we know for sure Unger was there at some point," Argo said.

"Really?"

"Yeah," Argo continued. "We found his credit cards and driver's license at the scene and his finger prints were all over the place." There was silence on the phone. Argo did not speak as he let the information sink in. "And he changed his appearance," Argo added.

"What?" Director Cicero asked. "How?"

"Cut his hair and changed the color."

After a moment, Director Cicero spoke. "It's time for a warrant."

"Yes, sir," Argo said, rubbing his forehead with his free hand as he spoke. He made sure there was a certain tone of indecisiveness in his voice. "I guess."

"You don't sound convinced." Cicero's voice sounded puzzled by Argo's reply.

Argo had been thinking about the crime scene ever since he had left DuPont. "Something doesn't add up for me, Boss," he declared.

"What, Leo?"

"I don't think Unger could have pulled off what I saw tonight alone."

"Okay." Cicero's voice trailed off.

"Here's the thing," Argo explained. "There are two dead bodies – one behind the bar and one in the center of the room. Both were killed by a small caliber gunshot to the head."

"Leo," Cicero said. "I know I'm a political appointee and not a criminal investigator, but what keeps Unger from walking into the place and firing two shots."

"Well," Argo said, having anticipated the question. "First, the shots were pretty damn accurate."

"You had me start with a low caliber," Cicero said, reminding Argo he was the first to take the new boss to the firing range. "You said they were easier to operate."

"Yes, sir," Argo replied. He shared a thought bothering him for a while. "But no one heard any shots, so I'm assuming the shooter used a silencer." Argo stopped, thinking the Director would catch his point.

"I'm not following you, Leo," Director Cicero prompted. "You're going to have to be more direct."

"Well," Argo continued, "David Unger was the Veep's advance man. We've got no record of him owning a gun or having any weapons training."

Cicero suddenly caught Argo's point. "Yet, he suddenly carries the right gun, with a silencer. And he operates it with deadly accuracy."

"Yes, sir," Argo said. He was pleased the Director caught his point. "I'll make an investigator out of you yet, Boss."

"Thanks," Cicero said appreciative of the compliment. "But I'll leave the detective part of the job to you."

"There's something else," Argo added.

"I figured there was," Cicero said. "Shoot."

"The second victim was beat up before he was killed," Argo said.

"And Unger wasn't the kind of guy who could beat someone up?"

"Good instinct," Argo said. "But it's more. In order to beat him up the way he did, he'd have to put down the gun. I mean the victim was busted up pretty badly."

"Unless there was someone else in the bar," Cicero completed Argo's thought. "I follow you."

"Precisely," Argo replied.

"Leo," Cicero replied. "You've got a great gut and I trust you implicitly. However, you realize the political implications here. I can't hold back on this one. I've got to get this to the Attorney General."

"I know," Argo said. He had carefully planned for this discussion to lead to this point. "But I don't want you to be surprised if I toss you a curve at some point."

"I appreciate the warning, Leo," Cicero replied. "Just make sure I'm your first call when something breaks."

"You got it, Boss," Argo replied

"Now get back home," Cicero said. "I appreciate what you're doing."

"Thank you, sir," Argo said. "I'll see you in the morning."

Argo heard the phone line go dead before hanging up his own telephone. He rubbed each temple with his index fingers. He pushed his chair back from the desk and stood up. "I'm getting too damn old for this shit," he sighed as he headed for the door to his office.

"G'night, Ally," Argo said on his way to the elevator.

"You too, Leo," Anderson replied. "Come on down anytime you want to slum with us common folk."

By habit, Argo reached into his pants pocket for his car keys. Pockets empty, he suddenly remembered he left his car with Louis in the garage. As he fished around in his pocket, he found the piece of paper the young reporter forced on him. He pulled the paper from his pocket and, without looking at it, handed it to Anderson. "Hey, Ally," Argo said. "Do me a favor."

"Anything for you," Anderson replied, taking the piece of paper.

"Take this and ask the folks from Public Affairs to give this guy a call," Argo instructed. "He had some questions and I promised to have someone call just to get him off my ass."

"You got it," Anderson replied.

Argo headed to the elevator bay and hit the down button before rubbing his eyes again. He was waiting to hear the 'ding' when instead he heard Anderson's voice.

"Hey, Leo," Anderson shouted out.

"Yeah?"

"Did you read this note?"

"Nope."

"Well, you better."

Argo reluctantly walked back into the office, and grabbed the paper from Anderson's hand. He gazed at the cryptic message.

"Have someone get a background file together for me on Gene Monks and the *Potomac River News*," he mumbled. When the bell rang for the elevator, he stuffed the note back in his pocket. Argo tried to decode the words in the note, but he was far too tired to try too hard. He was in no mood for word games. The elevator doors closed and he hit the button to the basement garage. A short drive and he would be home.

When the elevator reached the basement, the doors opened and Argo headed for his car. He was only a few steps off the elevator when friend Louis stopped him. Argo waved his hand in an attempt to ward off any discussion. "Get me home, amigo," he instructed.

"No can do, Papi," Louis replied, shaking his head apologetically.

Argo's mood was rapidly turning sour. "Don't mess with me, man," he said. "I'm too tired."

"I ain't messin' with chu, bro," Louis said sincerely.

"Then where's my car," Argo replied. "I need to get home."

"It's on the lower level," Louis said. "Secured until further notice."

"What? Why?"

"Your car's been bugged, mange."

Chapter 30

Duane Wallace joined the United States Park Service just out of college. Originally based at a remote Ranger station in the northwest, he initially enjoyed the peace and tranquility of having a national park as his home office. He was raised in a rural setting and the surroundings were comfortable. Soon, though, he grew bored keeping photo-snapping tourists a safe distance from bears and changing flat tires on RVs in the midst of buffalo herds. He wanted excitement. So when a spot opened up to work the horse stables on the DC Mall, he used his 4-H equestrian credentials to land the job.

Based along the Mall near the World War I Memorial, the stables are tucked into a small tree grove in close proximity to the Potomac River. There, the Park Service houses the horses used by the police to patrol the grounds surrounding the National Mall. When a Park Police officer returns a horse to the stable, it became Wallace's job to unsaddle, bathe and feed the animal. Before serving up oats, however, Wallace liked to take each horse for a short walk around the small marble bandstand located next to the stables.

He had the late shift this month, but did not particularly mind. The sounds of the DC night intrigued him. Hidden in his own personal forest, the cars in the distance paid him no mind.

"Come on, Cornbread," Wallace said as he led the horse around by its reigns. "One trip around and I'll get ya back to the stable."

Wallace walked the same steps so often he almost did not need the flashlight he used to illuminate his way. Step by step, he led the stallion, occasionally offering him a mint as a reward for good behavior.

The walk proceeded uneventfully until Cornbread suddenly halted. "Come on, boy," Wallace said as he snapped the reigns. The horse pulled back – spooked by something in their path.

When Wallace shined the light in front of them, he froze at the sight of a woman in a low cut white silk dress stained by fresh blood lying on the green grass in front of them.

Chapter 31

"You're sure those are the guys?" Tommy looked squarely at Unger as they paused near the front door of the bar. His brow furrowed and his eyes focused, Tommy's stare was purposeful. It was so intense and the change in Tommy's demeanor so sudden that Unger got goose bumps on his arms.

Unger glanced quickly back at the two men closing in on them, nodding nervously to confirm their identity. "Yeah," Unger replied. "You don't forget faces like those."

"You're absolutely sure?" Tommy reiterated his question. His voice was anxious, but steady. "Those are our boys?"

Unger was getting a bit frustrated with a line of questioning he considered inane and a waste of valuable time. "Yes," Unger repeated. "The little guy was at my kitchen table and the big guy was the one I fell over. Now, let's get the hell out of here."

"Not yet," Tommy said. He stopped just inside the front door and leaned against the antique table. As Tommy made some small talk with one of the patrons, he reached over and picked up a marble egg from a vase of decorative knick-knacks. He casually tossed it up and down in the palm of his left hand.

"Please." Unger was becoming panicked by Tommy's casual attitude in the face of impending danger. "Let's haul ass," Unger urged.

"Cool your jets, Ace," Tommy replied, his eyes becoming laser-focused on the marble egg.

Tall and Thick pushed his way through the dance floor, shoving men aside as he went. Short and Stubby followed closely behind. When they were about twenty feet away, Tommy looked at Unger. "Game on," he said.

"What?" Unger replied, confused and panicked all at the same time.

"Stand back, junior," Tommy said, winding up like a baseball pitcher. As Unger ducked out of the way, Tommy hurled the marble orb as hard as he could at the approaching pair. The egg smacked Tall and Thick on the forehead, just above the right eye. Tall and Thick let out a loud groan and then stumbled backwards, falling onto Short and Stubby. Men scrambled around on the dance floor at the sight and sounds of the altercation.

"Now, it's time to go," Tommy said, grabbing Unger by the arm. They both hurried through the front door. "Come on."

"Jesus," Unger said as they sprinted out to the street. "You hit the guy right on the head."

Tommy quickly cut right at the first street. "Yup," he said, beginning to pant a little as he ran.

Unger followed Tommy's lead, not yet daring to look over his shoulder. "Where did you learn to throw so hard?" he asked.

"College baseball," Tommy huffed. "LSU – four year, full ride." They headed around a corner and into a brick alley. Tommy pulled a set of car keys from his pocket and hit the unlock button. The red tail lights on a late-model white BMW flashed. "Get in," he instructed.

"Incredible," Unger gasped as Tommy started up the car. "You hit the guy right on the noggin."

Tommy jammed the accelerator to the floor and the tires squealed as he pulled out of the alley and onto the street. "Don't be too impressed, kid," Tommy said, looking in his rear view mirror as Short and Stubby rounded the corner with a dazed Tall and Thick stumbling behind. "I was aiming for his nuts."

Unger looked at him with a stunned expression.

"I always had a bit of a control problem," Tommy said matter-of-factly as he made a right turn. "I could have been All SEC, if I had just had a little more control. Well, control and a breaking pitch. I never really had a good curve ball either."

Tommy drove at maximum speed, darting in and out of lanes and making indiscriminate turns – left and right – until he was convinced they were not being followed by anyone. By the time he finally slowed down, they were on Constitution Avenue, near the Lincoln Memorial. Tommy pulled the car to the side of the road and turned off the engine. "Let's take a walk," he said as he tossed his cell phone on the front seat of the car.

"Not taking your phone?" Unger asked exiting the car.

Tommy shook his head. "We raised quite a fuss back there, kid," he replied. "It'll take 'em a while, but the po-po will soon figure out who gave your buddy the marble bean-ball. They'll be tracking my phone and license plate by the morning. We're on foot from here on out and without communication."

Unger and Tommy crossed the street to the dark and secluded walkways at the west end of the National Mall. The silence between the two was uncomfortable as they walked. Unger was the first to speak. "So, what happened to Jared?"

Tommy motioned the pair to a park bench. "Take a load off," he instructed as he sat down. "We've got a lot to cover."

Unger sat beside Tommy and watched as tourists made their way down a dimly lit path to view the Vietnam Veterans Memorial in the darkness of night. "So, what ..."

"Shhhh ..." Tommy cut him off. "Decompress for a minute." He looked in the direction of the Wall. "You know this is my favorite spot in all of DC," he said. "I always come here when I need to think."

Unger was jittery, shifting around nervously on the bench. "Why here?" he finally asked.

Tommy pointed to the Wall. "Because my dad's over there," he replied.

Unger hung his head. "I'm sorry."

"Don't be," Tommy replied. "I never really knew him. He was killed late in the war – I'm sorry – conflict. I was born during his second tour. I was angry growing up. Him never seeing me play ball ... wondering what he would think about his son being gay. It took several visits, but it was here where I came to peace with it all."

Unger found himself unable to reply and simply nodded.

Tommy acknowledged the nod and continued. "So, I come here when I need to think. It clears my mind. I feel like my dad is giving me one of those father-son talks we never had in real life."

Unger nodded. "I wish I could say I understand," he said. "But that would be a lie."

"Thanks," Tommy said smiling. He shifted his gaze to the flag pole between the Lincoln and Vietnam Memorials. "See the flag."

"Yeah," Unger replied while looking in the direction of the Reflecting Pool.

"There's an inscription around the base of it," Tommy said. "It implies the men and women whose names are on the Wall served honorably during some very difficult circumstances."

"Pretty humbling," Unger replied.

"So whenever I get caught up in the drama of my own life, I come here," Tommy said, looking up at the stars in the clear DC sky. "Somehow, after a few minutes on this bench, all my difficult circumstances end up seeming pretty small by comparison."

Unger looked up at the sky and pondered Tommy's words. "So am I your latest difficult circumstance?"

"Caught the reference, did ya?" Tommy smiled.

"So what happened to Jared?" Unger asked.

"Someone came to his bar this afternoon and killed him and his bartender," Tommy said.

"Damn it. It's because he was helping me," Unger said. He tried to say more, but words failed him.

Shifting on the bench to look at Unger, Tommy went on. "It was apparently a pretty grisly scene."

Unger put is head in his hands. "No," he said. "This isn't happening."

"I'm sorry, son," Tommy said. "But it is happening and you're right in the middle of it. The word in law enforcement is your prints were all over the place."

Unger looked up at Tommy with a pitiful look. "I stayed there for awhile."

"Yeah," Tommy replied. "I know."

"But I didn't kill anybody," Unger replied shaking his head.

"Yeah, I know you didn't."

"How can you know?" Unger said.

"It's a tight community," Tommy said. "Word gets around pretty quickly. From the fact those two boys were waiting there for you, I am going to assume, before he was killed, Jared let him know where you were supposed to be tonight."

"Or Charlie," gasped Unger, immediately taking in the implication Charlie Patterson might also be dead.

"Yup," Tommy responded solemnly. "I haven't heard from Charlie in several hours. Maybe he's fine – maybe not. But if something really bad did happen to him, I'm going to assume they'll find your fingerprints all over his office, too."

Unger nodded at the comment and returned his head to his hands. "Everybody I come into contact with is dying or in danger."

"Yeah," Tommy said, manufacturing a sarcastic laugh. "Just my luck."

Unger let the laugh hang in the air for a moment. "I don't understand why everyone is risking their lives to help me?" he said. "I won't blame you if you take off."

Tommy shook his head. "Sorry, kid," he said. "Just not my style."

"Thank you," Unger said gratefully.

"Anyway," Tommy continued. "It ain't gonna take a whole lot for those boys to figure out who I am. Everybody back at the bar knows me pretty well. I'm kind of a regular there."

"So we can't go back to your place," Unger said.

"No way, podna," Tommy said, again overemphasizing his friendly Cajun accent.

"Any ideas?" Unger asked.

"A few," Tommy rubbed the scruffy growth of his beard. "First, we've got to find out if Charlie Patterson is alive or dead – and fast." Over his shoulder he looked to the other side of the Mall where the red lights of emergency personnel were quickly gathering. "And now would be a good time to move along."

Chapter 32

Argo eased quietly between the sheets, trying desperately not to disturb Jane as he slipped into bed. Hoover – who was balled up at the foot of the king-sized mattress – looked up and wagged his tail once or twice before placing his head back down on his large paws to resume sleeping.

"I'm awake," Kline said softly.

"Sorry, babe," Argo said. "I was trying not to wake you up."

Kline reached to the bedside table, turned on the light and rolled back to face Argo. "I've been up," she said. "I couldn't sleep."

Argo leaned over and kissed Kline gently on the cheek. "I am really sorry about tonight," he said sincerely. "How long did they stay?"

"Not too much longer after you left," Kline replied before returning the kiss. "We had an after dinner port and they headed out. The Thompsons had a pretty long day themselves. They were tired and ready to get to bed."

"I wish I could have stayed until they left," Argo said. "It really was something I had to do – murder scene with David Unger's prints all over it."

"I understand," Kline said.

"I know you do," Argo laughed. "You make it too easy sometimes."

"And I've already been briefed," Kline snuggled in closer as she changed the subject. "I've been waiting up, but I didn't hear the garage door when you came in."

"Yeah," Argo said. "I parked on the street and came in through the front door."

"A bit overboard on not wanting to wake me up, don't ya think?" Kline asked.

Argo put his arm around Kline and pulled her in closer. "I wish I were as thoughtful," he replied. "But it's a little deeper. My damn car got impounded at headquarters and I drove home in a fleet car. I forgot the garage door opener in my vehicle."

"Your car got impounded?" Kline pulled back and looked up at Argo. "What happened? Did you have a wreck?"

"No," Argo responded. "My driving isn't that bad."

"Open to interpretation," Kline laughed. "So what's up?"

Argo tightened his lips. He knew they would normally never talk business at home, but Kline needed to know this information for her own safety. "Someone put a locator on my car."

"Why would someone track you?" Kline asked, truly puzzled.

"Good question," Argo nodded. "I've been asking myself the same question all the way home."

Kline let the information sink in a moment. "When was the last time your car was scanned?"

Argo had asked himself the same question, too. "Just before I left for LA," he replied.

Kline continued her interrogation. "And the car was in the garage all the time you were gone."

"Right," Argo knew where she was going. He did the math in his own head. "So someone bugged me in the last couple of days."

Kline thought about the implications before continuing. "Why would someone want to know your location?" she asked rhetorically. "Most people know we live together, and our address can be found by a sixth grader with two clicks on the internet."

"My thoughts exactly," Argo said. "Anyone who wants to follow me starts out already knowing where I live and work."

Kline did not wait for Argo to go any further. "Someone wants to know where you are between those times," she said.

"Precisely," Argo said smiling. "Good instincts, rookie."

"Hey," Kline said, punching Argo lightly in the ribs. "Don't forget I spent most of my adult life as an operative. I only crossed over to the analyst side after I got too damn old for the action."

"I know, I know," Argo said, grabbing her hand to stop any further assaults. "So, put your operative brain to work. What case am I working on?"

"The assassination of Vice President Shelby," Kline acknowledged, letting the information percolate in her consciousness. "Whoever is tracking you wants to know where you're traveling around the city."

"Right," Argo replied. "And who would want to know where I'm going?"

Kline decided to play the Devil's Advocate. "Press?" she asked. "It's the biggest story in the country right now. The media would certainly like to know where you are in the investigation."

Argo thought of the possibility of the press tracking him. "Maybe," he said. "In fact, I got a weird note tonight from a reporter who apparently knows my old pal Alberto De La Caverone."

"From the *Miami Herald*?" Kline replied.

"Yeah," Argo said. "Some young blog writer from DuPont wanted to talk to me. When I wouldn't give him any information, he handed me a note simply saying 'Alberto says Hola.'"

"Bizarre."

Argo agreed. "I know," he said "I'm going to go see him in the morning."

"You think he planted the device?" Kline asked.

"No," Argo said. "I may hate the press, but I don't think they're smart enough – or rather stupid enough – to track me for the sake of a story."

"I wouldn't put it past them," Kline warned.

"Too risky," Argo replied, but leaving open the possibility. "I just don't think he'd drop Alberto's name and then tail me, too."

"Makes sense," Kline replied.

"But I think this kid and I both have the same goal."

"What?"

"Finding David Unger is the key to finding out who killed Shelby."

"So you still don't think he did it," Kline responded. "I thought his fingerprints were all over the bar tonight."

"They were," Argo replied. "He was definitely there at some point, but he couldn't have pulled this one off. There had to be a second person at the scene."

"Someone helped him?"

"Maybe," Argo replied.

"Or what?"

"Or, someone came in after he left."

"The same one who planted the locator on your car?" Kline concluded.

"My guess," Argo replied as he gently ran his hand inside Kline's silk top. "Still, just to be safe, alert your security detail about the bug."

"I will," Kline replied as she felt Argo's hand running up her stomach and stopping on her right breast. "And just what do you have in mind now, cowboy?"

Argo smiled as he pulled Kline on top of him. "Collecting on a rain check."

Chapter 33

In a small roadside motel room on US 1 in Virginia near Ft. Belvoir, Tall and Thick was mindlessly tossing personal items into an Everlast boxing duffle bag. When Short and Stubby entered the room carrying two cups of coffee, Tall and Thick nervously snapped around.

"Calm down," Short and Stubby advised as he put one cup on the bureau where the television was located. The drapes were drawn closed, and the room was dark. Noises from the road were distant. "It's only me."

"Good," Tall and Thick replied. A large knot on his forehead marked the place where Tommy's beanball landed hours earlier. "I'm just a little jumpy tonight."

"Me, too," Short and Stubby said, peeking briefly out a small gap between the drapes and the window at the cars in the parking lot. Miles south of downtown DC, the motel was well hidden from the road. "Which is why we need to get the fuck out of here – the sooner the better."

"Do you think any of the people here will remember us?" Tall and Thick asked.

"This place rents by the hour," Short and Stubby replied. "No one here wants to remember who was in any of these rooms, but you need to put a move on it. I've aleady got my crap in the car."

Tall and Thick was moving slowly. "I think I have a concussion," he said, rubbing his head.

"Add it to the list," Short and Stubby laughed, before nervously sipping his coffee. "You've been punch-drunk for years now."

"But this one really hurts," Tall and Thick added for emphasis.

"I know pal," Short and Stumpy crossed the room and put his hand on Tall and Thick's shoulder in an effort to comfort him. Trying to sound sympathetic to his sidekick's plight was difficult. They were in this predicament because of several screw ups by the big man. *He lost the golden glove pendant. He came up with the idea to put a tracker on the car of an FBI agent. He got knocked loopy by a marble egg,* Short and Stubby justified to himself. *This is all on him.*

"I need a couple percocet," Tall and Thick replied as he zipped up his duffle bag.

"As soon as we get the room sanitized," Short and Stubby said, putting on gloves and grabbing a towel from the bathroom, "We'll find a gym in the next town. There's always someone with pills at a gym."

"I just want to get outta here."

"Yeah," Short and Stubby said softly. He tossed a pair of gloves to his friend. "So do I, pal. So let's get to work."

The pair quickly went about cleaning the room, thoroughly wiping down every surface with cleaner and tossing all sheets and garbage into a large trash bag they intended to take with them. Once they were done, the room smelled better than it probably had in decades.

"Alright," Tall and Thick said, picking up the garbage bag to take to the car. "The room is as clean as we're going to get it. Now let's roll."

Short and Stubby headed for the door, but stopped short. "Wait," he said. "Did you check under the bed?"

"Yeah," Tall and Thick replied. "That's the first thing I did."

"Well, do it again," Short and Stubby instructed. "We don't need another golden glove incident."

"I told you that wasn't my fault," Tall and Thick pleaded. "The kid ripped it off the chain."

"I know," Short and Stubby said, reassuringly. "We just need to be careful here. Let's double check."

When Tall and Thick was on his hands and knees looking under one of the beds, Short and Stubby approached him from behind and pulled his Sig Saur from his waistband. He took a deep breath before putting two silenced shots into the back of the man's head. Tall and Thick's body harshly collapsed from its prone position and lay flat on the floor.

It took a moment for Short and Stubby to regain his composure. Once his breathing steadied, Short and Stubby went to the door, opened it and motioned to the man waiting in the car at the end of the parking lot. Short and Stubby left the door slightly ajar and then he went over to nudge Tall and Thick's lifeless body with his foot. "Sorry, pal," he said softly. "I had to."

When the man from the car in the parking lot entered the room, he surveyed the scene. "Good," he said after observing the body. "I know this wasn't easy for you."

"No, it wasn't," Short and Stubby replied, "but I understand why it had to be done."

"You'll be compensated accordingly."

"Thanks," Short and Stubby said. He thought for a moment. "So what now?"

"Now I'll give you cover while you load the body into your car."

"Then …"

"Follow me to Maryland. There's an old boat dock on the Potomac River about a quarter mile from Inner Loop. I've got a fishing net in my trunk. We'll wrap him up and toss him into the river. By the time anyone finds him, I guarantee you'll be long gone."

Chapter 34

The buildings making up the Russian Embassy and Consulate in Washington, DC are located near the peak of Wisconsin Avenue on grounds known as Mount Alto. The location of a former veteran's hospital, it is one of the highest spots in the city. On its low side, the compound is leveled atop a tall stone wall. On the high side abutting quaint neighborhood homes, it is surrounded by a tall fence decked on top by foreboding razor wire. The vast grounds include administrative offices, apartments and even a school. With direct sight lines from the top floors of the building to the White House, the Pentagon and the Capitol, it is obvious the complex was built long before electronic surveillance was advanced enough to be a concern. The embassy has been cloaked in controversy, espionage and intrigue since the site was first picked in 1973.

When the Cold War was in full swing, the Soviets decided to move their embassy from a location next to the downtown Athletic Club to Chevy Chase. American officials insisted it be placed instead at Mt. Alto – perhaps because of a secret underground tunnel beneath it from which American intelligence could follow the activities of the officials there. Operations in the tunnel were one of the intelligence community's best kept secrets. The tunnel became not so secret when its existence was disclosed to the Soviets in 2001 by an FBI counter-intelligence officer turned mole, who is currently living out the remainder of his life in the confines of a federal prison.

The neighborhood where the Russian Embassy is located contains more than just trendy homes with passages to underground secret tunnels. The Vice President of the United States lives about a block to the east. And just up Wisconsin Avenue, the National Cathedral completes the triangle of notable buildings in Glover Park.

Oleg Kedrov quietly scooted over a bit on a bench in front of the National Cathedral when Jon Dosser approached. With a pat of his hand on the wood slats, he invited Dosser to sit with him. "It is a stunning building at night," Kedrov said in his heavy Russian accent, pointing to the top of the church. "Do you not think so, Mr. Dosser?"

"It certainly is," Dosser replied, looking upward as he sat.

"It is a shame portions of it fell following the earthquake," Kedrov continued, pointing at the fallen stones kept in the front of the building for tourists to observe. "Many of our teachers used to take our school children here on field trips. They would go up into the towers to get a view of the consulate grounds."

Caught up in the conversational nature of the discussion, Dosser asked, "Do you come to church here?"

Kedrov smiled at the inquiry. As a young KGB agent he advised Mikhail Gorbachev against lifting the ban on televising Russian Orthodox Church services. Later, he became trusted within the Central Committee of the Communist Party by orchestrating the downfall of well-known religious leaders, allowing them to keep their churches in return for certain concessions. "No," he said, shaking his head. "I am not what you Americans would consider a religious man."

Dosser silently winced, realizing the folly of his question. Kedrov was old-school KGB and Dosser awkwardly tried to recover. "I meant, did you come to Vice President Shelby's funeral here the other day."

"No," Kedrov knew Dosser had misspoke, but he decided not to challenge him further on the loathsome topic of religion. "The Ambassador handles such details, not me."

"Sure," Dosser replied looking downward.

Having gained the upper hand, Kedrov nodded. "You said you wanted to talk about Mack Wilson."

Dosser was glad Kedrov had changed the topic. He decided to get right to the point. "Yes," he said. "In fact, I'm here on behalf of Senator Wilson."

Kedrov looked at Dosser. "He is not a Senator anymore."

Dosser got the response he was hoping for. "No," he said. "He's not. He resigned following Shelby's death."

Kedrov waved his hand dismissively. "Which is why Mr. Wilson is of little value to me now," he said. "Senator Wilson mattered. Mr. Wilson is just another American citizen."

"What about Vice President Wilson?" Dosser replied quickly. "What if Mack Wilson held the number two spot in American government?"

Kedrov pondered the question. "Then you might have my attention, Mr. Dosser."

For a brief moment Dosser saw the hint of promise in Kedrov's eyes. "I can tell you President Rohman is likely to consider Wilson for Vice President."

"If such were the case, I would possibly change my opinion of a valued American public official like Mack Wilson," Kedrov said. He paused at the thought. "But this discussion is purely academic at this point. Your Congress is set to approve the pipeline, which is what everyone promised would never happen."

"It's more than academic." Dosser was going out on a limb. But he was considering it practice. If he could convince Kedrov that Wilson was in play, he might be able to convince Rohman to actually choose him. "Wilson's on the short list. Rohman nearly picked him the first time around."

Kedrov nodded. "Then I change my stance, Mr. Dosser. You definitely have my attention."

"Good, I was hoping a thoughtful man such as yourself would hear me out," Dosser said. He felt emboldened. "And I can help see Wilson gets the spot."

"Why do you tell me this?" Kedrov smiled slyly as he spoke. "Why did Mack Wilson send you here? Why did he not come here to talk to me himself?"

"Because he's scared," Dosser interjected.

"Scared?" Kedrov's voice boomed as he laughed out the words. "Of what?"

Dosser looked squarely at Kedrov. "You know what he's scared of," he replied. "He doesn't want to meet the same fate as Paul Shelby."

Kederov threw up his hands. "I have no influence over such matters," he declared. "American zealots plot to kill public officials every day."

"Agreed," Dosser said. "But we need to make sure the Russian zealots don't do so."

"I think I do not like this line of questioning, Mr. Dosser," Kederov said, his eyes narrowing with anger.

"Look, I'm not wearing a wire," Dosser said, holding his hands open to imply trustworthiness. "I'm not interrogating you. I'm not wired. We can go back to the Embassy and search me if you like. I'm clean."

Kederov pondered the offer momentarily. "Not necessary," he replied, waiting to see where Dosser went next.

Having overcome the momentary lapse in the conversation, Dosser continued. "So," he said, "Wilson needs to know if he's selected as Veep, the deal is still on."

"He is of little help to us now," Kederov replied. "It was a two person deal. Shelby was to influence the administration. We needed Wilson for the Senate."

"Wrong, Comrade Kederov," Dosser said boldly. "You needed Shelby. Shelby needed Wilson."

"And now Shelby is dead and Wilson is no longer in the Senate," Kederov replied. "Again, I fail to see the relevance of this conversation."

"If Wilson joins the administration, you'll have both in one man," Dosser continued. "Wilson will be your voice in the administration as well as your way into the United States Congress. In fact, he'll be President of the Senate. As number two, he can use his influence to kill the pipeline, or at least delay it for decades."

Kederov sat silently for a moment, letting all the information resonate. "And Wilson did not come to me with this personally because he is afraid."

"Precisely."

"Then why do you not have similar feelings?"

Dosser had anticipated the question. "Because you and I understand it was Shelby's idea to play both sides against the middle – to choose his own family farm and its profits over our deal. With Wilson you have a partner with no personal or political conflicts of interest, calling his own shots. And you'll have me by his side, reminding him of the correct path."

The big Russian contemplated the offer before rising from the bench. "Please give Vice President Wilson my best personal regards."

Chapter 35

There is a stark difference between the suites of offices reserved for members of the two chambers of Congress. Members of the House are confined to small, three-office suites where multiple staff members occupy a single room generally about the same size as the boss's personal space. Senate offices are much larger and have a plush feel lacking in those on the House side. In a typical Senate office, the Member's personal office and conference room are about the same size as a Representative's entire suite.

The difference in offices was not lost on Richard Thompson. Glancing up at the tall ceilings and windows covered by velvet curtains made him laugh. A strange set of circumstances surrounded his return to the public eye. No one quite understood his reasons for returning to DC and perhaps he did not even fully understand them himself. He felt he had some altruistic reasons, but he still could not help but be amused at the surroundings and the unlikely situation in which he had suddenly been thrown.

"Lot better digs than some damn inner-city, community college classroom," Michael Griffith huffed as he paced around the office. Griffith was nothing if not direct. He noticed his old fraternity brother was enjoying his new surroundings. "For the life of me, I can't understand why you left this life. You'd be in leadership by now. You could have an office in the Dome."

"Actually, Griff," Thompson started to reply "My cubbie back at the college ..."

"Cut the crap, Senator," Griffith swung around and faced Thompson, his unshaven face breaking into a smirk. "You aren't going to sit there and tell me you miss teaching."

"Actually," Thompson replied sheepishly, "I do. I miss the classroom."

Griffith shook his head in disbelief and looked like he was going to launch into one of his classic tirades when he started to laugh. At first it was just a chuckle. Then it quickly evolved into a belly-laugh. "You're one, sick, sonofabitch," he bellowed between laughs.

"I was actually thinking the same thing about you," Thompson replied, starting to get tickled at the situation himself. "I know it's hard in your world to believe elected officials really care, but there are still a few of us out there."

"I know, man," Griffith said, regaining his composure. "You ... Josh ... you pukes make it tough on people like me who are trying to make an honest buck off the dishonest enterprise of politics."

Thompson guffawed at the statement. "Honest buck?" he laughed. "In this town?"

"Sure," Griffith replied.

"The only honest buck in this town is made by the guy who shines shoes down in the basement. He works harder than anyone else in this building."

"Campaign money is honest graft," Griffith replied.

"You're ... you're an enabler," Thompson said, pointing his finger at Griffith.

"I sure as hell enabled you all these years," Griffith laughed.

"Yes, you did," Thompson said humbly. "And you know I've appreciated it all."

Griffith thought for a moment. "You've been trying to figure out where this leads you."

"Yes, I have."

"Join me when the term is done," Griffith suggested. "Get back into the game on the side of the candidate. Find ones you believe in and help them along their path."

"Hell, Griff," Thompson said, shaking his head. "I don't know the answers, man. I'm still wondering whether or not this was a good move for me and Ann. I don't know if I can convince any others to jump in."

"I know you think you were having an impact with your kids at college," Griffith replied. "But with me your reach could be broader. You'll have the chance to touch a lot more folks."

"I wish I could believe you," Thompson replied, breaking eye contact and looking out the window.

Griffith noticed the angst in his old friend's stare. "If I'm wrong about you returning, it will be over soon enough," he said. And then pointing to himself for emphasis. "And if the result is bad, I'll gladly let you and Ann put all the blame on me."

Thompson smiled and sat down at his desk, tossing aside the local section of the newspaper blaring a headline about a brutal double murder at a bar in DuPont Circle. "How do you do it, Griff?" he asked.

"What?" Griffith said with a bit of puzzlement in his voice. "Win? Hell, you've been with me long enough by now to know how I win. And what you've forgotten, I'll reteach you."

"No, man," Thompson said, putting his hands behind his head and leaning back in his chair. "How do you go around from one campaign to the next, jumping from candidate to candidate. Do you ever care if they actually live up to the voter's expectations?"

"It's a job," Griffith raised his greying eyebrows and shrugged his shoulders.

"Ever believe in your candidates?"

Griffith laughed. "Not part of the gig," he said. He paused and grunted acknowledgement. "Except you. I always believed in you. I never understood, but I always believed. Which is what you could bring to the table. There are a whole bunch of goofy true-believers like you out there. We could find 'em and elect 'em."

The Fat Man pounded on the frame of the solid wood door before unceremoniously walking right into Thompson's private Senate office without waiting for a response. "Why did you even bother to knock," Griffith laughed.

"Sorry, Griff," The Fat Man replied. There had always been a bit of natural tension between The Fat Man and Griffith. Both respected the other, but neither quite understood the other's intellect. "Formality is a force of habit."

"Well, knock it off," Thompson instructed. "We're not going to be here long enough to establish formality."

"I'll try," The Fat Man said.

"Next time just holler Olly Olly Oxen Free," Griffith said, slapping his knee in delight at his own joke.

"You're your own best audience, Griff," The Fat Man said sarcastically.

"And we can't yell in-come-free," Thompson laughed. "All the folks from the NSA might come crawling out from the walls." Thompson looked around at the spacious but sparsely-furnished office. "Can you believe how big these offices are?"

"We certainly have plenty of space," The Fat Man replied.

"If I would have had an office this big in the House, I would have considered staying," Thompson laughed.

"No you wouldn't have," Griffith replied.

"You came home at the right time and for the right reason," The Fat Man added, proud to have been part of the decision.

"Leave me to my fantasies," Thompson warned. Purposefully changing subjects to the dinner they had shared the night before, he said, "Last night was sure a lot of fun."

"Yeah," The Fat Man replied. "I was disappointed Leo had to leave early."

"Me, too," Thompson added. He leaned back in his chair. "I wanted to talk to him a bit more, but I was not nearly as bummed as Jane was at him walking out."

"It was a bit awkward," The Fat Man said.

"What happened?" Griffith asked.

"Leo cut out early on FBI business," The Fat Man said.

"Damn," Griffith replied. "Did Jane cut his nuts off? I'd sure hate to have her pissed off at me. She's one tough broad."

Having knowing Kline since her days as a CIA operative and having witnessed her in action, Thompson nodded in agreement. He stood up, stretched a moment and walked over to the couch. "I'd love to see you call Jane 'a broad' to her face," he said. "Still, she was annoyed. You could tell she was uncomfortable as soon as he got the call." He gestured for The Fat Man to sit down.

The Fat Man joined Thompson on the couch. "I don't know how Jane and Leo do it," he said. "My wife would have strung me up last night."

Griffith laughed at the statement. "Says the man who is temporarily living away from his family in DC," he said jokingly.

"I guess," The Fat Man replied, pondering the statement for a moment. "But for us, this is for a short time. Leo and Jane made this madness a lifestyle choice."

"Couples do what they have to do," Thompson said. He leaned forward and exchanged glances with both his friends. "Back when I was in Congress, I called home so much, I think Ann and I spoke more often than when we were living under the same roof."

"That's funny," the Fat Man laughed, running his hands through his scruffy beard. "Last night, I told my wife about an article in yesterday's *Journal* asserting married couples spend only seven minutes a day communicating."

"Yeah," Thompson said.

The Fat Man continued. "When I was done explaining the article," he said, "she told me I'd just used up two minutes of my daily allotment."

"Never forget who controls the agenda," Thompson added. "My life became a whole lot easier when I realized Ann was in charge."

"No joke," The Fat Man added a knowing smile. "Speaking of agenda," he said, "I met with staff this morning. MacNamara is almost done summarizing a bunch of the files Wilson was working on before he left."

"Good," Thompson replied, impressed The Fat Man mobilized the staff so quickly to accumulate the information. "What cha got?"

"He pre-filed a couple of amendments to the farm bill going to the floor next week," The Fat Man replied, shuffling through some papers in a portfolio. "None of them are really important to Kentucky, and most of them are rifle shots at specific industries."

"I suspect we can trace all of them back to PAC contributions," Thompson said.

"Dead straight," The Fat Man replied. "I can't imagine anyone back home really cares about ethanol subsidies in Iowa."

Thompson scratched his head. "Has Wilson called and asked us to take any of them to the floor?"

"Nope," The Fat Man said. "We've not heard from him at all."

"Well, I'm sure as hell not calling him," Thompson said. "If there's no Kentucky tie, toss 'em. If there's a link, do some background research. But don't make any promises. I want to know the full details on what I'm pimping."

"Right," The Fat Man said.

"You're going to disappoint a whole bunch of DC lobbyists," Griffith laughed. "Thank God you're a short-timer. I'd hate to be raising money for you right now."

"The pure joy of serving and not having a reelect to worry about," Thompson replied. "What else?"

"It seems Wilson had a pretty good constituent service operation," The Fat Man said. His finger wandered down to a note on his legal pad. "There are over a hundred active files transferred to our office. We kept most of Wilson's field staff in place. So the hand-off was pretty much seamless."

"Keep them going," Thompson replied. "We're the best governmental link to a distrusting public. If we can get Grandma her benefits, we're making converts one social security check at a time."

"Got it," The Fat Man replied. "All but one or two of his field staff have agreed to stay."

"Good," Thompson said. "Let's set up a conference call and schedule me to visit each of them over the first work period when I'm back home."

"Works for me," The Fat Man said. "They are a bit nervous. A visit from you will put them at ease."

"I need to let everyone know we're all in the business of constituent service," Thompson paused for a moment. "Me included."

"Roger," The Fat Man replied.

"What else you got me for me?"

"Well, I spoke with Maggie, who's covering all of Wilson's grant requests."

Thompson waved his hand in front of him. "Same thing as the floor amendments," he said. "If there's a Kentucky connection, follow up. If there isn't, cut it loose."

The Fat Man reached into a file folder and pulled out a letter. "I wanted to ask you about this one, though."

"What?"

"Have you ever heard of Longo International?" The Fat Man asked as he handed a letter to Thompson.

Thompson looked at the letter, noticing it was on Wilson's Senate stationary. "No," he said.

"No reason you should have," The Fat Man said. "They're a Sicilian construction company with operations in Minneapolis."

Thompson handed the letter back. "Why?"

"This letter," The Fat Man waved the letter, "is in support of an Ex-Im loan to Longo International to proceed with the geo-tech work on the pipeline."

Thompson winced. "Wilson hated the Export Import Bank," he said. "He thinks they're part of the Tri-Lateral Commission funding the manufacture of black helicopters."

"I know," said The Fat Man. "Which is why this letter stands out to me."

"What does this Longo International do?

"They engineer stuff," The Fat Man replied.

"What kind of stuff?"

The Fat Man shrugged his shoulders. "No earthly idea," he said.

"And there's no Kentucky tie?"

"None I can see," The Fat Man said as he placed the letter back into the file.

"Well, run it around the office with Wilson's old crew. See if we can establish a connection between Longo and the Commonwealth. If they can't come up with anything, cut it loose." Thompson thought for a moment. "No, if there's no tie, see if you can find Wilson. Maybe he can give us some insight."

"I'm already one step ahead of you," replied The Fat Man. "Wilson reached out to MacNamara yesterday. It seems Wilson's been holed up in some crash pad up by the National Zoo. He wasn't answering the phone this morning, so I sent Mac up there to wait him out."

"Mac?" Thompson said with surprise in his voice. "You're giving him nicknames now."

The Fat Man smiled. "Yeah," he said. "It turns out he's not a bad kid after all. I've been spending some time with him. I think if I work with him, he can get on the right track."

"You're a mentor now?" Thompson asked.

"A one man Boys Club of DC," Griffith echoed. "That'll make one helluva television commercial."

"Well, it's the old adage about leading a horse to water," The Fat Man replied. "I'm just leading him along the right path. Doing the right thing will be up to him."

Chapter 36

"It's the top of the hour in Washington, DC," said the morning drive disc jockey, with a voice sounding far too chipper for Leo Argo's tired and dour mood. "From the station bringing you the latest breaking news, along with traffic and weather on the tens."

Argo had been up late, and he was groggy as he drove the FBI loaner car into the city. The investigation into the death of Vice President Shelby was heading in a direction he did not like, but could not stop. His work hours were impacting his relationship with Jane Kline. And then there was the matter of the cryptic note in his pocket from some damn blogger in the city. He was simply in a major league grumpy mood. The last thing he needed this morning was the style of "happy news" so prevalent on talk radio. Still, despite the incessant cheerful jabber coming from the car's speakers, he turned up the volume on the radio.

"And that means it's time for the morning's headlines in our nation's capital," the chipper guy's female counterpart replied. Lori Loudon was the only reason Argo listened to this particular station. She was a seasoned radio journalist with first-class reporting abilities and a great set of pipes. "First up, Ben, Attorney General Rob Shumate has scheduled a press conference this morning at 10:00 a.m. regarding the Justice Department's investigation into the death of Vice President Paul Shelby," Loudon said matter-of-factly.

"What do you think, Lori?" Ben Bramlage, the male half of the morning drive duo, interjected. "Are they ready to start naming names?" But before Loudon could speak, the chirpy co-anchor answered his own question. "I certainly hope so. I can't understand why they don't have anyone in custody yet."

Loudon ignored the lead. "According to my sources," she said with authority, "Attorney General Shumate is ready to say who is behind Shelby's death. And all fingers seem to be pointing at David Unger, the Vice President's advance man."

"So Unger is in custody?" Bramlage led with the comment.

"Well, there seems to be a problem at Justice."

"Which is?"

"They seem to know who they want," she said.

"But ..."

"They don't know where he is."

"Well, what the heck is the FBI doing?"

Argo leaned to his right and changed the channel to a station more focused on local news. "I liked the news a lot more when they just told me the story," he instructed while shaking his head. "I don't need to listen to a damn conversation about how I'm screwing things up."

A new voice came over the speakers. "The overnight discovery of a dead body on the Mall has led to fears of a serial killer on the loose in DC," said the male voice on the radio.

"Good, a murder someone else is investigating," Argo said.

"Eerily similar to the crime scene for the unsolved murder of another transgender woman last fall in the same general area ..."

Argo leaned to his right and again flipped the dial to a classic-rock music station. "I need some white noise," he said aloud in the otherwise empty car. His head and shoulders moved subtly with the beat as Lou Reed sang about taking a walk on the wild side. "What's with all the transsexuals on the radio this morning, man?" Argo asked.

Gunning the car along the George Washington Parkway, he sang along to one of his all-time favorite tunes, even voicing in the familiar bass line. Looking out at the Potomac River and the yellow spring wild flowers blooming at the Lyndon Baines Johnson Memorial Grove, he reflected on the status of the case. Something was off about the rush to blame the death of Paul Shelby on David Unger, but he could not determine what was bothering him so badly. Evidence pointed to the involvement by the young advance man, but the connections seemed to flow together too easily. The investigation was moving so quickly, though, that Argo had no opportunity to change the direction. Like everyone else in the department, he was merely riding a wave at this point.

Nearly lulled to sleep by the drive, Argo was snapped awake by the chirping of his phone. Looking at the caller identification and seeing it was Proctor, he punched the answer button. "Argo here," he barked.

"Hey, Leo," Proctor replied.

"What's up, Proc?" Argo barked.

"Lots," Proctor said. "You sound like shit."

"Only because I feel like shit," Argo replied truthfully.

"You get any sleep last night?"

"Just enough to know I'm tired this morning."

"Really?" Proctor exclaimed in a surprised tone. "You left the scene ahead of me from what I remember."

"Yes, I did," Argo affirmed.

"Well, what happened, bro?" Proctor laughed "Madame Director summon you home so you two could get a little frisky?"

"Funny," Argo replied coldly. Unamused by the reference to his sex life, he flipped the bird at the telephone. "I stayed far too long at the office last night."

"The office?" he asked. "I knew you were going back to the Hoover Building, but you said you just wanted a secure line to call Cicero."

"My car got impounded," Argo replied disgustedly.

"What?"

Argo lightly bit his lip as he spoke. "Someone planted a tracking device on my car," he said. "Security found it when I pulled in off the street into the garage."

"No shit?"

"Yeah," Argo grunted as he merged onto the Roosevelt Bridge. He waved a thank you at the person who let him into traffic and continued. "It got impounded and I got a loaner."

"Sorry, bro."

Argo hated the way Proctor called him bro. It sounded so shallow. "Yeah," he said. "Just my luck. So what's up?"

Proctor went on in a very business-like manner. "Well, things lit up after you left DuPont Circle last night," he said.

"How so?"

"Yeah, man," Proctor continued. "There was a little shit-show at a bar about two blocks away from where we were."

"You're calling me about a bar fight?" Argo asked.

"There's more to the story."

"What happened?"

"Initial reports sounded just like a like a standard, run-of-the-mill dust-up," Proctor reported. "But the characters stood out."

Argo winced at the thought. "I assume you're about to tell me our boy was involved," he said.

"You got it," Proctor affirmed.

Argo shook his head. "So, what happened?" he asked.

"There was an altercation at a bar, and it involved someone who fits the new description we have of Unger," Proctor confirmed. "He ran out with a well-known patron of the bar."

Argo anticipated the answer to the question, but asked anyway. "Any idea where they are?"

"We traced the other guy's cell phone and found it abandoned in his car down by the Mall."

"And both are still at large?" Again, Argo knew the answer to the question.

"Affirmative," Proctor replied.

"I heard on the radio Justice is having a presser later this morning," Argo said. "I assume this is the subject."

"You got it."

"Thanks, dude," Argo said in a disgusted tone. Knowing he would be getting a call from Director Cicero and had little to provide in the way of answers did nothing to improve Argo's outlook on life. "This day just keeps getting better and better."

Chapter 37

The Newseum in Washington, DC is located on Pennsylvania Avenue near the National Archives. Although the facility is located within the single square mile that houses some of the world's most spectacular free museums, people stand in line to spend $20 per person to visit the venue where they can see the most important events of their lives through the eyes of the journalists who reported them.

In addition to the tourists who enter the museum through the front door, numerous business people head to the building for special events and educational training. Everything from public forums on the topics of the day to live television shows occur at the Newseum.

Charlie Patterson quietly rode along the Metro red line and looked at his watch. He was scheduled to speak at the Newseum about the impact of pending EPA regulations on the nation's construction cost structure. As he exited the train, he contemplated the questions he might face at the end of the seminar.

Focusing was hard. News of the brutal death of Jared Willis spread quickly throughout DC and rocked the gay community to its very core. Having lived in the nation's capital since graduating from college, Patterson watched the LGBT community go from underground to mainstream. He not only watched the change, but at times led it. Patterson hoped against hope the crime did not have ties to David Unger, but somehow in the back of his mind he was convinced it did. A random murder taking place immediately after Willis had interacted with Unger would be far too much of a coincidence.

Approaching the top of the escalator at the Archives Metro Station, Patterson squinted as he adjusted his eyes to the sunlight. He pulled his sun glasses from the breast pocket of his finely tailored blue suit and looked ahead at the last couple yards of his upward journey from the rails.

"Good morning, Old Top," Patterson said as he reached the apex of the escalator and stepped onto the concrete landing. About once a week, he grabbed breakfast at a small café behind the Navy Memorial. Such frequency over several years caused Patterson to become familiar with the local homeless asking for a bit of change. Old Top had positioned himself at the Archives stop for as long as Patterson could remember.

"Morning, Boss," the bald, homeless man with grey eyebrows replied in a cheerful mountain accent. "Ain't it a beautiful morning the Good Lord has made for us?"

"Absolutely." Patterson fumbled in his pocket for some change to give the man. When he discovered he only had a few coins, he reached in his back pocket for his wallet. Finding no singles, he soon produced a five dollar bill. "This ought to cover me for the next visit or two," he said jokingly.

Unaccustomed to larger denominations, Old Top eyed the bill with wonder. "Abraham Lincoln was always my favorite president," he said, snapping the bill before putting it in his cup. "Introduce me to Benjamin Franklin and it'll cover you for a lifetime," he laughed.

"You're offering discount plans, now?" Patterson chuckled a bit, thinking he was making a joke Old Top would enjoy. When the man sneered, Patterson did a double-take. It was contrary to his normal pleasant manner. "It was a joke, man."

Suddenly going silent, Old Top frowned and nodded to his left. "Ain't no joke, Boss, 'bout what's goin' on over there."

Patterson looked over at the two homeless men standing near the side of the plaza closest to the Lone Sailor statue at the Navy Memorial. There was something vaguely familiar about the duo, but Patterson shook off any attempt to make the connection. He turned back to Old Top. "You've got company this morning."

"Yeah," Old Top replied, indignantly slapping his knee. "And apparently these boys don't know this is my stop. I work here in the morning. Boys ain't got no respect for their elders."

"Everybody's got to get by somehow, my friend," Patterson reasoned.

"And leave me knawin' on day-old rye bread they serve at the shelter."

Patterson stuck out his hand. "You're a piece of work."

Old Top returned the shake. "I do what I can."

Patterson headed across the plaza towards the small coffee shop located opposite the street. He mentally reviewed the comments he was going to make at the Newseum in about a half an hour, when the two homeless men approached. Normally accustomed to giving to homeless people only after he had talked with them a few times, he held up his hand. "I gave my daily donation to Old Top," he said.

"I ain't lookin' for a handout," the taller of the two said in a heavy Cajun accent.

Patterson stopped dead in his tracks. "Tommy?" he asked, snapping his head around. He looked at the big man, who returned his stare with an embarrassed shrug of his shoulders. Patterson then shifted his eyes to the second homeless man. "David?"

"Hey, Mr. Patterson," David Unger, said making eye contact before looking down to the ground slightly embarrassed by this most recent intrusion into his protector's life.

"Sonofabitch," Patterson mumbled running his right hand softly through his hair. He looked around to make sure no one else had noticed them. "Wait here," Patterson instructed as he turned to walk into the café. "I'll get us some coffee."

"See," Unger said grabbing Tommy's arm, "I told you these clothes would work. Even Mr. Patterson didn't recognize us at first."

"Yeah. Great." Tommy looked at his tattered clothes. "I hope there are no pictures."

"Jared taught me how to fit in," Unger continued. "It's all about hiding in plain sight."

Patterson returned and set down three cups of coffee on the wrought iron table and pulled out a chair. "I sure as hell didn't expect to see you guys this morning."

"Things went *moodee* last night," Tommy said, shaking his head.

"How wrong?" Patterson queried.

"*Vary moodee*," Tommy continued. "We met like you planned, but me and David had to make a run for it on short notice."

"I didn't hear about it," Patterson said. "Usually word gets around pretty quickly."

Tommy nodded. "I'm surprised."

"Really?" Unger asked Tommy in astonishment. "He'd know about it?"

"Yeah," Tommy laughed. "It's a big town but a small community. I suspect everyone was too busy talking about Willis to give our incident that much attention." Turning to Patterson, he continued. "I was afraid the trail would lead them back to you, so we started to head to the metro stop by your office. Then I remembered you saying you were speaking at the Newseum this morning. We came here first."

"What exactly happened last night?" Patterson asked.

"The same two guys who were after David before were in the bar last night," Tommy explained. "They spotted David, so we took off in a hurry. But we caused a little dust up on the way out."

"He hit a guy in the head with a ceramic egg," Unger interjected.

Tommy shook his head as if to acknowledge none of what he had to tell was good. "We got out, made it to my car and put some distance between us and them."

Patterson scowled as he listened attentively.

"Then I ditched my car and headed to a homeless shelter to pick up some new threads." Tommy held up the collar on the ratty jacket he was wearing. "We hung out at the Archives Metro figuring we'd catch you here."

Patterson took it all in. "What happened to Jared?" Patterson asked, looking at David, who was in turn staring at the ground.

Tommy answered for David. "We're not sure," he said. "But I suspect he met up with the same boys we saw last night at the bar. This is way out of hand, Charlie. Isn't it time to go to the police?"

"I think so," Patterson said in agreement. He looked away, running through his mental rolodex of contacts. "But we need someone to broker the transfer for us. Everybody in DC wants a piece of you two. We need to start with someone who has ties beyond the police."

"And who you thinkin' about?" Tommy asked.

Patterson smiled as he came up with the right name in his head. "A friend of mine is tight with Leo Argo from the FBI," Patterson continued. "Joe Bradley. He's the Chief of Staff for Senator Richard Thompson. I know I can trust him to get us and our story in front of Argo."

"I've trusted your judgment so far," Unger said. "If it's time, then it's time." He was relieved at the thought. He was scared, confused and really tired of people jeopardizing their lives to help him.

Patterson looked at his watch. "But right now, I've got to run. I'm on at the Newseum in twenty minutes. You think you boys can stay out of trouble long enough for me to give my presentation?"

"I suppose so," Tommy shrugged.

"Yeah," Unger said assuredly.

Patterson rolled his eyes at the scroungy looking pair. "Good," he said. "Meet me back here in an hour and a half. I have an Uber car meeting me at the Newseum's business exit at 10 am sharp."

"Okay," they both said in unison.

Patterson pulled out his wallet and flipped two twenty dollar bills on the table. "And for God's sake, please quit cutting into Old Top's morning take."

Chapter 38

Despite his generally sour mood, Leo Argo chuckled to himself as he pulled up in front of the offices at the *Potomac River News*. Located in an old two-story on a side street in Cleveland Park, the converted store front made the operation look more like a five-and-dime than a newsroom. The large plate-glass windows gave a full view into the entire office. "Well, I wasn't expecting the *Washington Post*," he mumbled as he gazed at the unorganized grouping of tables, chairs, whiteboards and laptops. "But I sure as hell didn't expect *National Lampoon*."

Argo quickly spotted the reporter who had passed him the note, and started to walk in his direction.

Gene Monks looked up from his cell phone moments after Argo entered the room. He made apologies to the person he was talking to before terminating the call. A large grin spread across his face and he looked at his watch. "I expected you'd be here earlier," he said. "Alberto said you're known for being early."

"I had a rough night last night," Argo said, sticking out his hand.

Monks returned the handshake. "It looks like it," he replied, pointing at Argo's bruised eye. "Up late watching the ball game? Your eyes are so dark, it looks like you got punched."

"Why is everyone obsessed with my eye?" Argo said somewhat grouchy. It was a friendly meeting, but there was no reason to get into details.

"In any event," Monks said. "I'm glad you came by this morning."

Argo looked around the room at the various people typing away on the stories of the day. "Why don't we take a walk?" he suggested.

"Good idea," Monks replied. He went to the door and held it open for Argo. Once they were outside, he headed in the direction of the main drag. "Alberto speaks highly of you. He says you're a hard ass, but a good man."

"How do you know Alberto anyway?" Argo asked. He was a bit curious at the connection.

"We've known each other since college," Monks said. "He was the editor of the school paper and I was one of his writers. He worked his way up to the *Herald* and I went corporate. When cuts started, my job was one of the first to go."

"So you went from a corporate desk to a store front?" Argo asked.

"It's not quite so simple," Monks said. "There were a few other steps along the way, but I found a bunch of damn fine writers and devised a way to sell advertising for a hybrid print/on-line product. It's not AP, but it's making a difference in our small part of the world."

Argo shrugged his shoulders. "I guess I never really thought about it in such a micro context." They walked a few more steps. "But if Alberto wants to send me a message, why is he going through you? Why doesn't he just call me?"

"The beauty of being a blogger versus main stream media," Monks replied. "Alberto writes with a lot of practical restraints on him in Miami. Working with over zealous attorneys manages to keep a lot of things in reporter notebooks that will never see the light of day."

"I suppose you've asked me here to talk about one of those things?" Argo asked.

"Yeah," Monks said as his cell phone rang. He looked at the number and sent it to voicemail. "I hate these damn things."

"Me, too." Argo seconded the sentiment. "And I hate to be so to-the-point with a friend of a friend, but I'm really kind of busy today."

"Sure," Monks said. "So Alberto's been working on an investigative story about countries with banking secrecy laws. I agreed to be one of his sources by going to Belize and setting up a few accounts. You know, just to see how the system operates."

"Got it," Argo said.

"Well, it turns out the country's bank secrecy laws aren't quite so secret."

"So I understand," Argo agreed. "I have heard if you spread a few US dollars around, bank loan officers will tell you everything but account balances."

"Yeah," Monks continued. "I found one of those chatty bankers."

"Good use of your money, I take it?"

"Oh, yeah," Monks replied. "He gave me the names of a couple of corporate giants who will have a very hard time explaining their accounts."

"It sounds like you've done some good work on Alberto's story," Argo said. "But what does this have to do with me?"

"The banker also gave me the name of a few politicians who had accounts with balances in excess of a million dollars."

"Like?"

"Like Kentucky's Mack Wilson."

Chapter 39

Getting up from the café table, Unger looked around the Navy Memorial plaza. Businesspeople were making their way through the hustle-and-bustle of yet another work day in the nation's capital. The monument is unique in that it not only borders Pennsylvania Avenue, but also provides a wide walking path heading north towards the Smithsonian's National Portrait Gallery. Unger watched as men in dark business suits with cuff linked white shirts looked at their expensive watches. Women in dresses and tennis shoes carried leather briefcases. All of them showed blind indifference to each other's presence. None of them realizing the two homeless guys just out of their eye line were DC's most wanted.

"So what do you want to do for the next hour or so?" Unger asked Tommy nervously.

"I don't know," Tommy replied, fiddling with the two twenties he had put in his pocket.

"We could just sit around here for a while," Unger replied. "We've got forty bucks and I'm still hungry."

"Too high ticket," Tommy mumbled. "Homeless folk don't eat where these people do."

"Darn," Unger exhaled in a sigh. He poked Tommy in the belly. "Easy for you, though," he joked. "You got a bit more insulation than me."

Tommy ignored the playful prodding by Unger. He was staring intently over towards the Archives Metro Station, where Old Top was talking to a DC police officer and pointing in their direction.

"Hey, sorry man," Unger said, thinking he had pissed Tommy off. "I was just kidding. I mean I would probably be better off if I chucked a few pounds."

The officer looked at Tommy and Unger, and he headed in the pair's direction. Tommy knew the guy was going to hassle them, so he cut Unger off in mid-ramble. "Maybe we should just keep moving," he said softly.

"Why?" Unger asked.

"Because we're about to have a third for breakfast." Tommy nodded towards the approaching cop.

"Crap," Unger said.

Tommy started to walk calmly in the direction away from the Metro station. "Follow me," he said. "And don't start running until I do."

"Okay."

"And when we do," Tommy continued. "We're going to split up. You head up towards the Portrait Gallery to the right."

"Why?"

"Because I'm going to get him to follow me up Pennsylvania."

"How?"

"Shut up and listen," Tommy instructed sternly. "I'm getting him to follow me."

"Okay," Unger nodded.

"You head north, and circle back around. Lay low and meet Charlie at the Newseum."

"And you?"

"I'll meet you there, too." Tommy wanted to add 'I hope,' but did not. He really did not need to actually utter the words. It was implied in their eye contact. He smiled softly and then suddenly and without warning, Tommy smacked Unger hard on the back of the head. "You crazy," he shouted, before slapping him again. "I ain't gonna show you my knife." And Tommy started a mad dash up Pennsylvania Avenue.

As soon as Tommy started running west Unger headed north. He did not have to run far because the police officer immediately gave chase to the crazy man yelling about his knife. Once clear of the scene, Unger slowed his pace immediately as people on the plaza diverted their attention to the scuffle in the distance. In an instant, he blended in to the crowd – just another homeless guy wandering around the streets of DC.

Unger looked up ahead at each side of the street, his senses in overdrive. When he concluded there were no police around or interested, he proceeded. Slowly, he disappeared under construction scaffolding covering the sidewalk and turned right on E Street. Once out of the eyesight of anyone on the plaza he leaned back against the wall of a building to try to stop his legs from shaking. He looked across the street at a large clock outside a bank, realizing there was still an hour to kill before he met Charlie.

Around the corner on Sixth Street, Unger noticed the stage door to a theater was propped open. He looked around nonchalantly before ducking into the entrance. He could hear actors who were practicing their lines on stage as he found a safe, dark spot in a stairwell, just off stage left.

Unger's heart was beating so loudly he was sure the actors on stage could hear it pound. So he curled up in a ball and tried to slow his breathing. Just as he was starting to feel relaxed, he heard a voice. "What the hell? I've told you street people a thousand times you aren't supposed to be in here."

On the other side of the plaza, Tommy made a run up Pennsylvania Avenue crossing Eighth Street to the tree-lined court in front of the Federal Bureau of Investigation. As the DC officer followed in close pursuit, several uniformed FBI officers guarding the perimeter of the building drew their weapons and converged on him. Tommy turned to cross the street, but he knew he was out of room to run. As quickly as the chase had started, it was over. Tommy looked up, dropped to his knees and put his hands behind his head.

An FBI uniformed police officer grabbed Tommy's shoulder and shoved his chest to the concrete. Planting a knee into Tommy's back, he instructed the big man to remain still and cooperate.

"Ease up, Ace," Tommy replied, wincing from the pain. "I ain't gonna put up a fight."

Howard Jenn, one of the uniformed FBI agents, walked over to the DC cop. He recognized the face, but had to look at the name badge for his name. "What you got going on here, Gorman," he asked, pointing down at Tommy on the ground, who was being cuffed with plastic ties.

"I found this gentleman down on the Navy Memorial," he replied as he tried to catch his breath.

"Short run," Jenn laughed. He shook his head as he glanced over at Tommy being patted down. "The dummy ran in the wrong direction, I guess."

"Yeah," said Gorman. "It started when one of the regular homeless guys complained this guy was taking some of his regulars."

Jenn knew the beat. "Old Top?" he smiled.

"Yeah," Gorman replied.

The FBI man nudged Tommy with the tip of his shoe. "Dumb ass," Jenn admonished. "You're better off trying to steal from Director Cicero than taking a customer from Old Top."

"So it seems," Tommy grunted as the other officer pulled him to his feet.

Gorman continued his story as two DC police cars pulled up to the scene. "So I start to walk up to him, and he slaps some other poor guy across the head. Then he starts yelling about a knife and takes off running."

"He's clean," the FBI agent who had searched Tommy declared.

"No knife?" Jenn asked.

"If he had a knife, he tossed it," the agent replied.

"No," insured Gorman. "I was too close. He didn't dump anything."

"Doesn't matter to me," Jenn said. "He's all yours. And we wrapped him up all nice and tight for you."

"I didn't have a knife." Looking at Jenn, Tommy smiled. "I'd rather go with you guys."

"I'm sure you would," Jenn said smiling. "Been in the DC holding facility once too often I suppose."

"I've never been there before in my entire life."

"Sure you haven't."

Tommy squared to Jenn and in a very business-like voice said, "I need to see Leo Argo."

Jenn was stunned a homeless man would know the name of anyone in the top brass at the FBI. He put his hand up to stop the approaching DC officers.

"Run my prints," Tommy said sincerely. "Agent Argo will be looking for me."

Walking up and putting his face in Tommy's, Jenn asked, "How do you even know his name?"

"I know more than you think," Tommy said, looking up confidently.

"Yeah? What?"

"I know where to find David Unger."

Chapter 40

Residents of the apartments near the national zoo have a natural alarm clock – lions. In this neighborhood, people spend the morning listening to the powerful roar of the lions. Like roosters crowing the dawn of a fresh day, the lions announce the arrival of each new morning. And as the time for feeding gets closer, the roars become louder and more frequent. By the time breakfast arrives, everyone in the neighborhood is wide awake.

Andy MacNamara shivered as he walked up to the entrance of former-Senator Mack Wilson crash pad. The roaring seemed surreal in the setting of an urban neighborhood. He ducked inside the building and tried not to draw attention to himself by walking straight to the elevator. Once on the 8th floor, he located Wilson's unit and began knocking. He tapped lightly at first and then increased the volume to pounding when Wilson did not answer. When a woman peeked out from behind the chain of her neighboring door, MacNamara decided it was best to try Wilson's cell phone in order to roust him. There was no answer there either so he headed back to the elevator.

When MacNamara pushed the elevator button to return to the lobby, he smiled at the visions of Wilson's portly frame passed out on his bed, snoring as loud as the lions next door. When he found the supervisor's apartment, he knocked.

"What you need, man?" said the old fellow in a sweat-stained t-shirt as he opened the door.

"I was supposed to pick up someone from number 838," MacNamara said, pointing upstairs and trying to express some sense of urgency. "I banged on his door and tried calling his cell phone, but he's not answering."

"So what do you want me to do about it?" The man scratched sleep from his eyes.

"Well, this is really important," MacNamara said pleadingly, trying to win the man over.

The man shrugged his shoulders in an indifferent manner. "So?"

"So, can you go up and let me in?" MacNamara pleaded.

The man laughed. "Are you kidding me, man?" he asked. "I just can't go around letting people into apartments. They'll string me up by my toes."

"No?"

The old man shook his head. "No way."

MacNamara anticipated the refusal and went to 'Plan B.' He reached in his pants pocket, pulled out his cell phone and started dialing.

"What are you doing, man?"

"I'm calling the Secret Service," MacNamara replied.

"The Secret Service …"

"Yeah," MacNamara said confidently while gritting his teeth in mock aggravation. "The guy upstairs was due at the White House over an hour ago. He's a real big wig. When he didn't show up on time, they sent me up here to get him."

"No shit?"

MacNamara stuck out his thumb and raised it to his lips. "But the guy likes to drink a bit. They figured he's passed out and maybe I could get him up and going. You know, save everybody some embarrassment."

The superintendent was nodding as MacNamara spoke buying the whole story. "Damn," he declared.

"What's your name, mister?" MacNamara asked calmly.

"Kunal," the superintendent answered. "Why?"

"I need to get the Secret Service here to break down the door," he said calmly as he turned his back on the superintendent. "I'll need to tell them who to ask for when they get here. Thanks anyway."

"Now, hold on," said Kunal, holding up his hands and pondering the problems a visit from authorities could cause for others in the building. His phone would be ringing off the hook in no time.

MacNamara was dialing the number for local time and temperature when he paused and looked up. He decided to lay it on thick. "Andy, here," he said, mimicking a conversation on the other end. "Yeah, I couldn't get him up. You'll need to send a battering ram."

It sounded outrageous, but Kunal was buying it. "Mister," he said as he followed MacNamara.

"What?" MacNamara said as he put his hand over the phone's microphone.

Kunal looked at the floor and shuffled his feet. "I suppose I could open the door for you," he continued. "We could peek inside. But if your friend isn't there, we lock it back up."

MacNamara thoughtfully pondered the offer. "Let me call you back," he said to no one on the other end of the phone. He clicked the device authoritatively and shoved it into his pants pocket.

"But, man, if I get in trouble, you got to cover for me."

"Okay, fair enough," he said. "I have a pretty good idea he's just sleeping off a bad night. You'll actually be keeping him out of trouble. He'll be grateful."

"Meet me out at the front lobby."

In the front lobby moments later, Kunal appeared behind the glass of the receptionist desk. Looking at the registration book, he ran his finger down the registry. "838," he mumbled. "Looks like your friend had a visitor after hours last night."

"Really?"

"Yeah, people need to sign in after 10:00 at night. Name of Jacquie Cracker," the old man smiled and rubbed his chin. "I remember her coming in. I was outside smoking a cigarette. She's a tall lady in a pretty white dress. Came in with a guy in a suit and tie."

"What time did they sign out?" MacNamara asked.

Kunal looked at the registry. "Don't know," he said. "They didn't sign out." Kunal thought about the implication that the woman could be a prostitute and the man her pimp. "You sure you want to go up there?" he asked laughingly.

Having procured transsexual hookers for Wilson in the past, MacNamara smiled at the thought. In fact, he was pissed at Wilson for the added hassle arising from Wilson's failure to open the door and MacNamara looked forward to any added embarrassment he would cause his former boss. Better yet, a surprise trip to Wilson's love den would be one more thing for MacNamara to hang over Wilson's head. "Yes, sir," he smiled. "Even more reason to go up and wake the happy couple."

"Okie-dokie," Kunal giggled.

MacNamara held his index finger to his lips as if sharing a secret. "The folks at the White House don't need to know about this," he said and winked.

"Alright then," he said, picking a pass key from the wall. "Let's head upstairs."

Kunal led the way to the elevator. Hitting the button for the eighth floor, Kunal mumbled while the doors closed. "Man in bed with a she-male hooker and I'm gonna swing open the door," he said. "I gotta be outta my damn mind."

"Trust me," MacNamara said in a soothing voice. "You're doing the man a big favor. Better for me to find him with some bimbo than the Secret Service."

When the floor bell rang, Kunal went to the door of 838 and knocked loudly. When there was no response, he placed the key in the door, turned the latch and gently pushed open the door. He looked at MacNamara. "You go in," he said nodding. "I'm waiting out here."

MacNamara slowly walked into the front room of the apartment. "Senator," he said in a tone somewhat less than a shout. "Senator Wilson, you up yet?" He laughed to himself at the unintentional sexual double-entendre.

Despite promising to stay behind, Kunal followed MacNamara cautiously into the apartment. "Senator?" he said. "Damn. Man must be important."

"Come on, Senator," MacNamara said, approaching the door to the bedroom of the apartment. "It's me, Senator. You guys get some clothes on and I'll come in."

Nothing.

"Knock on the door," Kunal instructed, pointing to the bedroom.

Looking over his shoulder at the superintendent, MacNamara smiled. Ten minutes ago, he was not going to let him in the room. Suddenly he was giving instructions. Adding a bit of drama to the situation, MacNamara reached down and slowly turned the doorknob. "Ready or not," he sang out. "Here I come. I sure hope you're not doing the same thing."

When he pushed open the door, Kunal let out a high-pitched scream and ran from the room.

MacNamara looked at the bed mesmerized by what he saw. Senator Mack Wilson's lifeless blue body lay in an odd prone position. A hypodermic needle and rubber tube lay on a table next to the bed. Stumbling backwards until his motion was stopped by the wall, MacNamara dropped to his hands and knees and began to puke.

Chapter 41

Charlie Patterson's resume included high-level work in two administrations and informally counseling several others, so he rarely lacked for words. He spoke often at events because he laced his institutional knowledge of government with personal stories of the people he worked with over the years. While many in DC come across as incessant name droppers, Patterson was sincere and believable. He exudes the essence of DC access. Whenever he spoke, the audience got the idea that powerful people dropped Patterson's name when they gathered.

Patterson's appearance at the Newseum was not his finest performance. He normally wowed his audience with stories of governmental access and influence. Today his mind wandered to the death of Jared Willis and the woeful predicament of Tommy and Unger. He knew it was time for Unger to turn himself in. However, he also knew once Unger was in the hands of the authorities, he had little, if any, control over the outcome. He was conflicted and the disengaged manner in which he went about his comments reflected his mood.

Finishing the speech, he skipped the normal social chit-chat and headed down to the lobby. Glancing up and down Sixth Street, he could see no sign of Tommy or Unger. As concerned as he was by the fact his two cohorts were absent, he bristled because his Uber car had not yet arrived. He looked at his phone for the app to locate his driver, when he noticed a cream Cadillac Escalade a half block away flashing its headlights. Patterson looked both ways, crossed the street and headed toward the car. When he approached, the driver rolled down the window.

"Mr. Patterson?" the driver asked.

"Yes."

"I'm your driver," he replied.

Patterson poked his head in the open window. "Why didn't you pull up to the Newseum?" he asked.

The driver laughed. "Because your luggage asked me not to."

"My luggage?"

"Hey, Charlie," David Unger said meekly, sticking his head up slightly from the cargo portion of the vehicle located behind the back seat.

Patterson exhaled heavily and closed his eyes for a moment. Then he opened the door and slid into the back seat. Putting his arm onto back of the seat, he looked back over his shoulder into the cargo area. He was surprised to see only Unger. "Where's Tommy?" he asked.

"No idea," Unger replied. "There was a problem and we had to split up. We were supposed to meet back at the Newseum when you were ready. But he hasn't shown."

"Which, I guess, begs the question," Patterson said. "How the hell did you end up in this car?"

"I can answer that," interrupted the driver. "I'm a part time actor over at the theater up the street. I drive Uber to make ends meet until I'm discovered. I found your friend here hiding in a stairwell."

"I ducked into the theater after Tommy and I split up," Unger interjected.

"Anyway, the driver continued. "I was ready to call the cops until he mentioned your name."

Patterson leaned forward. "I'm sorry," he said apologetically. "Do I know you?"

"No, sir," the driver said. "But I sure know you. Every gay man in DC knows you – at least by reputation. You know," he stammered a bit. "You're the Queen Mum."

Patterson smiled at the reference. "Don't be embarrassed," he said. "I'm not offended by the nickname."

"Good," the driver said. "Anyway, when your friend told me he was waiting to meet you, I agreed to park near the door so I'd be the closest Uber driver to the Newseum when you came out. But he wanted to make sure you were alone before we signaled you."

"Thanks," Patterson replied. He reached and patted the man on his shoulder. "And I'll make this ride well worth your while."

"No need, sir," the driver said smiling. "I just can't wait until I tell all my friends I drove you around today. You're a legend around here."

"Thank you," Patterson replied sheepishly. "I'm sure you're being far too kind. But I would like to enlist your services for the remainder of the day. Money is no object. However, I do need your discretion."

"Discretion is my middle name," the driver assured.

"Good," Patterson replied. He handed a business card over the driver's shoulder. "Let's head to my office first."

"What are we going to do there?" Unger asked.

"Wait," Patterson replied.

"Wait?" Unger was confused. "For what? I thought you said it was time to turn myself in."

"It is," Patterson nodded. "But, we've got to get the timing down just right. So we'll wait until the lunch crowd clears out of the 116 Club."

Chapter 42

Theodore Roosevelt Island is a small nature preserve located in the Potomac River directly between Georgetown and Rosslyn, Virginia in the shadows of the Watergate complex. Originally a plantation, it was the spot President James Madison ferried to during his escape from the British invasion of DC during the War of 1812. President Teddy Roosevelt declared the island a national park and a statue of the Rough Rider stands along one of the many hiking trails intersecting the island.

Stationed about a mile away at the Pentagon, Lt. Col. Carson Collins loved the island for many reasons. He used the trails as a place to rehab following an injury he sustained during one of his deployments to Afghanistan. He loved finding natural solitude so close to the city. Just a year earlier, the trails proved just rugged enough to relearn walking with a prosthetic leg. The demons no longer haunting him, he now loved the island for something entirely different – fishing.

Walking along the boardwalk with his fishing gear in one hand, he wrapped his other hand around the hand of Levi, his young son. The sun felt warm and the brackish smell from the backwater marsh along the down-river portion of the island filled their nostrils. As young boys are prone to do, Levi was filled with questions.

"Do you think we'll catch anything today, Daddy?" Levi asked with excitement.

"I sure hope so, son," Collins replied.

"We gonna go to our 'honey-hole?'" the young boy continued. "We always catch something at our special spot."

"We'll go there last," Collins laughed. "Remember, we need to hit our best spot right as the tide starts to come in. Low tide is when the striper hit."

"Oh, yeah," Levi said, his eyes darting around as he spoke. "I forgot. So where we gonna go first."

Collins smiled. "Well, we've never fished the rocks before. I thought we'd try there first," he said. "Let's see if they're biting down by the rocks."

"Okay, Daddy," Levi said with solid determination. Suddenly, a raft of ducks causing a commotion near the Virginia shoreline caught the boy's attention. "Hey, look at those birds back there."

Collins laughed at the boy's comment. "Yup," he said. "And what kind are they?"

Levi looked a second time. "Mallards," he said. Then looking at his father for some sort of affirmation, he said, "Right?"

"Affirmative," Collins said, reaching down and scuffing the boy's hair. "Good call, son."

Levi looked again and pointed towards the shore. "But what's over there, Daddy?"

"What?"

"The lump of stuff up against the shore they're all fighting around." Levi looked in amazement as the birds fought around what appeared to be a rather large sack of potatoes.

Putting his hand above his eyes to shield his face from the sun, Collins replied, "I'm not sure, son." Collins pulled a set of binoculars out of Levi's Spiderman backpack. As he zoomed in on the lump, his heart skipped a beat.

"What is it, Daddy?" Levi asked, sensing his father's anticipation.

Collins put his arm against the railing of the boardwalk in an effort to steady himself. Struggling for a quick lie, he dared not tell his son he saw two lifeless bodies wrapped in a large fishing net. He raised the binoculars a second time. As best he could tell one body was short and stubby while the other was tall and thick.

Chapter 43

Thompson bounded up the steps of the Hart Senate Building two at a time, racing to his office to deal with The Fat Man's crisis of the day.

Known for the melodramatic, The Fat Man liked to turn the smallest incident into the brink of nuclear war. Maybe it was the trial lawyer in him, but he could turn into a field general at the drop of a hat. And like most great leaders, people often followed him into whatever war he declared. And Thompson always marveled how he usually won. But because The Fat Man sought a resolution of war so often, Thompson usually took his initial declaration with a grain of salt, waiting for a more detailed plan to develop.

But when The Fat Man called the Senate floor requesting Thompson return to the office immediately, his voice sounded different – harried maybe – but certainly uncharacteristic. It was just as well. Thompson did not particularly like the floor. The Senate is often referred to as the world's most exclusive fraternity. When around the other Senators Thompson felt like the unwanted pledge, accepted by the others because they needed the dues. He was allowed in the frat house and shown the rituals, but he was not really accepted as a member. He was an outsider and others let him know it.

As he looked over the wall into the courtyard of the Hart Building, Thompson quietly hummed "Accidently Like a Martyr" to himself. Sure, it was one of Warren Zevon's strange love songs, but the chorus seemed oddly appropriate. He stumbled into this role as Senator. Martyr was a bit extreme, but it served to make a point. The song fit his current mood.

Thompson ducked into the side door to his office as he wondered what could have The Fat Man so riled up. When he entered his private office, his old friend looked oddly at him and shrugged his shoulders. "Sorry to drag you from the floor," he said.

"Not a problem," Thompson replied. Looking around the room he saw Charlie Patterson sitting alone fiddling with his cell phone. More confused than before, Thompson crossed the room and shook Patterson's hand. "Good morning, Charlie," he said, looking at his watch. "Sorry. Good afternoon. I guess I missed lunch."

Patterson stood to shake hands. "Take this call and I'll handle lunch," he said, looking at his cell phone before handing it to a confused Thompson. A Facetime call was in progress. When he looked at the screen, Patterson continued, "Senator," he said. "This is a bit unconventional, but meet David Unger."

Thompson shot a look at The Fat Man.

"Yeah," The Fat Man replied. "THAT David Unger."

Thompson was taken aback. He took his jacket off and walked to his desk contemplating the impact of what was happening. As he placed his jacket on the back of the chair, he looked at The Fat Man. "Clear my calendar for the remainder of the day." The Fat Man started to speak, but was silenced when Thompson raised his hand. "I have to take this in for a minute."

Thompson shook his head. Then, then looking at Patterson, he said, "This is more than a bit bizarre."

Grimacing his agreement, Patterson jumped in. "Senator," he said. "We've known each other for a long time."

"And our friendship allows you to put me into direct contact with a felon?" Thompson replied. After pausing for a few seconds, he went on. "No," he said looking at the young man on the cell phone screen and reconsidered. "You put me in contact with the most wanted man in America."

The Fat Man saw Thompson was quickly working himself into a rage. "Alleged felon," he interjected.

"What?"

"While we were waiting for you, Charlie told me a story I'm inclined to believe," The Fat Man said. Thompson's eyes were sharp and narrow as he listened. "I don't think this kid is responsible for the death of Vice President Shelby."

"Come on, Joe," Thompson replied. "This is out of our league. Even for you, a conclusion like that is a stretch."

"I don't think so." The Fat Man argued. "The story is pretty compelling."

Patterson jumped back in. "Senator," he said, before pausing and dropping all formality. "Richard, this kid is not the one responsible."

"Then who is?"

"I don't know," Patterson said shaking his head. "But it isn't him."

"Alright," Thompson said, "so what's his story?"

For the next hour, Patterson repeated the story to Thompson, who in turn, peppered him with questions as if interrogating a witness in court. When they were done, Thompson looked at The Fat Man. A quick exchange of glances was all the pair needed to agree something did not add up with the story being told in the press.

"So what do you want from me?" Thompson said, and then in a leading manner asked, "I suppose you want me to meet with him?"

"No," Patterson said. "I'd like for you to set up a meeting with your friend Leo Argo," he said, holding his hands open. "David will turn himself in, but only using you as a go-between for the FBI."

"Joe," Thompson asked, "your thoughts?"

"It gives you cover," The Fat Man replied confidently.

"Meeting with an alleged killer gives me cover?"

The Fat Man continued undaunted. "You're acting as a go-between for a surrender. Even if he turns out to be guilty, you're the one who helped find him."

Thompson thought for a moment about the implications of his decision before answering. "I'll do it," he said, handing the phone back to Patterson. "How do you want to proceed?"

"I have Unger in a secure location within walking distance," Patterson replied. "Let's go there. You can meet him and convince yourself of his sincerity before you call Argo."

"Sounds like a plan." Thompson said, turning to leave.

The Fat Man stood up and started to walk out with the pair. "I need to cancel a call first," he said.

"Who?"

"Jon Dosser," The Fat Man replied. "His name popped up on a document in this Longo International. I called him this morning and we scheduled a second call for later. He said he'd be glad to look at whatever we found in Wilson's files. So I may go meet him."

Thompson thought for a moment. "Stay behind," he instructed.

"What?"

"This meeting is in my official capacity," Thompson said, not really sure if it was or not. "At least that's going to be my story. And as it's in my official capacity, I get immunity." He put his hand on his friend's shoulder. "You could lose your license. Make your call. Go to your meeting."

"You're the boss," The Fat Man replied, confident Patterson would protect Thompson's interest.

Thompson headed to the door. "Dinner tonight?"

"Sure," The Fat Man replied. "I'll head to the Capitol Hill Club as soon as I'm done with Dosser."

Chapter 44

Argo stared through the one-way glass at the big homeless man handcuffed to the metal chair in the FBI's main interrogation room. He listened to the distinctive Louisiana Cajun accent as another man asked him question after question.

"I'll waive all my rights," the man shouted. "As soon as I get to talk to Leo Argo." Knowing there were people on the other side of the glass watching, Tommy looked at the mirror on the wall. "Hear dat?" he repeated. "I'll talk as soon as I get to Argo."

Argo kept trying to place the face and voice. "I've never met this guy before in my life," he said to Director Cicero, who was also observing the interrogation.

"That's what I suspected," replied Cicero. "But while you were getting here, I had someone run his prints." He handed Argo a clipboard with a printout attached to the top. "His name is Thomas Kryon. Other than a ten year old DUI in Baton Rouge, he's got no record. He's employed and he's worked a whole bunch of jobs in DC. He's not Donald Trump, but he's certainly not a homeless man either."

Without looking up from the clipboard, Argo spoke. "Nice work, detective," he said jokingly.

"You hang around the hallways enough and you pick up a thing or two," Cicero replied, trying to hide his delight at Argo treating him as a colleague instead of a political appointee. "And you'll be proud. I never once called him a 'perp.'"

"This is good stuff," Argo replied, flipping more pages. Once he was done, he looked up. "Anyone else know we got him?"

"I spoke with the director of the Secret Service earlier," Cicero said. "They think he was driving the escape car last night for Unger. They're sending Proctor over to watch the interrogation. He should be here in about half an hour."

Argo winced at the thought of the Secret Service knowing the development. He cooperated, but only to a point. This investigation deserved anonymity and he trusted no one outside the agency. Yet, he did not want to chide the Director for speaking too freely. "Did you tell them about my meeting this morning?"

"No," Cicero shook his head. He could tell Argo was not pleased the Secret Service knew they had a new lead. "I know you don't trust Proctor, Leo, and neither do I. Our motivation in this investigation and his are entirely different."

"He's just a weird guy," Argo said, haltingly. "He seems to want a suspect, regardless of the circumstances."

"I had to tell them, Leo," Cicero replied. "POTUS is on all of our asses over this case. I have direct orders from the Oval Office to report."

"Okay, I understand." Argo did not understand or agree, but he said it anyway. He placed the file on a ledge in front of Cicero.

"Leo, I know most people around here think I'm just a political hack appointed by the President," Cicero said, putting his hand on his subordinate's shoulder. "But I've got pretty good instincts, too. I had to do what I had to do. You've got some time alone here."

"Then I don't want to wait any longer."

"I concur," Cicero said, appreciating the situation they both shared. "I'll leave if you want me to."

"Only if you need plausible deniability," replied Argo, using the phrase coined in the Watergate era for when aides dared not tell the President of their actions so he would not have to lie at a later date.

"I'll stay and take my chances," Cicero said as he watched Argo walk from behind the glass into the sterile interrogation room. Tommy looked up as Argo walked in. Their eyes locked.

"Unstrap the man," Argo instructed. They continued to eye each other while another officer cut away the plastic cuffs. Tommy's eyes were red and puffy. He looked like he'd been through a wringer and he appeared very ill at ease in his borrowed street clothes. Once free, the big FBI agent ordered the others away. "Now then," he said. "Everybody haul ass."

"Thanks," Tommy replied, rubbing his wrists after they were freed. He waited until all the others left the room. "Your buddies are not nearly as accommodating."

"I'm Leo Argo," He flopped his badge on the desk to verify his identity.

Tommy glanced at the credentials in the wallet and shoved them back across the table top. "I assumed as much," he said. "You're a big dawg here. When you talked, those other boys listened."

Argo was having trouble sizing up his adversary. Tommy was awfully calm for his circumstances. He noticed Tommy wiping some white crust from the corner of his mouth. "You want a bottle of water?" he offered.

"And some vodka to go in it if you have any," Tommy said half-jokingly. "I've had a bad morning."

Argo got two bottles of water from the table behind him and handed one to Tommy. The other he opened and took a sip. He was well aware the clock was running. He sat down across the table. "We don't know each other, do we?" Argo asked.

"Not unless you frequent alternate-lifestyle clubs around DuPont Circle," Tommy responded. He had purposefully run towards the FBI building only hours earlier with a plan to be captured and he hoped, make his way to Leo Argo. Now in front of Argo, he could not resist testing him a little bit.

"No," Argo said, smiling at the inference. He knew the man was toying with him, but he decided to play along just for a moment. "My girl and I don't tend to go to dance clubs anymore."

"Well, you should sometime," Tommy said. "Let me know when you're headed there and I'll buy the first round."

The two stared at each other for a few seconds, each daring the other to look away. "Why are you asking for me, Tommy Kryon?" Argo used his full name for two reasons. First, he wanted the man to know he knew his identity. More importantly, he wanted to indicate the time for games was over.

Tommy understood the implication of Argo's sudden change in demeanor. He sat up in his chair and wiped the cocky smile from his face. "We don't know each other, but we do have a mutual friend."

"We have a mutual friend?" Argo asked with a smirk.

"Joe Bradley," he said, remembering the name Patterson had mentioned earlier in the day. "Chief of Staff for Senator Richard Thompson."

Argo stood up at the mention of The Fat Man's name. He usually did not let a witness see his emotion. But hearing Bradley's name in the mix got the best of him. He put his hands on the table and leaned forward. "Okay," he said menacingly. "You have my attention."

Tommy started to speak, but Argo interrupted him by putting his index finger to his lips momentarily. His eyes narrowed and shot forward. "And by attention," he said, "let me go one step further. I'll be blunt. If any harm comes to Joe Bradley, I'll fucking kill you myself." Argo paused for effect. "We on the same page?"

A quick nod was all it took to let Argo know Tommy believed him. "Cool down, Ace," he replied, his Cajun accent seemingly heavier in the response. "The 'mutual friend' line was just a turn of phrase. I've never met the man. I wouldn't know him if he walked through the door."

The understanding complete, Argo sat back down. "Then by all means continue," he instructed.

Tommy went on to explain his odd journey to the FBI's interrogation room. Argo never wrote down a single word of the conversation. He did not have to or want to. What the man was describing fit another piece into a puzzle Argo had been putting together for days. The manner in which he met David Unger intrigued Argo. And the description of the men who approached Tommy and Unger in the bar sounded much too familiar for Argo to conclude it was a mere a coincidence. He was sure it was the two men he met at the boxing gym – the men who likely pegged his car with a tracking device – the owner of the Golden Glove pendant he found at Unger's apartment.

Tommy continued with his story, which Argo interrupted only occasionally with a clarifying question. At one point, Tommy caught Argo glancing at the glass window. "You want me to tell them, too?" he exclaimed, pointing at the two-way glass.

"There's nobody back there," Argo responded. But before Tommy could respond, the door to the side room gently opened. Argo looked at his watch hoping Proctor had not arrived early.

"I'm talking to him," Tommy informed the person entering the room by pointing at Argo. "I've got no business with you."

FBI Director Cicero walked towards the pair. "Hi," he said, sticking out his hand to Tommy. "I'm Bob. I run this place."

Argo was not sure what was happening until Cicero looked at him. "I don't want deniability," he said, "plausible or otherwise – not when I have the truth staring me in the face."

Argo was pleased to see the sincerity in Cicero's eyes. He was not sure what Cicero's plan might be, but he decided to let the boss take this wherever he wanted.

"Two things," Cicero said, raising his index finger to indicate the first. "The Vice President's wife is a friend of mine. You don't find many friends in politics and very few of them reside in DC. I considered her one of the few Inside the Beltway people I ever truly liked or trusted. The Vice President's faults aside, I owe it to her to get this right."

Tommy nodded in appreciation of his frankness. "Never met the man myself," he said. "Probably wouldn't be too helpful right now to say I didn't vote for him either."

"Quit while you're ahead," Argo instructed.

"Seemed like we were all being honest," Tommy shrugged.

Argo shut Tommy up with a menacing stare and then looked at Cicero. "Okay, so you're telling me we're both in this up to our nuts," Tommy declared. "So, what's the second thing?"

Cicero looked at Argo. "Proctor is in the building," he replied blandly.

Argo slapped his hands together. "Damn," he cursed softly. "I was afraid he'd make it here before I got done. He got here quick."

"Who's Proctor? Tommy asked.

"The end of your line," Argo replied. "Now shut up."

"He just pulled into the parking lot."

"So our exclusive interrogation just ended."

Cicero thought for a moment. "Maybe not."

"What do you have in mind?"

Cicero smiled. "Well you know me, the simple political hack I am ..."

"We've been through this already, Boss ..." Each quickly interrupted the other.

"I've just determined the detention of this homeless man is purely a local matter," Cicero said, holding up his hand to demand silence. "I'm making an executive decision. Agent Argo, please transport him downtown to the DC holding facility for processing."

"Thank you, Mr. Director," Argo said, smiling at Cicero's directive.

Putting his hand on the agent's shoulder, he added, "I mean it, Leo."

"What?"

"Processing," he said. "I want him in your custody at all times. Deliver him on your timeline, but deliver him."

Argo acknowledged the order. "Yes, sir," he said.

"Now get a move on," Cicero added "You don't have much time to play with here. I'll head down and delay Proctor. He'll report up the chain of command pretty quickly. They'll have more people looking for you than Unger." Cicero turned and quickly left the room.

Before Tommy could stand up, Argo grabbed him by the collar of his shirt. "Try to run and I'll shoot you," he warned. "Got it?"

"Yeah," Tommy replied. "I found you, remember. I know I'm up to my ass in alligators. Trust me. I didn't risk it to have you shoot my – might I say fine – ass."

"Now turn around and let me put these on you then." Argo said as he pulled a pair of handcuffs from the latch on his gun holster.

"Now there's a sign of trust," Tommy replied, rolling his eyes.

"I'm transporting you, remember," Argo said flatly. "I don't want to walk you through here unsecured." Argo snapped the cuffs on Tommy behind his back. "It'll look weird. Just keep quiet and tight. Follow my lead and I'll take the cuffs off when we get clear of the building."

"Got it," Tommy acknowledged.

Argo loosely held Tommy's arm as they headed out of the room towards the elevator. When the elevator doors opened, another person approached. Argo indicated his disapproval. "Prisoner transfer," he said. "This one's an express to the garage."

When the doors opened in the garage, the pair headed straight to the small space where Louis worked. When Argo approached, Louis smiled a big toothy grin. "*Que pasa*, Leo," he asked. "I got your car all ready to go. No more bugs on this baby. It's clean."

"I appreciate it, *mejo*," Argo said. "But I can't use my regular ride right now."

"Damn," he replied. "I even washed it for chu. Your Crown Vic hasn't been this sparkly since it left the factory."

"It's not I don't appreciate it," Leo said. "I'll come back and pick it up before I head home tonight. But for right now, get me some wheels from our impound lot. Make sure there are no government plates on it."

Tommy was casually watching the exchange when he heard the bell on another elevator ring. Before he knew what was happening, Argo grabbed him roughly by the cuffs and shoved him down behind a parked car, out of the line of sight of the opening doors. "Quiet," Argo whispered in his ear.

Nearby, Argo could hear Scott Proctor getting his car keys from Louis. "You seen Leo Argo?" Proctor asked, his voice agitated.

Louis laughed. "Chu just missed him, mange," he said.

"Fuck," Proctor declared.

"Left here about five minutes ago in his Crown Vic."

Proctor proceeded to his own service car and left rubber as his car headed out the garage exit. Once Argo was sure Proctor was clear of the building, he tugged Tommy to his feet and back over to Louis. "I owe you one, pal," he said.

"Anything for chu, Leo," Louis replied. "Now let me go find chu a car."

"Next time, give me a little warning," Tommy said. His arms still cuffed, he worked his shoulder up and down as much as he could. "I've got a bad rotator cuff."

"Follow my lead," Argo warned. "Or your rotator won't be the only thing hurting."

Chapter 45

The Lincoln Cottage is located in a remote corner of northeast Washington, DC, near the Maryland border. On two hundred and fifty acres of land known as the Soldier's Home, it is the centerpiece of an active military base dedicated to the housing and care of US veterans. President Lincoln used a cottage on the grounds as his Summer White House, commuting on horseback every day to Pennsylvania Avenue. He wrote the first draft of the Emancipation Proclamation there and visited the day before his death at Ford's Theater.

Although currently considered an active military installation, portions of the grounds are open to the public. Most come to tour Lincoln's summer home. Walking the grounds in front of the cottage takes visitors back to a point in time when the Lincoln children ran around the lawn playing games while their father met with military leaders to discuss war strategy.

The other portion of the base open to the public is not as historic, but just as unique – a golf course and driving range. Located a driver and a three iron from the front lawn of the Lincoln Cottage, it is one of several urban golf courses in DC.

As instructed, Jane Kline left her security detail at the front check point of the Soldier's Home and drove her fortified black Escalade into the parking lot of the pro shop alone. Cars zipped along the road just outside the tall electrified fence to her right, oblivious to the meeting about to take place. Kline wondered if Oleg Kederov understood all the times their paths came close to crossing when she was on the operative side of the CIA. Once a well-connected insider in Russia,

Kederov's banishment to the United States was punishment for some internal fall. Intelligence was certain Kederov was looking for a way back into the Kremlin's good graces. Kline was wary of meeting with a man she was certain had pulled the trigger on several KGB-ordered hits.

She exited the car and walked up to the driving range to find Kederov hitting golf balls. Actually, the word "hitting" seemed a bit of an overreach. Cursing at them seemed more appropriate. The chunky little Russian would hit a ball and swear at its banana-like path through the sky. He looked up as Kline approached. "Good afternoon, Madame Director," he said, lining up another shot and then taking an awkward swing. "*Robho*," he sneered as the ball cut sharply right.

Kline smiled at Kederov's obvious lack of sports prowess. His swing, poorly conceived and poorly executed, reminded her of films of President Richard Nixon whiffing at golf balls in the seventies.

"Do you play golf, Madame Director?" Kederov asked.

"I did several years ago," she said. Pausing, she pointed to the metal of her prosthetic leg. "But now I seem to pull everything left."

"I am sorry," Kederov said in a tone anything but apologetic. "I forgot about your unfortunate injury."

"Not a problem," Kline replied. "It's okay. I never really had the patience for the game."

"It is a damning sport, really," Kederov replied. "No matter how hard you try, you are never satisfied with how you play. I practice. I play. I stink. Yet, still I come back for more."

Kline chuckled. "I feel the same way about fishing, except in the end I suppose you can't cook and eat a golf ball."

Kederov rolled another ball in front of him. Following a big, deep breath, he took a mighty looping swing. The ball went along a similar left to right path as the previous one. "*Cyka*," he cursed again in Russian

"I suspect you didn't invite me out here for a golf lesson did you, Comrade Kederov?" Kline asked, watching the curving flight of the ball. Her patience was growing thin.

"Director Kline," Kederov smiled. He loosened the Velcro on his golf glove. "Always one to cut to the chase."

"Always," Kline replied.

"Well then," Kederov said, tapping his club on the ground. "I should have anticipated a quicker transition to business."

"We are both people who value our time, Comrade," Kline replied. She hobbled over to his golf bag and pulled out a club and made a casting motion with her arm. "Now if this were a fly rod, we'd relax a little before talking." She paused for emphasis. "But it isn't and you need to get to the point."

Kederov knew his adversary possessed the upper hand. It was time for business. He put his club back into the bag and pointed to one of the benches behind the hitting area, Kederov waiting for Kline to be seated before he joined her.

"You know my circumstances," he began.

"Some," Kline replied. "I'm sure there is more to your story than I know." She wanted to see how far he would go with his explanation.

Kederov smiled humbly at Kline's coy response. As he expected, she made this difficult. Eating a little crow was expected. "I was sent to America on special assignment," he said, looking at the ground.

"And ..."

"And we both know such a depiction of my arrival on US soil is a lie," he said. "There was no promotion. I did not come here of my own accord. I was banished."

Kline nodded at the admission. "Our intelligence has told us as much," Kline said, letting him up a bit. Kederov was a better killer than he was a bureaucrat. Still she was not quite sure where he was heading. She decided to just let him talk.

"Well," he continued, knowing he must reveal his true motivation. "I was hoping to earn my way back home."

"Show value again?"

"Yes," Kederov said. "I had many places where I could make my mark. Counter-surveillance was never my strong point. I had other skills not as useful as they used to be. So, I went the political route."

"I never really viewed you as a political type."

"Which is why I was able to get away with much of what I accomplished," Kederov said proudly. "You and your people never suspected my involvement."

"Involvement? In what?"

"The pipeline," he said. "Your country's success in developing it is the biggest threat to our control of Eastern Europe. I figured out a way to slow down the process."

Kline thought she understood the reference. American politicians on the left were doing enough on their own to kill a north/south pipeline. But she knew Russia was behind several of the major contributions to environmental groups opposing it. "You've not hidden your opposition," she said. "But contributions are hardly illegal."

"I went further," he said.

"Okay," she said haltingly. He had her attention.

"Unfortunately, my operations put me in the middle of a controversy with Cold War level consequences," he said. "The current state of this operation will cost me what is left of my reputation in Russia." He paused and looked skyward. "It may cost me my life."

Kline cocked her head and leaned forward. "Go ahead."

Now it was Kederov's turn to play offense. "First, I seek political asylum and protection," he said.

Kline was stunned at the request. She did not expect this from their meeting and she struggled not to show any reaction. "You know it doesn't work quite so easily," she said. "I can't offer either unless I know what we're talking about."

Kederov decided to play his trump card. "I had no role in the death of your Vice President," he said. "But I believe I can supply you with information sufficient enough for you to draw certain conclusions." Kederov took off his glove and pulled a handkerchief from his back pants pocket. He wiped the sweat from the deep creases in his brow. When Kline failed to respond, he looked up, "Now do you know what I am talking about?"

The silence was deafening. Initially, many in the CIA suspected a Russian connection, but Kline personally discounted it early. Maybe she was wrong. Maybe Kederov was being too quick to deny responsibility. She said nothing.

Kederov smiled and continued. "There are those in your government who will soon be looking to blame me. I bribed people, but killed no one. When all of this becomes public, despite my protestations to the contrary, I will likely be called home."

"To explain it to your superiors," Kline said.

"Now, Madame Director," Kederov smiled. "We both know what will happen to me when I return to Russia. I am so far in, explanations will not matter. There will be no balloons for my welcome home party, but there will be lots of loud noises."

"Okay," Kline replied. She had seen Kederov's look before – the desperate look of a man who would do anything to stay alive. She believed him. "I'll run it up the chain of command. I'll need a little more information though."

"Dah." Kederov looked directly at Kline and chose his next words quite carefully. "Have you ever heard of Longo International?"

Chapter 46

"I gotta take this call," Leo Argo said in an unapologetic tone. Seeing Jane Kline's number appear on his cell phone as he drove up Pennsylvania Avenue towards the Capitol got his attention.

"Fine by me," Tommy replied. "Just don't forget I've got dinner reservations tonight at the city lock up."

"Lighten up," Argo chuckled at the reference. "It's my significant other."

Tommy shook his head in disgust. "Breeders."

"Hey, babe," Argo said into the phone as he raised his finger to his lip to silence Tommy. "What's up? ... Yeah ... Well, I've got someone in the car with me."

"You can let me off at the next corner, if you really want to," Tommy said, pointing at the approaching intersection.

"You talk," Argo instructed. "I'll listen." He shielded the phone from his passenger and listened intently as Kline explained details of her meeting with Kederov, concluding with the revelation Jon Dosser, the Vice-President's Chief of Staff, was the man behind the death of Vice President Shelby.

"Damn," Argo exclaimed when she finished. "I was way off base on this one. Keep me in the loop."

"Problems at home?" Tommy asked as they headed up to the Hill.

"None of your damn business," Argo replied, his phone ringing a second time.

"Ga lee," Tommy laughed his Cajun slang. "She is persistent as a pole cat at a popcorn festival."

Argo rolled his eyes. "That doesn't make any sense," he shook his head, looking at his phone. He didn't recognize the number, but answered anyway. "Argo here," he said. His eyes grew wide as the caller filled him in. "You've got to be kidding me," was all he could reply.

"Who dat?" Tommy asked. "Your old lady again?"

"A friend of mine," Argo replied. "He says he's with David Unger, who wants to turn himself in." He paused for a moment. He was starting to like Tommy and decided to rib him a bit. "And if you ever do meet my partner, don't call her my old lady."

"Why?" Tommy howled and slapped his knee. "You afraid she might kick your ass?"

"No, I'm afraid she'll kick yours."

Argo sped past the Senate office buildings and headed north on a side street. He angled the car into a narrow spot in front of what could best be described as an old corner speakeasy, about a block from the Hart Building. The green cloth awning in front of the building had the number 116 across it.

"What the hell is this?" Tommy asked.

"The 116 Club," Argo replied. "It's a private club with a very limited number of high-profile members."

"And David is in there with all those big shots?" Tommy asked with surprise in his voice. "Dat ain't very smart."

"The 116 is only open for lunch," Argo said as he opened the door to let Tommy enter first. Although he found Tommy both amusing and straight forward, he was still in official custody. He needed to make sure Tommy did not run. "They've been shut down for a couple of hours. Your good friend is waiting for us inside."

"Good friend?" Tommy laughed as he looked back at Argo holding the door. "Damn. One little kiss and suddenly we're good friends. I'd hate to know what you'd be calling us if I'd ... well ... you know."

"Fine," Argo replied as the closed the door. "Does accomplice to premeditated murder sound better?"

Tommy's head snapped forward. "Naw. Friend is good. Let's stick with good friend. That works for me."

The inside of the 116 Club was dark, but not because the place was closed for business. It's always dark inside the 116 Club. It's simply part of the place's weird charm.

Richard Thompson greeted Argo when he came through the door. "Hey, Leo," Thompson said, sticking out his hand. "I didn't expect we'd be seeing each other again quite this quickly. Who's this?" he asked, looking at Tommy's clothes. "You traveling with plain clothes protection these days."

Returning the handshake, Argo glanced at Tommy. "A friend of Mr. Unger's," he said with a stern look at his prisoner. "Meet Senator Richard Thompson."

"A pleasure, sir," Tommy said, knowing it was not the time to say something snarky.

Introductions made, Argo looked at Thompson. "Just how the hell did you get dragged into this?" he asked.

"Long story," Thompson replied. "But you'll end up hearing it all in a few minutes." He led the way to the stairs near the back of the dining room. "Unger is upstairs waiting for us with his lawyer, Charlie Patterson."

"He's lawyered up already? He hasn't even turned himself in yet."

"Patterson is a friend of mine," Thompson said. "I trust him implicitly. He's not here to stand in the way. He's here to facilitate you finding the right man – the man who actually killed the Vice President." He turned and led the pair up the narrow stairs to the Club's private dining room.

When they entered the room, Unger could not withhold his excitement at seeing his protector. "Tommy," he shouted as he stood up. "You're okay. I was afraid something happened to you, too." Unger crossed the room and grabbed Tommy in a fierce hug.

"Yeah, you ain't got the best luck with new acquaintances these days," Tommy laughed as he returned the hug and then thumped Unger on the back. "But when we split up, I knew where I was headed. I remembered the name Charlie dropped. So I ran to the FBI building and started acting like a local loony. Once they had me, I started repeating the name 'Leo Argo' until they let me talk to him."

"By the way," Argo inserted himself into the reunion, addressing himself to Unger. "I'm him – Agent Leo Argo of the FBI."

Their eyes met and they stared at each other for a moment. Unger took a deep breath at the thought of what he was about to reveal. "Well, I'm the guy you've been looking for," he replied. He was nervous and shaking, but tried to sound confident. "I'm Vice President Shelby's advance man. I'm David Unger."

Patterson stepped in and introduced himself to Argo. "Senator Thompson had nothing to do with any of this until a couple hours ago. I went to him to set up this meeting."

"Okay," Argo said, accepting the explanation. "So what's your official capacity?"

"For the time being, let's assume I'm representing Mr. Unger. He'll have proper representation later. But after you hear and confirm his story, I hope it won't be necessary."

"Then you're telling me I can question him?"

"Be my guest," Patterson replied. "I set up this meeting so he could lay everything on the table. But before we go to the Hoover Building, I want you to talk to him here."

"I don't usually operate the way lawyers tell me to," Argo said. "But as a courtesy to your relationship with Senator Thompson, I'll agree to your ground rules, for now." Kline's call had set his mind going in a direction other than Unger anyway. Heading back down Pennsylvania Avenue would only make unraveling the story harder. *Too many eyes behind the mirror,* he thought. "But I control the agenda from here on. If he starts bullshitting me, the game is over. He's under arrest and I'm turning him over to the wolves."

"Agreed," Patterson said. He looked at Unger, who also consented.

"Thank you, Leo," Thompson interjected.

Everyone sat down and Argo began a detailed interrogation of Unger, starting with when he arrived at the White House from college and continuing right on down to a description of where he had been hiding over the last several days. Although Unger would occasionally look at Patterson for a reassuring glance, he answered every question with a surprising level of candor and detail. The drama wore on into the late afternoon. With his knowledge of what Kline had already told him over the phone, Argo eventually steered his interrogation into a detailed review of Unger's relationship with Jon Dosser. The line of questioning piqued Thompson's attention and he leaned forward in his chair.

When a question about Longo International was posed, Thompson literally stood up. "What does Longo International have to do with this?" he asked hurriedly.

"Not your turn to be asking questions, Senator," Argo replied, acting a bit out of instinct. He closed his eyes at having made such a gaffe. "I'm sorry. I didn't mean to be so short with you."

Thompson's eyes looked worried. "No, it's okay. I just know the name – Longo International," he said.

Argo turned his attention from Unger to Thompson and pointed to the door of the private dining room. "Step out in the hallway with me a second." Once out of earshot of the others, he leaned in and asked in a low voice, "What's up?"

"Mack Wilson is somehow tied up with Longo International."

"Slow down, Richard," Argo said, ignoring formality. "I know some things about Longo I'm not at liberty to share right now, but linking Wilson with Longo is a pretty serious charge. What's the connection?"

"Joey found some old files on Mack Wilson's computer about Longo International," Thompson said, running his fingers through his hair. "They were hidden in plain sight, word files marked as .exe files. You know our friend the computer geek. He found them. One of my staff, a guy named MacNamara, is still pretty close to Wilson and he knew where Wilson has been staying. I sent him there earlier this morning to ask about them."

"What are in the files?"

"I have no idea," Thompson said nervously. "Joe was looking into them. He had a call scheduled with Dosser to discuss them."

"Call Joe and find out what's going on," Argo instructed as he pulled out his cell phone and dialed Proctor.

"Where the hell are you?" Proctor asked. "I've been looking all over town for you."

"I've been holed up in a little private club by the Senate," Argo said quickly getting to the point. "Do you have any idea where Mack Wilson is now? We need to bring him in for an interview."

"Oh, yeah," Proctor said. "Wilson's real easy to find, but he won't do us much good."

"Why?" Argo started to pace nervously. "Where is he? We really need to get him in custody now."

"Then go to the morgue," Proctor replied. "Wilson is dead."

"What?" Argo gasped.

"As a door nail," Proctor continued. "A former staffer of his found him a few hours ago. He overdosed during a drug-laden dalliance with a hooker. According to the staffer, he had a thing for trannies."

The phone call was abruptly interrupted by Thompson grabbing Argo's shoulders to get his attention. "We got a problem," Thompson said, his eyes wide.

"Hold on," Argo said, hitting the mute button on his phone.

"The scheduler at my office says Joe's on his way to a meeting with Dosser," Thompson said, visibly agitated. "They've got no idea where, but are going to try and run him down."

"Fuck me," Argo grunted. "Stay on it," he instructed Thompson. Argo thought for a minute. The reference to the transsexual hooker had grabbed Argo's attention. Recalling the morning radio report about the body of a dead transsexual on the National Mall, he remembered Wilson's name being mentioned in connection with the earlier discovery of a different body – also a transsexual. He was not yet sure how it all fit together, but two dead transsexual hookers found at the same place were more than mere happenstance.

Argo unmuted the phone and turned his attention back to Proctor. "You said Wilson was with a tranny last night, right?"

"Yeah," replied Proctor.

"You sure?" Argo repeated, hurriedly.

"Pretty sure," Proctor said. "I have a witness that saw her enter the building."

"Alright," Argo said, not ready to let Proctor in on the information Kline had supplied to him about Dosser. "I'm not sure how, but I think the same person may have killed Wilson and Shelby. The two investigations should be merged."

"What the hell are you talking about, man?" Proctor asked.

"Look," Argo said. "I'll share all my information later, but …"

Thompson interrupted Argo's call for a second time. "This doesn't make any sense," he said.

"What?" Argo asked. "You got something else?"

"The office can't get Joe to answer his cell phone," Thompson said.

"So, maybe he put it on silent," Argo said.

"Maybe," Thompson said, "but one of the staffers heard him say he was meeting someone at the Lincoln Memorial. I've got to believe he's meeting Dosser."

Argo shut his eyes at the news. "Proc," Argo said slowly and with determination. "Now I'm certain, the two investigations are one."

"You've got to give me something more," Proctor pleaded.

"I can't," Argo said, gesturing at Thompson to get everyone together. "And if I'm wrong, I'll take the heat."

"Roger that," Proctor said.

"Just meet me down at the Mall with a small Emergency Response Team. Our killer is headed there right now," Argo said.

"Unger," Proctor said excitedly. "You've located David Unger."

"David Unger is with me," Argo replied. "But he's not the one who killed Vice President Shelby. Take your ERT unit and set up a perimeter around the World War I Memorial on the Mall ASAP. But don't make a move until you spot Jon Dosser."

"The Vice President's Chief of Staff?"

"Consider him armed and dangerous. He's our Number One suspect."

Chapter 47

The glow from the Lincoln Memorial lit the sidewalk as The Fat Man jumped from the taxi cab. He made his way from the drop off area and looked up the mountain of steps leading to the statue of America's 16th President.

During a long phone conversation, The Fat Man and Dosser spoke extensively about the files staff were reviewing about Longo International. The Fat Man was delighted when Dosser agreed to take a look at the documents. The meeting location was certainly odd, but fit into Thompson's philosophy of encouraging staff to explore the city. It had been years since The Fat Man had been to the Lincoln Memorial. Now at the bottom of the long flight of steps leading to the top, he let out a heavy sigh, rethinking his decision to meet at such a random location. Huffing and puffing, he started the ascent to the top.

Once there, he saw Jon Dosser standing in the predetermined location and approached. "Hi," The Fat Man said, sticking out his hand. "I'm Joe Bradley. Senator Thompson's Chief of Staff. I appreciate you taking the time out to deal with this for us."

Dosser returned the shake, but not the greeting. "It's quite an exceptional statue," Dosser said softly as The Fat Man moved to his side.

"Yes, it is," he replied. The Fat Man found Dosser's cool nature odd, but attributed it to his high position in the administration.

"It's actually two separate visions of Lincoln," Dosser continued, his voice almost monotonic in nature.

"What do you mean?"

Dosser put his left hand up to cover half of the statue. "Do this," he instructed. "Cut it in half." When The Fat Man complied, he continued. "One part is Lincoln at war," he said. "His hand is in a fist. His leg is drawn under his body. And there's a bit of a frown on his face."

"Wow," replied The Fat Man at the observation.

Dosser changed hands. "Now look at the other side. His leg is outstretched. His hand is relaxed and he's almost smiling."

The Fat Man mimicked Dosser's actions. "Amazing," he declared.

With The Fat Man lulled into artistic observation, Dosser asked the hard question. "So, Mr. Bradley, do you have the documents about Longo International. I'll be glad to look at them for you."

"Well," The Fat Man said repeatedly holding one hand up after another to gaze at Lincoln, "I found some files hidden on Senator Wilson's hard drive as .exe files."

"Fascinating," replied Dosser.

"Yeah," The Fat Man continued, fascinated by the sculptural details of the Lincoln Memorial. "He was apparently supporting some Sicilian company trying to get the geotechnical work on the pipeline." Instead of handing the file to Dosser, he quickly walked to the left of the statue and peered up at Lincoln's face.

Dosser followed in close pursuit. "A Sicilian company, you say? Longo International was foreign?"

"Yes, Longo International." The Fat Man continued to peer at the statue. "Palermo," he said, before turning and walking to the other side of the statue to observe its details.

"Interesting," Dosser said, increasingly anxious to see the files as he followed behind. "Have you talked to Senator Wilson about Longo International?"

"Not yet," The Fat Man said.

Dosser breathed a short quiet sigh of relief. "I've heard no one knows where he's been hiding out over the last week or so."

"I do," said The Fat Man nonchalantly.

"You do?"

"One of our staffers who used to work for Wilson knows he had an apartment up around the zoo. I sent him up there earlier today to talk to Wilson."

"Heard from him yet?"

"Nope."

"Mr. Bradley," Dosser said as he cut off The Fat Man's latest crisscross. They both stopped and made eye contact. "I believe you wanted me to look at some files."

"Oh yeah," The Fat Man said, pulling a couple of papers from his coat jacket and handing them to Dosser.

Dosser was stunned by the documents, which while coded, broke down the payments made by the Russians and the disbursements to fictitious names for Shelby, Wilson and Dosser. *"Wilson was dumber than I ever imagined,"* Dosser thought to himself. *"It won't be too long before someone figures it out."*

Dosser turned and looked down the darkened Mall. "You know, Joe, if you like my observations about the Lincoln Memorial, you'll love my tour of the World War I Memorial."

Chapter 48

Richard Thompson could almost count the seconds in fragments. He nervously tapped his foot on the floor of the car and stared out the window as they drove. Horrible thoughts of The Fat Man lying bleeding and in pain or dead ran rampant through his mind. As hard as he tried to put them out of his mind, he could not stop the morbid cycle of thoughts haunting him. Silently blaming himself for whatever ill fate had befallen his friend, Thompson bit at his fingernails. He made The Fat Man come to DC, after all. This was not the gig he signed up for.

Patterson, Unger and Tommy all sat silently in the back seat.

The car was quiet, but Argo knew what was going through Thompson's mind. Similar scenes played out in his imagination. "He may not even be there, yet." Argo said softly. "Let's not jump to worst case scenarios." Argo did not believe his own words, and he was sure Thompson did not either.

"Yeah," Thompson replied half-heartedly. Patterson put his hand on Thompson's shoulder for support. "I'm sure he's fine," Patterson said when Thompson glanced backwards.

As they sped down Independence Avenue towards West Potomac Park, Argo kept a watchful eye on the scene ahead of them – or more accurately, the lack of any scene whatsoever. Despite the call to Proctor requesting him to surround the monument, he detected absolutely no movement in the distance. The ERT was good, but he expected to see something. But the reality was no people. No extraordinary movement. Nothing.

"I don't like this," said Argo, throwing the car into park about fifty yards from the WWI Monument. "Stay here," he told Tommy, Patterson and Unger in the back seat. All three readily agreed.

Argo glanced at Thompson. "The same goes for you," he said. "Wait here until I check it out."

Thompson heard the order, but it did not register. He threw open the door and hopped to the pavement. With the headlights of Argo's car silhouetting him from behind, Thompson sprinted towards the monument. He barely heard Argo yelling at him to stop. Eyes dashing from side-to-side, at first he saw nothing.

Thompson froze in his steps when he spotted Jon Dosser emerging from behind one of the monument's pillars with The Fat Man in his grasp. Dosser shoved The Fat Man to his knees and stood behind him, the point of a brass-knuckled, serrated blade knife with its tip pointing at the side of The Fat Man's throat. The Fat Man was pale and shaking.

"Stop right there, Agent Argo," Dosser warned. Recognizing the other person from the news broadcast he watched with Wilson, he added "You too, Senator. Everybody slow down."

"You okay, Joey?" Argo shouted, his gun drawn and aimed at Dosser.

The Fat Man cleared his throat. "I think so," he said in a faint voice.

"Drop the gun, Argo," Dosser instructed.

Argo stepped closer and steadied his aim. "Not a fucking chance, pal."

Dosser shook his head at Argo's approach. "You know the problem with most people who slit throats with knives," Dosser said. "They slash the knife across the throat. Sometimes they don't go deep enough to reach the jugular vein." He held the tip up slightly. "They taught me in the military if you plunge the blade into the middle of the neck and then push forward, you can't miss."

Thompson shot a fearful look at Argo and then back at Dosser.

Dosser picked up on Thompson's anxiety. "Want to watch it happen, Senator?" Dosser asked.

"No," Thompson said in nearly a whisper.

"What's that, Senator?" Dosser raised his voice. "I didn't hear you."

"No," Thompson shouted firmly. "I don't want to see that happen."

"Good," Dosser replied, his hand readjusting its grip on the knife. "Then tell the agent to drop his weapon." When no one moved, Dosser pressed the point of the blade into The Fat Man's neck. A small drop of blood appeared. "I'm not fucking around here."

Despite his better judgment, Argo lowered his gun and considered his options. Keep Dosser talking until the ERT arrived was all he could come up with. "No," he said, tossing his gun to the ground. "None of us wants to see what it looks like."

"Smart move," Dosser said smiling.

Back in Argo's car, Tommy, Unger and Patterson were silently watching with wide- eyed anticipation. Tommy broke the tension by reaching for the door.

"What are you doing," Patterson asked.

"I'm outta here, man," Tommy replied as he slowly opened the door.

David grabbed his arm. "Tommy, don't take off."

"This ain't gonna turn out well, Ace," Tommy replied. "You're a good kid, but I gotta do what I gotta do."

"You'll be cleared," Patterson said, adding to Unger's encouragement to stay.

"By who," Tommy replied. "Those boys are about to die. I ain't gonna join 'em."

In front of the memorial, the negotiation between Argo and Dosser continued. "So how do we do this?" Argo asked.

Dosser pondered the question. "Well, I know you're not going to just let me walk out of here with him."

"You're probably right," Argo said, raising up his hands in surrender. "Then, how about trading me for him?" he asked.

"Are you kidding me?" Dosser replied. His eyes were steely cold.

"No," Argo replied. "I'm your only way out of here tonight. Let me be your hostage and I'll talk to Director Kline about including you on whatever deal she cuts with Kederov."

Dosser blinked at Kederov's name. His cover story was fully exposed and his potential for escape compromised with the CIA involved. He thought about the offer. "Where are your cuffs?"

Argo exhaled as he slowly unlatched them from his belt, holding them up with one finger. "Right here."

"Good," Dosser shouted, gesturing to a point at Argo's right. "Now put them on Senator Thompson."

"Not the deal," Argo replied immediately. "It's me or nothing."

"You're not in a position to negotiate," Dosser said. "I want him."

"Not happening."

"It's my only offer. That guy for this one." Dosser pointed the knife back and forth between The Fat Man and Thompson for emphasis. "I walk out of here with the Senator. When you guys offer me a deal with CIA buy-in, I let him go."

"No," Argo repeated.

"It buys you twenty-four hours," Dosser shouted.

Thompson turned and walked over to Argo. The look in Thompson's eyes told Argo all he needed to know. "No damn way, Richard," Argo insisted.

"It's okay, Leo," Thompson said, holding his hands passively behind his back. "I need to do this.

"I can't."

"He's my best friend," Thompson said softly. "I've got to do this."

"It's too big a risk."

"But one I need to take," Thompson assured Argo. "If you don't cuff me, I'm just going to walk up there without them. He's too amped up right now. The cuffs will actually help to defuse the situation."

"No."

Thompson placed his hand gently on Argo's shoulder. "Think of it, Leo – I could never go to a ball game again if something happened to him."

Argo offered no response but a heavy exhale.

"Cuff me, Leo." Thompson held his hands out in front of him. "Do it."

"This is insane," Argo said, snapping the cuffs around Thompson's wrists. "I'm going to jail for doing this, you know. I'm handing a US Senator over to a known killer. This won't look good on my resume."

"You are acting on my direct request," Thompson said.

"But I don't take orders from you," Argo argued, turning Thompson around to face the memorial. Argo started to add something about a dead man not being able to confirm stories," but thought better. "Be ready to move," he whispered. "Whether it's now or later, I'll get you out of this somehow. I promise."

"You damn well better," Thompson said. "Or you'll have to answer to Ann and Jane." Thompson walked slowly towards the steps of the monument. "Better you answer to them than me," he said to himself.

When Thompson was about ten feet away from the steps to the memorial he could see The Fat Man was visibly shaking. "You don't have to do this," The Fat Man implored.

Stopping just short of the steps, Thompson looked at The Fat Man. "Yeah, I do," he said, looking to Dosser. "He's on his feet before I start up the steps."

"Okay," Dosser replied, putting a hand under The Fat Man's armpit to help him stand. "Now, you walk up."

Thompson inched up the steps, in an effort to keep Dosser as calm as possible. When Dosser released The Fat Man's arm, Thompson gestured his approval. "Walk away, Joe," he said and The Fat Man started forward.

Suddenly, the dull thud of a shot muzzled by a silencer came from the tree grove to Thompson's left side. Before he could do anything to see the exact place of its origin, Dosser's shoulder snapped violently to his right. His body whipped backwards, and he dropped his knife in the process. Dosser careened off one of the pillars before his momentum caused his body to roll off the bandstand. Thompson lunged up the steps, shoved The Fat Man to the marble floor and covered him with his body.

From the darkness of the trees surrounding the memorial, a shadowy figure emerged. "I told you I'd be here, Leo," came a voice.

"Proctor?" asked Agro, squinting through the night's haze. "Damn man, I never thought I'd be so glad to see your sorry ass."

Coming into the light, Proctor approached smiling broadly. A Sig Saur with an attached silencer dangled at his side. "I couldn't let you come to the party by yourself."

Argo looked at Thompson and The Fat Man. "You two okay?"

They both nodded affirmatively, Thompson helping his friend up before placing his cuffed wrists on his shoulder. He looked back at the man from the trees. "I don't know who you are, but I am damn glad to see you," Thompson said to Proctor.

"Me," Proctor sneered. "I'm your worst fucking nightmare." In an instant, Proctor's expression changed. His eyes narrowed, he lowered his gun and fired a single muzzled shot into Argo's knee.

"You piece of shit," Argo shouted, pain shooting through his leg. On the ground, he looked in the direction of his gun, which was about five feet away and then he looked in the lighted area under the dome of the memorial, where both Thompson and The Fat Man stood startled.

"Don't do it, Leo," Proctor said, pointing the gun towards Thompson. "Killing a Senator will just be another notch for me."

Argo pulled at his leg. "What the fuck is going on here, Scott?" he asked.

"I'm doing my job," Proctor replied.

"Your job?" Argo panted through clenched teeth. "Since when is shooting the good guys part of your job?"

"Yeah," Proctor said, waving the gun nonchalantly around. "It's kind of funny isn't it? I mean, me shooting you."

"I'm not laughing," Argo replied.

"I have lots of jobs on my detail, Leo," Proctor calmly explained. "And tonight my job is the advance man."

"Advance man?"

"That's what I'm calling it, anyway," Proctor said. "I'm here in advance of all the agencies that will be looking into this grizzly crime scene, coordinating all law enforcement efforts to make sure the investigation runs smoothly. I came up with the new title for myself when we were at the kid's apartment. "

"You're with Dosser on this?"

"No, no, no," Proctor insisted, cocking his head at the reference. "Dosser is a greedy pig. I blame this all on him as much as anyone. Pigs get fat and hogs – well, you know."

"I don't understand." Argo replied, still holding his leg from the pain.

"Nor should you," Proctor laughed. "Shelby was greedy, too. He just couldn't choose between profits for the family farm or quick ill-gotten rubles. I think the rubles would have been a bigger take, but he was so damn proud of that farm. Greed versus pride – so many deadly sins – and then another hog to the slaughter."

"So you killed Shelby?"

"No, that was Dosser," Proctor said. "He had the military background to create the pen bomb. And I never had that kind of access. But his death was inevitable. If Dosser hadn't killed him, the Russians might well have. Dosser merely hurried the process."

"Wilson?"

"That's the beauty of greed," Proctor said. "Dosser was so interested in his own gain, he took care of the Senator for me, too. All I had to do to protect the institution of the presidency was to make sure it all fell at the feet of the man Dosser was setting up."

"David Unger," Argo suggested.

"Aren't you the smart one," Proctor said sarcastically. "Dosser did all the heavy lifting. I merely completed the puzzle for him."

"You're insane," Argo grunted through clenched teeth.

"Oh, 'insane' is such an accusatory term, Leo," Proctor said, scratching his temple with the barrel of the gun. "An ugly word that implies an impure motive. I'm a protector."

"What?"

"I'm protecting the presidency," Proctor said, looking at his watch. "But enough of this idle chit-chat. In about two minutes this will be a horrible crime scene, littered by dead bodies left in the ugly wake of David Unger's madness and his plot to kill the Vice President."

"Someone will figure it out, Scott," Argo insisted.

"Hardly," Proctor replied. "The White House and the press are so damn anxious to find a killer it'll be over before you know it."

"It won't work."

"Sure it will," Proctor insisted. "I'll give all the credit for landing Unger to the late-Leo Argo, horribly killed in the line of duty. You'll be hailed a hero – posthumously, of course. They'll have a big ceremony for you. I bet Cicero even names a room at the Hoover Building after you." He paused and chuckled. "The Leo Argo Memorial John."

"What about Kederov and Unger?"

"What of them?"

"They know the story."

"You think people are going to believe an old commie and a queer," Proctor laughed out loud. "Fucking priceless." He quit laughing abruptly. "Goodbye, Leo. I hate to off you. You're a good guy, but the story doesn't work with you in the ending."

As Proctor lowered his aim at Argo, a rock about the size of a baseball hit the rogue Secret Service Agent on the side of his head. The impact dropped him to one knee. Momentarily stunned, the gun slipped from Proctor's grasp.

"What the fu …" was all Proctor got out before Tommy hit him with a solid body blow from the side. The two rolled in the grass and struggled on the ground as Argo crawled to his gun. Suddenly, a muffled shot echoed across the Mall. When Proctor stood up with his Sig Saur in his hand, Argo fired four shots into him.

"Check on Dosser," Argo shouted to Thompson as he crawled toward the twitching body of Scott Proctor.

Thompson ran to the side of the bandstand to check. "He's not here."

"What?" Argo said, tossing Proctor's weapon to the side.

The Fat Man joined Thompson and peered into the darkness of the grove. "He's gone, Leo," he shouted. "There's nobody here."

"Shit," Argo said. "He must have been wearing Kevlar. We'll get him later."

Unger and Patterson ran from the car to Tommy's side and looked down at the blood streaming across his shirt. "Dat time I was aiming for his head," he coughed, blood coming from his mouth as he spoke. "Best bean ball I ever threw."

"You're going to be okay, Tommy," Unger pleaded, placing his hand under the dying man's head. "I swear."

"Don't swear, Ace," Tommy smiled weakly. "It's not your style."

"But ..."

"It's the bottom of the ninth and two outs," Tommy continued. "Damn, dat was a good toss, wasn't it?"

"Yeah," Unger choked. "Right on the money."

Tommy tried to speak, but life was quickly draining from his body.

"Thank you," Unger said, his voice choking with emotion. "You saved my life. You saved all our lives."

As Tommy took his last breath, Unger leaned forward and kissed him on the forehead. "Your dad would be proud."

Chapter 49

The peak day of DC's cherry blossoms is either bloom or bust. If cold spring rain is falling, the petals turn brown almost as soon as they hit the ground – becoming just another slippery substance along the sidewalks surrounding the Tidal Basin. But in the right circumstances, a warm breeze flows across the water to pick the blush petals gently off the trees. On those days the blossoms float through the air as if a sweetly fragrant snow is lightly blessing the nation's capital. Such was this day.

Senator Richard Thompson, The Fat Man, Charlie Patterson and David Unger walked for about thirty yards taking it all in. Jane Kline pushed Leo Argo in a wheel chair about five yards behind. They walked about a hundred yards before any of them spoke.

"This is beautiful," said Unger, gazing around to view the cherry blossoms, but also secretly hoping no one recognized him.

Thompson caught the uncomfortable glances. "Calm down, son," he advised. "It's DC and you're yesterday's news. It's all over. *Carpe diem.*"

"And the smells," The Fat Man added, taking a deep breath. "Seize the smells, too." He was proudly wearing a gold chain around his neck with a gold boxing glove pendant dangling from it, a gift from Argo. It was not the one Argo recovered in Unger's apartment. That one was still at FBI headquarters. The one the Fat Man wore was one of the many Argo had won as a kid.

Unger smiled and drew in a deep breath. "It is pretty awesome."

Thompson looked over his shoulder at Kline. "Thank the CIA for the weather," he said jokingly.

"You're welcome," Kline replied, laughingly.

"I don't get it," Unger said as they walked. "I thought Jon Dosser was a good guy. I trusted him."

"Turns out he wasn't," Argo interjected and looked knowingly at Kline. "According to a well-placed source, Dosser stumbled into the deal between Shelby, Wilson and Kederov and forced himself into the payoff. When the transaction started falling apart because of Shelby's family loyalties, Dosser killed him to get Wilson's attention."

"That's bizarre," Thompson said.

"He got more than Wilson's attention," Argo continued. "The assassination scared Wilson so badly, he resigned – something Dosser never anticipated."

"I guess he also never anticipated Wilson was a bigger squish than Shelby," Thompson opined.

"Precisely," Argo replied. "And when Joey called to say he had documents from Wilson's files, he had to sever all connections to those files."

The Fat Man reached up to the patch on his neck where Dosser used his knife to draw blood. "I'd appreciate if we'd discontinue the use of the word 'sever.'"

"What about the two guys who were waiting for me at my apartment?" Unger asked. "I never want to see them again."

"You won't," Argo assured Unger. "They were associates of Proctor. We found their bodies on the south shoreline of the Potomac River with bullets in their brains." Argo tapped his leg. "The slugs matched the ones fired into my leg from Proctor's Sig Saur."

"What about Proctor?" The Fat Man asked. "He's the weirdest connection in this entire story."

"I never felt totally comfortable around Proctor," Argo said. "And I guess my instincts were dead on. He believed it was up to him to protect the integrity of the presidency."

"Big calling," The Fat man replied.

"He was committed to the cause," Thompson said.

"I'm still upset about Dosser, though," Unger added.

"That you misjudged him?" Argo asked. "It happens all the time in this town. People aren't always what you hoped for."

"No," Unger replied. "I'm pissed he got away."

"Let it go, David," Kline spoke up for the first time. "And go on with your life. Jon Dosser will get his someday."

EPILOGUE
(six months later)

Jane Kline sipped morning coffee from her kitchen table while reading an article from a Belize City newspaper for the third time. According to the account, a man possessing forged American credentials was killed after removing a large sum of cash from the national bank. A stocky man with a Russian accent was being sought by police as a person of interest in the case. Witnesses recounted the Russian followed the man into his small rented flat, but disappeared thereafter.

"Yup," Kline said to herself as she put her coffee cup down on the table. "He always was a better killer than a bureaucrat."

"Come on, boy," Leo Agro encouraged, leading Hoover into the foyer from his morning walk. They both entered the kitchen seeking water. "Anything good in the paper today?" Argo asked, pouring bottled water into Hoover's bowl before turning the container up to his own lips.

"Nope," Kline replied, tossing the paper onto the table. "Just the run-of-the-mill morning briefing stuff."

"You've got a smile on your face," Argo replied. "You look — well, satisified."

"Let's just say one of my new assets just earned a big gold star today," Kline said. Changing the subject, she reached down and felt Argo's knee. "How's the leg feel?"

"Great," Argo said, grabbing her hand and holding it lovingly. "Two good wheels between the two of us. We're a helluva pair."

"I like our odds," Kline said smiling.

"Me, too," Argo said, taking another sip of water while he leaned against a kitchen counter. "It's a blessing in disguise really."

"You think?" Kline winced slightly at the thought.

"Think of it," Argo continued. "I was nearly timed out at the Bureau anyway. It was time for me to move on. The work-related injury gave me a reason."

"And an annuity," Kline added.

"You're starting to sound like a bureaucrat," Argo teased, touching Kline tenderly on the tip of her nose.

"Maybe," Kline offered, playfully biting at his finger as he quickly pulled it away. "But I'm still not sure this new gig is the right job for you."

"Come on, babe," Argo pleaded. "Opposition research is the latest gold mine in politics. Campaign houses need people to find dirt under candidate's fingernails. It'll be just like FBI work, minus the people shooting at me."

"You're just not the political type," Kline replied. "That's no insult. Neither am I."

"That's the beauty of it," Argo said. "I don't have to be political. That's on everybody else's plate. I just dig up the dirt. And besides, Griff is paying me a hefty salary to do it."

"I know," Kline said. "And that's one of my concerns. I'm having trouble seeing you and Michael Griffith working together."

"Not so hard to envision, is it?" Argo replied.

"Well, not without you ultimately killing him," Kline laughed.

"I know," Argo replied, "but Thompson will be at the company when he finishes up his term. He's going to be leading this new venture. I suspect I'll be dealing with him more than Griff."

"That's a relief," Kline said. "You know, the not killing Griff thing. I'd hate to only see you during conjugal visits at a federal prison."

"Three hots and a cot," Argo said. "Not so bad."

"Seriously, babe," Kline continued. "You think you'll be happy looking into the past of people trying to get elected to office?"

"Yeah," Argo replied. "It won't be heavy lifting, but everybody has a past. It'll be up to me to uncover it."

Acknowledgments

As I have learned from past efforts, books are not written entirely by the author. A lot of people along the way contribute to the creative process. I have several mentors and imaginative folks around me who add to the final product and I want to thank them all for being fans, supporters and friends.

Rod Pennington continues to be a guiding light in my personal and professional life, gently reminding me when my writing (and eating) go astray. The memos Mark Morris writes to me on each book are funnier than anything I'll ever put on paper and twice as insightful. Steve Smith has had an impact. Jon Deuser is more than a bad guy in my novels – he's a great friend with an English degree. Jim and Kathy Brewer, Sheri Fuller and Debbie Strietelmeier are loyal readers and good editors. And the real Fat Man, Jeff Landen, has made me a better writer and person than I could ever be on my own.

My friends all know I write where there is lots of activity, but I can't determine whether it's driven by my ADHD or my love of Guinness. In either event, thanks to the folks at the Dubliner in DC, Ireland's Four Courts in Arlington, VA, the Capitol Hill Club in DC and the Red Zone in Ft. Mitchell, KY, for keeping the words (and Mitcher's) flowing for me. My wife finds it disturbing that all the bartenders at these establishments know me by name, but I appreciate you letting me hang out at your rails from time to time. Coffee works too, so thanks to Biggby's in Ft Mitchell, KY, Roebling Point Book Store in Covington, KY, and Joseph Beth in Crestview Hills, KY, for keeping caffeine and power strips at the ready.

Best of luck in life to Levi Richard Carson. Your dad Curtis loves you (and I'm kind of proud of you both). There is a great world ahead of you. Enjoy it.

No book is ever complete without a cover and Kevin Kelly does them better than anyone. He is the most talented person I know, and

I am always honored when he takes time out of tossing fine art around the world to piddle around with my covers. Kevin is aided this time by a great photo we discovered on-line by Brandon Kopp.

My publicist Debbie McKinney keeps me in front of more people than I deserve to be. Maybe this will be the book of mine she actually reads. And my publisher Cathy Teets at Headline Books is the greatest. In a day and age when authors complain about their publishers, I can truthfully say I love mine.

Finally, to my best friend and harshest critic, Linda. I could never do this (or anything else, for that matter) without you.

* * *

Books by Rick Robinson

The Maximum Contribution
Sniper Bid
Manifest Destiny
Writ of Mandamus
Strange Bedfellow
Alligator Alley
America's Got Talent Winner Landau Eugene Murphy Jr:
    From Washing Cars to Hollywood Stars
      (with Landau Eugene Murphy Jr.)
Killing the Curse (with Dennis Hetzel)

Opposition Research by Rick Robinson, coming 2016